Praise for Carlee Boccacci and her work:

"I loved reading *The King: Torn Between Worlds*, and literally could not put it down. The heroine of the story is a likable character who has a strong voice and had me rooting for her from page one. The novel is a tale full of intrigue, humor, mystery, and romance… Elements of fantasy and the fairy tale setting make this a worthwhile read. The story is unique, interspersed with elements found in the classics such as *Anne of Green Gables* and *Pride and Prejudice*. These elements, mixed with a fantastical setting, seamlessly flow together to create a captivating escape from reality.
Two thumbs up for *The King: Torn Between Worlds*, by Carlee Boccacci."
- Tamara Grantham, author of the *Fairy World MD* series

"Carlee is feisty, passionate, and not afraid of a good fight. It reflects in her writing."
- Barry Friedman, writer/comedian/*Tulsa Voice* columnist

"Carlee Boccacci is a first class storyteller whose imagination is so pitch perfect that her characters' fantasies become our realities."
- Teresa Miller, author of *Means of Transit*

"This delightful fantasy will enchant you from the first page to the last."
- William Bernhardt, *NY Times* Best-Selling author

The King
Torn Between Worlds: Book 1

Carlee Boccacci

The King
Torn Between Worlds: Book 1
Copyright ©2016 Carlee Boccacci
CreateSpace, Charleston SC
Cover Art by Eric Vogt
ISBN: 978-1530452927

This book is a work of fiction. Names, characters, places and incidents are the product of the author's imagination or are used fictitiously. Any resemblance to actual persons, living or dead, business establishments, events or locales is entirely coincidental.

No part of this book may be reproduced, scanned, or distributed in any printed or electronic form without permission. Please do not participate in or encourage piracy of copyrighted materials in violation of the author's rights. Purchase only authorized editions.

Carlee Boccacci

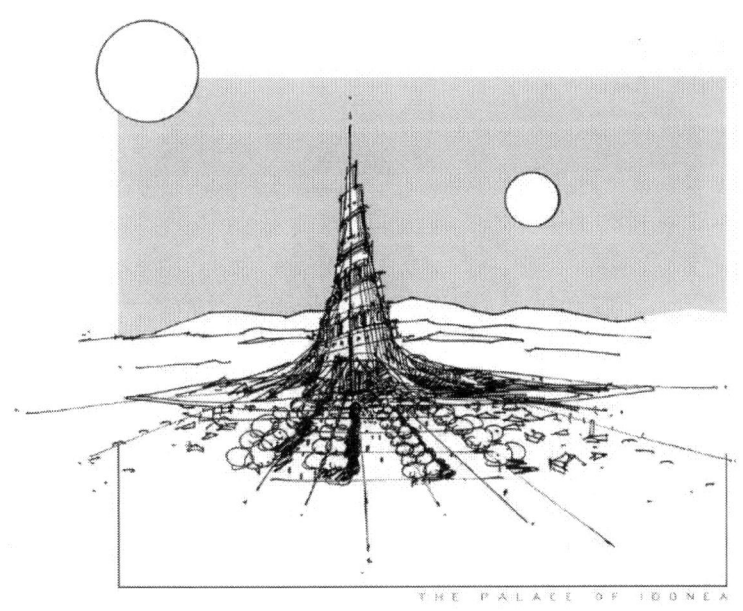

THE PALACE OF IDONEA

For Erika, my biggest fan, greatest supporter, and dearest friend.

Prologue

Arkin couldn't listen to the agonizing screams anymore. But he didn't dare leave her side. The healer told her to scream. He said it would do her more harm if she tried to be discreet. This was not the time for restraint.

"It is all right, Ingrid. Breathe. Breathe. The child will be here soon." The healer turned to Arkin and instructed, "You must fetch some water and clean cloth. It is time." As he turned back to a laboring Ingrid, Arkin obeyed his commands.

Arkin left his wife to gather the items. He took a quick glance out of a dirty window in his small house. One might believe it was the middle of a bright sunny day judging by the light streaming in through the glass. But it wasn't. It was the middle of the night. The light was coming from the palace. The palace burned. And Arkin had started the fire. They would be coming for him. Very soon.

Arkin knew it was not customary for the father to be present for the birth. But he did not know how much time either he or Ingrid had left. So, he hurried back into the bedroom where his wife was beginning to deliver their baby. He set down the blankets he found and flew to Ingrid's side to hold her hand. "It is all right, darling. You can do this. Our baby is coming. You can do it. Push, my love. Do not stop. I am here with you."

The King

Arkin held his wife's hand and she squeezed his. He used his other hand to wipe the sweat from her brow. He looked into her eyes, and he saw despair. "Do not give up now, Ingrid," he said to her. "You are too strong to stop now."

She took a deep a breath, as deep as she possibly could and said, "Arkin, you must…you must protect the child."

"We will. Together. You and I," he said.

"No. Not me. I will not…"

She could not finish. The baby would not wait a moment longer. Ingrid screamed and grasped her husband's hand and the edge of the bed. When the baby arrived, the healer quickly cleaned the newborn infant, wrapped it up in a blanket, and handed it to Arkin.

"It is a girl," the healer told him. "Now, I must go."

Arkin stood. "What? No. You will stay. My wife must be cared for."

"I delivered your child. I gave your wife a special tonic to bring relief from her pain and accelerate her healing. But it may be too late for that. It is all I can do. I am not willing to stay and lose my life. I can see the flames at the palace from here. If you have any hope of survival, you will do the same and flee. They will be coming." The doctor looked from Arkin, down to the baby. "They will be coming for all of you." With that, the healer grabbed his bag, and left the house.

Arkin turned to his ailing wife. He looked only at her ashen face. He could not stand to see the blood covering the bed. Arkin knew that she wouldn't survive this. Even if the healer had stayed, there was not much hope. He sat down beside her as she took breaths that grew more shallow. He gently handed her the baby. Ingrid smiled weakly. She looked into her daughter's eyes and caressed the tiny fingers.

"Arkin?" she said.

"Yes."

"What will you call her?" she asked.

"I...I do not know. But we can think of a name together. Let me clean you up. You just rest and I will take care of you."

"Arkin listen to me." She looked at her husband with a look of determination. "You must go. Now. Take her and go." She handed the baby back to her husband and looked away.

"No, Ingrid. I will not leave you."

"If you stay, we will all die. They will be here at any moment." She glanced toward the door.

"Then we will all go."

"Do not be a fool. I am dying tonight, one way or another. But I will not die with you and my child. Now, go."

"But...where? Where can we go? Haldor will find us."

"You know where you must go. Follow the plan. Take the Bridge to Earth and leave. It is all worked out. Hide. Hide our daughter. They must never find her."

Arkin nodded. "They will not find us." He bent over his wife and held her to him for a brief moment. "Ingrid, my dear, I will love you always." He released her and sat up. The life in her had left.

There was no time for tears. That could come later. At that moment, Arkin had to go. He had to run for his life and the life of his daughter.

The front door burst open and Arkin whirled around, clutching the baby in his arms. But running in through the door was only a small boy, about eleven or twelve years old.

"Sir. You must go. The king has sent his soldiers and they are on their way here. I can help you. Let me take you to the Bridge. I know a shortcut through the woods."

Arkin sprang into action. He filled a small bag with a blanket, some bread, a small jug of milk; and at the last moment, he returned to his wife's side to remove a thin gold bracelet from her wrist and placed it in the bag. He grabbed a dagger from the bedside table and slipped it into his belt. Then he quickly dressed and swaddled the baby. When he had his few precious items with him, he rushed out of his house, leaving the lifeless body of his wife behind.

"This way, Sir," said the boy, motioning with his hand. Arkin followed him into the tall trees behind the house. Only the light from the burning palace lit their path. The boy ran in and out between the trunks of the trees as if he had done it every day of his life. Arkin kept up as quickly as he could. He trusted the boy to take them to safety. The boy was the son of Ingrid's brother, and wanted them to stay alive. He was the only one who could help them now. Arkin's other family and friends were continuing the chaos at the palace that he, himself, had started. If Ingrid had not gone into labor, Arkin would be there fighting with them.

They reached the top of a hill and were about to descend the other side, but Arkin stopped briefly to take one look back at his house. From this height, he could see only the roof. Smoke was still drifting from the chimney. But no one inside could feel the warmth of the fire. The pathway leading to the house was quickly being obscured by shapes. Dark silhouettes of tall soldiers carrying swords headed toward the house, their shadows dancing in front of them on the ground. Arkin was thankful that his wife was already dead. They wouldn't be able to cause her any pain when they found her.

"Sir, we are almost there. We must hurry."

The urgency in the boy's voice made Arkin refocus his thoughts back on his mission. He needed to get himself and his daughter to safety. They half ran, half slid down the hill. Once they made it to the bottom, it was a straight shot to the Bridge.

Arkin ran. He didn't know where the energy was coming from. Maybe anger, maybe desperation -- but wherever it originated, he used it to run as fast as he could to the entrance of the Bridge. Once they arrived, Arkin looked down at his infant daughter and rubbed his thumb tenderly over her pink cheeks. "We will be okay. I will take care of you." The baby's blue eyes looked at her father, and she wrapped her tiny fingers around his thumb. Arkin smiled, one tear escaping and rolling down his cheek.

"Okay, Sir. My mother told me to give this to you. It has a contact name and location. They are waiting for you and the baby." The boy handed a small slip of parchment paper to Arkin.

Marianne Logan
Guthrie, Oklahoma
United States of America

At the very bottom was an address. That was where he was headed once he got to Earth. That was where he and his daughter would begin their new life in hiding.

"Are you ready, Sir?"

Arkin held his daughter close to his chest, and stepped onto the Bridge. "Yes. I am ready."

The boy pushed a few buttons on the control panel and, as the beam from the Bridge began to form, Arkin looked at the boy and spoke to him. "Thank you, Arthur. You have saved our lives." Then Arkin looked up to the sky.

And everything went dark.

Book 1

Chapter 1

"Annie! Watch out!"

I looked down just in time to see the bike courier speeding right towards me. My quick pivot and spin to get out of the way would have earned a 9.2 at the Winter Olympics.

"Geez, Annie. Keep your eyes in front of you. Stop staring at the sky."

"Yes, ma'am."

"Don't call me that."

"Yes, ma'am, Erika." I shot my best friend a grin and she rolled her eyes at me.

We continued walking in a comfortable silence. We both had the same destination in mind and didn't need to be distracted by conversation while fighting pedestrian traffic on the busy New York City sidewalk. We both breathed a little sigh of relief when we walked into the coffee shop. We made it our goal to come here every morning before work. It was our time to collect ourselves and have some girl talk before our day began. It was a relaxing place for us. Quiet, cozy, and the smell of coffee woke us up just as much as actually drinking the stuff did.

"So," Erika began, "how's it going with Jake? Is he still making wedding plans without your permission?"

"Oh my gosh, I can't stop the guy. I haven't even said 'yes'."

"Are you going to?"

I shook my head. "Don't ask me that. It's too early and I haven't had any caffeine yet."

Erika laughed and went to order our Vanilla Lattes. Venti, please. After she left the table I let my eyes wander to the window. Outside, it was a grey morning and people were hustling to get to work. No one looked up to smile at the others passing by them. No one called out a greeting to wish another a nice day. Everyone stared straight ahead, determined to get to their destination as quickly as possible.

I could never help but wonder why. Were their lives full of cash registers, written reports, presentations, and water coolers really fulfilling? Did they wake up every day excited about getting to work? Maybe they just endured it so they could go home to their families and enjoy the fruits of their labor watching movies on their fifty-two inch flat screen. Or perhaps they were saving up to take their dream vacation to Hawaii with their wives or husbands. Whatever the goal or reward, there they were on a Tuesday morning, barreling to work, with no smile to be seen up or down the block.

I guess I sighed a little too loudly. Erika made a face at me as she sat down with the two steaming mugs.

"What now?" she said. "Let me guess. You are trying to figure out why you bothered to get up today? Or maybe you are trying to understand what the purpose of life is? Oh, wait, no. This time you are longing for the day your prince will come and take you, his blond haired, blue eyed princess, away from all this normalcy. That's it, isn't it?"

I knew she was just being sarcastic but I replied anyway.

"But Erika, don't you ever wonder what else is out there? I mean...this can't really be it, can it?"

"Annie, my dear, sweet sweet friend," she took my hand and patted it. "You've got to stop this. We are born, we grow up, we earn money to buy nice things, we enjoy our friends, we grow old, we die. It's up to you to find the meaning of your own life and find the happiness where you can. There is nothing else out there. Keep your mind - and your eyes - on the ground. You'll drive yourself crazy if you don't. Anyway, isn't my friendship bringing you the most joy you could ever have?" she teased.

We drank our coffees, chatted about the upcoming day, and when we were finished half an hour later, we gathered our things. As I was picking up my jacket I heard Erika gasp.

"Hey, Annie," she said in a low whisper. "Isn't that your stalker? Look, across the street, next to the subway entrance. What is up with that guy?"

I nonchalantly turned my eyes in the direction she had described. And there he was. My stalker. I had seen him about twice a week at that point. It had become a game for Erika and me to try to guess where and when I might see him next. I had just seen him the day before, so I wasn't expecting the next time to be so soon. And yet, there he was. He was wearing his usual tailored long black coat with a sea green scarf. He had on a white button up shirt, black tie, black slacks and black shoes which seemed too shiny for the dirty sidewalks of the city - almost as if he actually floated rather than walked on them. His shoulder-length, straight black hair was untouched by the autumn breeze. And his eyes...

His eyes were staring straight at me.

"I don't know, Erika, but we'll be late for work if we don't get going."

I picked up my purse and put my arm through my jacket's sleeve when I froze. My stalker was walking across the street...straight towards the coffee shop. I looked at Erika. "Sit back down. Sit back down. Now." I grabbed my own chair, sat down and pulled my almost empty coffee mug in front of me and glared at my stunned friend until she did the same.

"I thought we were late. What are you doing?" she asked as she slowly reached for her chair.

"He's coming."

"What? Who? Your stalker?" She looked towards the window.

"Don't look. Pretend we're still talking. Pretend we're normal."

"I kinda thought I was," she said as she lowered herself into her chair. "Jury is still out on you, though. What is your problem?"

There I sat, one arm through one jacket sleeve and the other sleeve dangling to the floor as the door to the coffee shop opened and in stepped my stalker. What was he doing? Was he going to come talk to me? Ask me out on a date? Grab my purse and run? I was determined not to make eye contact. I stared down at the lukewarm remains of my latte like it was the most amazing thing I had ever seen. I repeated *do not look up, do not look up* about twenty times in my head before I just couldn't stop myself from sneaking a peek. By that time, the man had already ordered his drink and was sitting with one leg crossed over the other in an arm chair by the window. He had not come to talk to me. He had not tried to ask me out...or even grab my purse and run.

I was kind of disappointed.

"He's just minding his own business and reading the paper. Can we go now?" Erika was getting frustrated, I could tell. I'm still not sure why she has continued to be my friend all these years. I can be trying at times, or so she says. As does my boyfriend...and my mom...and my little sister. Hmm... Maybe there was something to that. But I would think about that later.

"Yes, let's go. Sorry." I slowly stood and finished putting on my jacket, peeked at my stalker, grabbed my purse, peeked at my stalker, pushed my chair in, peeked at my...

"Annie, for heaven's sake. Stop stalling and let's go."

"Yep. Coming."

We walked out of the coffee shop without one more glance towards my mystery man. Well, maybe just one - or six. But he didn't look up at me. Not once. Why was I upset? I didn't even know who this guy was. Most likely he just happened to live near me, work near me, and enjoy the same coffee. Of course we would run into him often. That happens, right?

The problem was, I started looking forward to catching a glimpse of him. Besides seeming out of place at times, he was very alluring. Enchanting, even. It was kind of exciting. A stranger, a mysterious man who was watching me...*me*...as I went about my daily life. *He must be fascinated with me!* I would think to myself. And why not? I am a pretty fascinating person.

But then he had been right there, in the same place as me, and hadn't said a word. Hadn't even glanced in my direction.

I sighed. There went my source of excitement for a while.

The rest of the day was uneventful as usual. I spent eight hours (not counting my thirty minute lunch break) at a cash register, taking people's money in exchange for hours and hours of reading pleasure. I worked at a small bookstore and while I myself have always loved reading good books, selling them is not quite as thrilling. I had, however, considered more than once that I might like to own my very own bookstore someday.

That was my great ambition in life (if you could call it that), to own my own bookstore, own my own apartment, and maybe have a family someday. My boyfriend, Jake, was very ready to jump to that last part. He and I had been together for over three years. We met through mutual friends and really hit it off. We moved in together after dating for a couple years, and he talked marriage ever since. Usually it's the girl that scares the boy away with talk of commitment. But our relationship wasn't usual, I guess.

It wasn't that I didn't love Jake, because I did. But sometimes you need more than love – despite what John Lennon might say. I felt like Jake was my roommate rather than the love of my life. I wanted excitement; I wanted romance. The most exciting thing Jake and I had ever done was take a couple of rock climbing classes the year before with some friends. And last month he brought home a dozen roses and made dinner. That was really nice until he pulled out the box. Yep, the ring box. Before he could even open it and get down on one knee I ran to the bathroom claiming that I drank too much wine. I stayed in there over an hour. I even wondered if the bathtub might make a comfortable bed.

He tried a few times to get the marriage question out and I'm now an expert at finding just the right excuse for the moment. Once I even screamed that a woman outside was being mugged and beaten right in front of my eyes. I had to help her. Call the police for the love of God! Oh the injustice! Pretty sure he didn't buy it, but I ran out the door just the same.

I avoided him whenever possible that last month (which is hard to do when you live with someone) and he seemed to get the hint. I knew it was breaking his heart that I wasn't ready to marry him, but I couldn't say 'yes' to him just to keep him happy. That would make me miserable.

After work, Erika and I walked to a nearby pub for an end of the work day drink. We usually did that about once a week or so. The pub was pretty busy at that time of the day. Lots of business men and women were enjoying happy hour before heading home. Erika and I grabbed a small table in the back. We were further away from the noisy crowd making it easier to talk.

"Okay, Annie, admit it," she began once we were seated.

"Admit what?"

"You have been moping all day."

"I have not," I refuted.

"Have to, and I know why," she said slyly.

"What? Why?"

She smiled. "You're sad because he didn't talk to you."

"Who didn't talk to me?" I knew exactly who she meant, but I thought I should play dumb to throw her off the scent. She was a little too right on track.

She sat back in her chair, crossed her arms and said, "Your stalker. He didn't talk to you in the coffee shop and it has ruined your whole day, hasn't it?"

"What? You're crazy."

"Am I? Or am I absolutely correct? You wanted him to talk to you. You look for him almost everywhere we go. You kinda want him to be your knight in shining armor."

"Oh, shut up." I waved off her accusation. Correct or not.

She continued. "But what about poor Jake? He will be heartbroken." She frowned at me and put on her best sad face.

"Oh my gosh, Erika, stop it!" I threw a crumpled up napkin at her and we laughed.

"Okay, okay. But seriously, what's wrong with Jake? Why won't you say 'yes' to the guy?" she asked me.

I sighed heavily and said, "Nothing's with him. It's just…there aren't any…it's not…I don't know. It's not what I've been looking for, I guess."

"Well, if you're looking for Mr. Perfect, you will be looking for a really long time," she said.

"Yeah, I know. But I want to be with someone who I can't live without, you know? And someone who can't live without me. I want someone who wants to be near me as much as he can, and someone who I want to be near. But the thing with Jake is…well…seeing him for an hour every night before bed is really enough for me. And that's not passion. That's not real love, is it?"

"Annie, that doesn't sound good. Jake is ready to marry you tomorrow and you are talking like you are ready to end it today."

"No, I'm not. I'm not." The second time I was saying it more to myself than to Erika.

Then Erika leaned forward and looked me in the eye. "Annie, what's going on? What do you want?"

"I don't know. I want…" I shook my head. "I need to just stop complaining. I mean, I have a great life, great friends and family. I think I need a little more time to be…just me before I take the plunge and become someone's wife."

I looked at Erika and she didn't seem satisfied.

I told her, "I'm fine. I promise. But thank you for your concern. I really appreciate it."

She finally smiled at me and said, "That's what I'm here for. To look after my Annie."

We spent the rest of our time talking about work. As I listened to Erika, my mind wandered back to what she said earlier about my stalker. She was completely right, and that bothered me. It absolutely had ruined my day that he hadn't talked to me in the coffee shop. Part of me really thought he would. But why had I thought he would? And why had I wanted him to? I didn't have any idea who this guy was or if he really was following me. But there was something about him. Every time I saw him, it was like I was seeing someone that I had met before, but couldn't remember when or where. He was familiar. Somehow, I knew him.

"Well, since it's getting late and I'm pretty sure you stopped listening fifteen minutes ago, I should probably head home," said Erika, waking me up from my thoughts.

"Huh? Oh, no, I was totally listening," I lied.

"Uh huh, sure. Then what did I just say?" she asked.

"Umm, you were saying how you are the most wonderful and forgiving friend a person could ever have, and that I am so lucky to have you."

She laughed. "Close enough. Let's go."

Erika lived just between the pub and my apartment, so I walked her to her place first, before I walked the last few blocks home by myself. I tried really hard not to look for him on my way home. And I tried even harder to convince myself I didn't care.

I heard the TV on in the living room when I opened the front door to the apartment. I could tell by the program that was on that I was home later than usual. I had been walking a little more slowly recently. Even taking the long way home. You know, just taking in the sights, breathing in the fresh... well, breathing in the air of the city. Truth be told, I didn't want to give Jake much time to talk marriage before I could go to bed.

"Hey. I'm home," I called.

"Hey, babe," said Jake. "I brought home a pizza if you want any. Everything on it...except onions, of course."

"Thanks, sweetie. I'm starving."

We sat in front of the television and quietly ate our pizza together. I asked him about his day. He replied with the same answer I got almost every evening.

"My day was fine. I got some leads on some new clients, so that's good. Tyler said I should be up for a promotion soon." Tyler Freeman was Jake's boss at the accounting firm where he worked. Yes, Jake was an accountant. Thrilling.

I gave the same response I always did.

"That's great, sweetie. Maybe when you get that raise we can start saving for my bookstore."

"Yeah. Maybe so."

Then we watched the news, and after that I claimed major sleepiness and headed for the bedroom.

"Hey, Annie?" said Jake.

Uh-Oh. Here it comes. "Yeah? What's up?" I said.

"I talked to my mom today."

This was not going to end well. "Oh yeah?"

"Yeah. She told me that there is a two bedroom apartment opening up in her building and it's really spacious. There's an office area that we could turn into a playroom."

"We only need one bedroom. And I don't think you have enough toys to fill an entire playroom. Unless your Star Wars action figures count." This was my way of playing dumb and trying to turn this awkward situation into a moment of hilarity. It didn't work. Guess I'm not always as funny as I think I am.

"Well," he continued "I was thinking more for when there are three of us. Or even four."

"Are your parents moving in? Because I really don't think that's the best idea. Anyway, you like your parents even less than I do, so really--"

"Annie..." he sighed and dragged his hands down his face. "Annie, listen to me. When are we going to sit down and talk about our future?"

There it was.

"Jake, you know I love you, but I'm just--"

"No, Annie, I don't know that. Not anymore. Something's wrong. There's something you're not being honest with me about. Is there someone else?"

"Jake, there is nobody but you. I do love you. I just need more time. There are things I want to do before I get married."

"Like what? Buy your bookstore? Go on a European Cruise? Fly to the moon? How long do you expect me to wait?" He got off of the couch and walked to the window.

I sighed. "Can we talk about this tomorrow? I'm too tired. We are both tired and shouldn't have these conversations before bed. No one goes to sleep happy."

"Annie, I just...I just want us to be together forever." He turned from the window and looked at me. "I love you."

"I know, Jake. I love you, too." I crossed the room and gave him a kiss. "Goodnight."

Then I went into the bedroom, changed into some shorts and a tank top, and climbed into bed.

This was my life. Twenty - six year old Annie Watts. Works at bookstore, has aimless conversations with boyfriend, may or may not have mystery stalker, drinks coffee. Something would have to change...and soon...or, like Erika said, I would drive myself crazy.

I went to sleep that night thinking about my mystery stalker. I first noticed him about six months before. I had only seen him a few times that first month so I didn't think too much about it. But then I started seeing him weekly, in different places, and he was always looking right at me. But he seemed to stay far enough away that I would have to make quite an effort to confront him. I chose, instead, to make up stories about who he was and what he wanted. It was more fun and less creepy that way. And even though he hadn't taken his opportunity to talk to me earlier that day, I still couldn't help but feel like he was, in fact, watching me for some reason.

Thinking about that made me look forward to the next day. Would I see him again? Would he be watching me? Would he try to talk to me? What would I even do if he did? I imagined he might open by saying something like, "Hello. You are so fascinating that I just can't keep from following you around all day. Please will you run away with me to an island that I own because I have millions of dollars and want to spend all of them on you?" And my reply would be something like, "Well, sure!" And we lived happily ever after.

It was all well and good to ponder these things while lying safely in my bed, but I had to wonder. If I ever did meet him, would it be anything like I imagined?

Chapter 2

Wednesday morning started off bright and sunny. Jake had left a note for me on the kitchen counter before he left for work.

Sorry about last night. I just can't stand the thought of not being with you forever. Let's go out to dinner tonight. You pick the place.
Love you. Jake

I had already decided we would go to my favorite Thai food restaurant for dinner. Jake took me there on our first date. Nothing like going back to the beginning to rekindle a dwindling flame. I had heard that somewhere and it made some sense.

"Good morning, Erika." I greeted my friend as she closed the door to her building behind her.

"Hey," she said. "The sun is out today. That's nice. Now if only I were laying out on a beach instead of on my way to work."

"Well how about we find a puddle to lay next to? Strip down to our undies? Think we might get arrested?" I said.

"You are welcome to try, Annie. I think I'll just stand by and watch to see how it goes."

"Ah, maybe tomorrow. I don't feel like going to jail today."

"You do seem to be in high spirits. Had a good night last night?" she asked.

"No, actually, last night was terrible. But the sun is out today and I have a date tonight. Jake is taking me to my favorite restaurant. And you know how food makes me so happy." I grinned.

"Oh yes. I still have no idea how you are so thin with the way you eat."

"Good genes, my friend. Good genes."

We made our stop at the coffee shop, spent four hours selling books, took a quick lunch break at a sidewalk cafe down the street, and then four more hours at work. And not once did I glance around to search for my stalker.

Okay, that's a lie. I may have glanced a time or two...but that's all, I swear.

As Erika and I walked out the door of the bookstore to head back home, I tripped on a loose piece of sidewalk and took a nose dive towards the concrete. I caught myself with my hands (which hurt pretty badly) but was thankful I hadn't fallen on my face. As I picked myself up, I froze as I realized I was looking at a pair of black shoes standing right in front of me. Shoes that seemed too shiny for the dirty city sidewalks. I continued to gather myself up off the ground, all the while staring wide eyed at the familiar black slacks, long tailored coat, and the sea green scarf. I finally made my gaze turn up to his eyes...and whaddya know? His eyes matched the scarf.

    I was paralyzed in that moment. I was frozen and yet at the same time I was swimming in those sea green eyes. The bright sun was beaming down on me while I butterfly stroked my way through his warm green gaze.

    "Annie? Annie? Annie!" I heard Erika calling my name from somewhere far away. It took a while for me to realize she was standing right next to me.

    "Wha...what? Yeah. I'm here." I still wouldn't look away from the man in front of me. Not even sure I could if I tried. Erika grabbed my arm and pulled me towards her, away from the stranger, and that helped yank me out of my trance...literally.

    "Annie, let's go," she said in as demanding a voice as she could manage. I looked at her and then back at the stranger. This was the moment I had thought about dozens, no, hundreds of times. My mystery stalker, the man who was, no doubt, fascinated with me, was right there. I couldn't just walk away. But what should I do? What should I say? Should I run away and forget about it?

    I didn't have a chance to do or say anything (or run for that matter) before he spoke to me.

    "You have been looking for me, Annie. So here I am. Are you happy I have come?"

I blinked a few times. "What? That's not what you're supposed to say."

He cocked his head to one side. "I am sorry. What is it I am supposed to say?"

I flinched. *This isn't one of your imaginary conversations, Annie. This is real. Pull it together.* "Nothing. I... Hey, how do you know my name?"

"I know a lot about you, Annie Watts. And I have decided that it is time we finally meet." He held out his hand. "So, shall we go?"

I reached for his hand when I thought better of it and pulled it back. "No. I mean, where? Where are we going? No, I'm not going anywhere with you. I don't even know who you are."

He smiled at me then. A smile that could only be described as mischievous...and I liked it. "My name is Rali. And I think you, Annie, are one of the most beautiful creatures I have ever seen. And quite fascinating."

I knew it.

"Thanks, um...Rali, was it? Like, Raleigh, North Carolina?" I tried not to look him in the eyes for fear of losing all self-control.

"Yes. Sounds exactly the same," he said.

"So, Rali, you said something about me looking for you?"

"Yes. You have been looking for me," he answered.

"Right. Wrong. I mean, that's not what's happening here. See, you've been stalking me for quite a while now," I said. "I haven't been looking for you."

He looked confused. "Did you not look for me this morning on your way to work?" he asked. "Did you not glance my way several times at the coffee shop?"

And I thought I had been so smooth.

"Do you not look for my face in passers-by? Do you not constantly search the skies hoping that I will come and take you away?"

"How do you know I was looking for you? Maybe I was looking for someone else. My boyfriend, maybe." He chuckled at this suggestion. I continued, "And anyway, you started it. You were looking for me first." Not my most mature moment. "So don't stand there and tell me that I... Wait, what?" The last thing he said had just registered. "What does looking at the sky have to do with you? How do you know why I look...I mean...I'm not searching for you in the sky. That's ridiculous. Who does that?" I laughed nervously and looked at Erika. She rolled her eyes.

"Well, Annie, I am sorry to hear that. I had hoped that you might come willingly," he said.

"Come willingly? Where? Where are you trying to take me? And just knowing your name doesn't mean I trust you. I still don't know you." This was not at all going as I imagined it might while lying in bed the night before. Which was quite disappointing.

Erika jumped in. "I'm so sorry, sir, but we need to get going. It was very nice to meet you." She grabbed my arm and pulled me away from my stalker (who now had a name...Rali).

I began to move in Erika's direction, her hand still around my arm, when a powerful force pulled me back in the other direction. It felt like an airplane door had just been opened at thirty thousand feet, and I was being sucked towards the opening. I didn't have time to react or fight against it. It happened so quickly. I was smashed against him so suddenly. He wrapped me in his arms. But this was no loving embrace. I was being taken. But not taken into a getaway car or taken at gunpoint. No, we launched straight up into the air as if thrusters were attached to our feet. I watched Erika get knocked to the ground by the force of it all and the next thing I knew, I was looking down at her from ten feet above...then twenty...then forty...and then I couldn't see her at all. I was rocketing through the sky so quickly that I couldn't make out anything below me. I was above the clouds with nothing to hold on to except Rali. At that moment I pondered whether it would be better for me to try to wriggle out of his grip and fall to my death (not that I could) or just hang on for dear life. I was trembling so much I feared Rali may lose his grip on me before I could decide. But soon, I saw a bright light ahead of us. *This must be what death is. Rali is the angel of death and he is taking me to heaven...hopefully.* The bright light spread out across the darkness of space like a blanket, and as soon as we entered it...everything went black.

    The rumors are true. Before you die, your life flashes before your eyes. I saw myself as a little girl, running around the backyard of our tiny house in Guthrie, Oklahoma in my pink bathing suit. I jumped back and forth through the sprinkler while my mom and dad watched and laughed. I ran to my mom and grabbed her hand, pulling her towards the spraying water. She fought me but just barely. I always won with my mom.
    As the memory of the three of us laughing in the yard began to fade, I saw myself as a young teenager. I was sitting on the living room floor with my little sister who must have been about nine years old. She was crying. I was trying to explain to her that when someone dies, they don't ever get to come back to us. We never get to play with them or hug them

again. When someone dies, they leave us forever. Then I saw my mom, dressed all in black, come pick up my sister and carry her away, looking at me with sad, disappointed eyes as she left. All my family members had come to our house. There was my aunt, my two older cousins, and my dad's parents. Yes, I remembered. This was after my dad's funeral.

As that scene went dark, I saw a blurry shape begin to form. It was a building...what building...I couldn't quite see it yet...there it was...the library at the university in New York where I spent most of my time as a college student. I could see myself through a window, nose in a book, no one else around. The light in the library was so dim except for the lamp on my small table. Another person was there in the library now...a man...standing behind me. But who was it? I couldn't remember. One of my professors? No. It wasn't. This man was standing so close to me. Why didn't the girl in my memory sense him? The man turned away from her...and toward me. Outside the window looking in. I knew this man. And he knew me. He had been watching me for a long time. The man I saw in my memory...was Rali.

I woke up coughing on a hard, cold floor. I wasn't dead, though my lungs wouldn't fill with air fast enough and anytime I could manage to get a breath, my body quickly coughed it back out. I rolled onto my back and tried to relax. I took slow, shallow breaths to try to re-teach my body how to breathe. My eyes couldn't focus on anything. It was so bright. I couldn't tell if I was inside or outside. It was warm, but I could feel a cool breeze coming from somewhere. I must be in an abandoned house, I thought, or somewhere inside, next to a window. I tried to remember what had just happened. I had been at work, then Erika and I left. I fell. I was talking to someone, and then I was here.

But where is here? My eyes starting working again, slowly but surely. There were two people standing over me, looking down at me. I heard them talking about someone named Annie...oh, that was me. Then I heard another voice which was familiar to me. It was soothing. It was comfortable. Where was it coming from? I studied the faces above me as they came into focus. I didn't recognize either of them. I heard that voice again.

"Annie? Annie. You are all right. You will feel weak for a little while. But you will soon regain your strength," said the soothing voice.

"What? Where am I? What happened?" I asked the voice.

The voice replied, "You are with me, on Idonea."

"Ida who? And who is 'me'? Who are you?" I asked between slow breaths.

He chuckled before answering, "It is me, Rali. I have brought you to my home."

I lay still, allowing my vision to recover before looking around. When I was able to focus, I sat up slowly. I saw him standing with that same smile he had shown me earlier. Only this time I didn't like it so much. He was no longer a distant stalker I fantasized about, but a real life abductor.

He wore different clothes. He was wearing a long silver vest made of...was that metal? Underneath was a long-sleeved, black-linen shirt. His pants were still black, but this time they were leather. He wore a matching black leather belt around the waist of his vest. And black shiny boots. He seemed to prefer his shoes to be clean and sparkling.

"You. I remember you. Rali. You were there, right? You were there on the sidewalk. Is that where we were? It was you I was talking to when Erika...Erika?" I looked around frantically and didn't see my friend anywhere. In fact I didn't see anything familiar...not even remotely. I was in a small building with long open windows which were allowing the sunlight to pour onto the floor. The floor itself seemed to be made of gold. The door, like the floor, must have been made of gold. There was a large round opening in the ceiling above me which bathed the room in dazzling light. The warm rays of the sun bounced off every surface and made the whole room sparkle. It was radiant. It was magical. It was...not New York.

I tried getting on my feet a little too quickly and ended up back on the slick, cold floor. The two people who had been standing over me grabbed my arms to help me up. As soon as I was on my feet and standing on my own, I turned to face my abductor.

"Where are we?" I asked in as strong a voice as I could muster.

"I told you," he answered. "We are on Idonea. This is my home."

"Idonea? Where is that? Somewhere in the Mediterranean? How did you get me here? How long have I been gone from home? How do I get back?" I asked, my body shaking from fright.

"Idonea is my home. It is far from New York, not even close to the Mediterranean. I carried you here. You have been gone for about twenty minutes Earth time. And to answer your last question...you do not get back."

"What? Wait...what do you mean 'Earth time'? Time is the same everywhere."

"Not here," said Rali.

"Here, where?"

"On Idonea."

"Yeah, I got that. But if I've only been gone for twenty minutes, I can't be far from home. Right? So you can easily take me back. So let's get going." I was on the verge of either crying, fighting, or screaming for my mommy.

There was that chuckle again. Then Rali said "I cannot and will not take you back. We are not close to your home."

"But you said we have been gone only twenty minutes. Are we still in the City? If you take me back now, I won't even call the cops. Just...let's go. Come on." I tried sounding confident to hide the growing terror inside me.

"Annie, we are not in the City. We are not even on Earth. We are on Ido--"

"Oh my gosh, if you say it one more time I'm gonna do something really mean…and bad." Where was my college - level vocabulary when I needed it?

"Listen, Rali, I don't know what your problem is, but you can't keep me here. It's…it's illegal. It's kidnapping. You could get arrested." That'd scare him. "Okay, I am walking out this door and calling the police from the first phone I see. And you'd better not dare try and stop me." I hoped the fierceness and the growly tone of my voice would convince him that he really shouldn't mess with all one hundred and thirty pounds of me.

I walked carefully towards the door. He didn't move. I stared directly at him as I put my hand on the doorknob. He stared right back. I turned the doorknob, still watching to see if he made any move to stop me. I opened the door to freedom, dug in my heels and off I went...SMACK into the hardest man - shaped wall that I had ever encountered. I rubbed my poor nose and backed away from the person in front of me. He was tall (over seven feet for sure), he was broad (as broad as 5th

Avenue), and he was strong. The worst part was that there were about twelve of him. And they were all wearing gold colored armor and carrying swords in their belts. They were the most beautiful and frightening thing I had ever seen in my life. I backed away from the doorway as the small army of men marched in single file and surrounded the inside of the room. Then, as if commanded by the same inner voice, they all drew their swords and pointed them at me. Well that was about all I could take. I ran as quickly as I could back to Rali and dove behind him. I wrapped my arms around him tightly and held him against me as a shield.

    If they were gonna kill me they'd have to take him down, too.

Chapter 3

With my head plastered against his back, I felt his laugh before I actually heard it. Why did Rali think my impending doom was funny? I sure didn't. I peeled myself off of him and tried not to notice how rock solid his body was.

I failed miserably.

"Annie, they are the Royal Bodyguards. They are not here to hurt you. In fact, they are here to protect you."

"What? Then why do they want to stab me with their swords?" I looked at the army and they were returning their swords to their belts.

"They are merely saluting you. Giving you their respect as their possible future queen," he informed me.

"They have a funny way of showing it. Next time try saying 'Hey, we salute you and you have our respect.'" I suggested. "And what's this about future queen?"

"You have been brought here to be considered as a candidate to marry the king and become the next queen of Idonea. But it is not set in stone. There are others who--"

"Ok, wait wait wait. Back up the truck," I interjected.

"Truck? What truck? I see no truck." Rali looked around confused.

I shook my head. "Nothing. There's no truck. It's an expression, just...never mind. Okay, listen. Here's what I know so far. You grabbed me, we flew through the air, I woke up here, I am attacked by your Bodyguards--"

"They were saluting--"

"Whatever. Anyway, then you tell me I'm supposed to marry some guy I've never met and be the queen of wherever I am? Is that right? Did I miss anything, Rali?"

"You may be queen of 'wherever I am', also known as Idonea. There are others who desperately desire to be queen. You will have to be much more appealing to the king than they are."

I stared at him for a really long time. I was so confused. But I was even more angry. I didn't know what to say. What could I say? "What in the world are you talking about? What is going on? Where am I? And if you say 'Idonea' one more time, I swear--"

"Annie, Annie," he jumped in. "Calm down. Let me explain. You have been brought here so that you may begin a new life in a new place. This place is called Idonea. We are not on Earth anymore. I have brought you to a new planet, far from your own. This is your chance to build a new life, possibly as the queen. You will love it here, Annie. But you have to give it a chance. Let me show you around."

I just about fainted. "You mean I'm not...You're seriously trying to tell me that we are on a different planet?" Should I laugh or cry? "But...how is that possible?"

"I will explain it all later. Right now I would like to show you your new home. Or would you prefer it if I took you to your room in the palace where you will be staying?" asked Rali.

My legs started to shake and Rali caught my arm as I started to fall. "I don't understand," I said.

"Here, Annie. Let me take you to your room. You should rest."

"No, I...I can't really be here. I must be dreaming. That's it. I'm having a nightmare," I said as I removed my arm from Rali's grip.

Then, to show me that I was, in fact, not dreaming, Rali pinched my arm.

"Ow!" I retaliated by shoving his arm away. *Oh wow, that is one lean, muscular arm.* I thought maybe I should shove him again just to make my point clearer, but before I could, he said, "Come, Annie. You should get some rest. It has been a big day for you."

I stood as tall as I could. "No, you are taking me straight to the king. There is no way he is going to keep me here. He wasted his time having you come and fetch me for him. Come on. To the king!"

Rali stared at me as if he couldn't believe I was ordering him around. He was probably fascinated by my command of authority. I grabbed his arm (yes, I had found another way to touch his arm again) and started pulling him towards the door. Of course Rali couldn't take me back home. The king had commanded him to go to Earth and bring me back. Rali would only take me to Earth if the king commanded it. And I was going to make sure he did. Somehow.

We headed towards the door and the bodyguards followed. As soon as I stepped outside that building I knew Rali had been telling the truth. I was not on Earth anymore. Besides the overwhelming beauty I saw in front of me, I noticed two small suns in the sky. I was pretty sure Earth just had one. No wonder it was so bright here. To the left of me I saw a silvery blue river gently flowing downstream. On the right were tall leafy trees which created a forest where some creatures that looked an awful lot like deer were grazing. Colorful birds of all sizes flew through the air above me.

This was paradise. Maybe I actually had died and gone to Heaven. I looked up ahead of me and saw what I figured must be the Kingdom of Idonea. From that distance I could see many small buildings and houses along a winding path that led to what had to be the palace.

The palace itself seemed out of place. The buildings and houses could have been lifted right out of a fairytale. They looked quaint and from long, long ago. The palace, however, rose high above the kingdom and seemed transported from a time way in the future. It was the color of the sunlight and sparkled radiantly. I was mad at myself for how desperately I wanted to see inside it.

"Well, Rali, lead the way," I said. And Rali obeyed. We started towards the kingdom. I decided I would use this time to get as much information from Rali as I could. I needed to know what I was up against.

"So," I began, "What is the king's name? What do the people call him?"

"King Valiar is what 'the people' call him. 'Your Highness' and 'My King' are also acceptable. His friends and close servants, however, call him something else," he answered.

"I'll stick with King Valiar, thanks. I have no desire to be a close friend of his. Is he a good king? Is he kind? Is he reasonable?"

"Depends on who you ask," he said.

"I'm asking you," I said quickly.

"Well then, I would say he is a very good king. And kind to those who are kind to him," he said with a grin.

"Of course you would say that. You must be a very loyal errand boy to him." That was my way of trying to insult him. I hadn't forgotten that it was Rali who actually physically abducted me and took me from my home. Not the king, even if it was his idea.

Rali only laughed at my comment. I was trying to insult him and he laughed at me. He was getting more and more aggravating by the minute.

"How long has this king been the king?" I continued.

"About twelve years now. The previous king died and left his son to rule. That is how it has been since the formation of this kingdom."

"I'll confess, I thought that you were a king when I woke up and saw you standing there."

Rali chuckled. "You think the king of all of this would leave it just to bring you here? That sounds risky."

"I said I 'thought'. Past tense."

He nodded and I continued my questioning.

"So when did this kingdom come into being?" I asked.

"Over a thousand years have passed since then. There were not as many Idoneans then as there are now. We have grown."

"That tends to happen," I said.

"Yes. I suppose it does. They were eager to fill this planet with people." He smiled and looked sideways at me. I ignored him.

"Well, the king sure has a nice place here. Can't deny that."

"He will be pleased that you approve of your new home," said Rali.

"This is not my new home. The king will send me back to my home. He has to."

"Well don't tell him that. This king does not usually feel like being generous to those who demand things of him like that."

All right, this was good. I was getting tips. What else could Rali tell me?

"How should I ask him? Should I start crying and begging? Or should I try bargaining? What could I trade, anyway? Does he like shoes? I could offer my shoes. I don't like wearing shoes anyway. Too uncomfortable. But these are awfully nice. They could be a gift for his new queen. They're Blahniks. My mom got them for me. I would never spend that kind of money on shoes. Or maybe I should threaten him. I took a kickboxing class once."

Rali smiled as I rambled. If I wasn't so angry at this man I would find that smile incredibly attractive. But I was angry at him. So nope, no attraction at all.

After I finished talking, Rali said, "I think you should be yourself. Make your case before the king however you think best."

We continued walking in silence. I gave up trying to get information from him. Instead I took in the sights. I wanted to be able to describe this place in detail when I got back to my own planet.

The King

As we approached the gates to the kingdom I felt a little nervous. What if the king denied my request to be sent back home? Impossible. Why would he want to keep me here? I didn't want to be here. I didn't want to be his queen. And apparently he had women dying to marry him. Surely he would rather pick one of them. And he would probably be annoyed with Rali for throwing a wrench like me into the works. There was no way he wouldn't let me go back to Earth. Nope. I would be heading home in less than an hour, I was sure of it.

Pretty sure.

We walked through the gates and there were the little buildings and cottages that I had seen from far away. They were all very simple but cozy looking. They were side by side with little space in between. I spotted large yards with green grass and colorful gardens behind some of the cottages. The small buildings themselves were made mostly of brick and stone, though a few were built with logs. Some of the cottages were far enough apart that I could catch glimpses of the silvery river and a low grey stone wall built along the opposite side of the water. Above us, there were wooden signs hanging over shop doors advertising their various goods. As we passed by them, they rocked and squeaked in the breeze. I glanced in some of the windows which displayed what the stores had to offer.

Then there were the people. So many people walking up and down the streets. But it was nothing like the city where I was from. These people walked slowly, as if they had all the time in the world. Their world, not mine. Many were walking while holding hands with another and looking in shop windows. Others were standing in groups, talking and laughing. They wore clothes that fit the scene. The women wore long simple dresses that looked handmade and comfortable. The men were in baggy trousers and loose tunics. It was a happy sight. In fact it almost made me forget about my important mission.

     Almost. I looked around at all these pleasant looking villagers and then one by one, they noticed me and my entourage. Some quickly bowed, others seemed too confused to do anything at first, but finally ended up bowing like the others. Wow, I guess they had been told their (maybe) future queen was coming today. I liked this way of showing respect much more than the way the bodyguards had done it. I smiled politely at those that made eye contact but tried to stay focused on my mission. To convince the king to let me go home.

     It took us about fifteen minutes to walk from the gates of the kingdom to the palace. And what a sight. I strained my neck looking all the way to the top. Large balconies jutted from the sides of the palace. The outside walls were decorated with intertwining gold and silver latticework. Guards stood at the entrance and bowed as we entered. I was trying not to act like a tourist, but at the same time I wished I had my camera with me. When we stepped inside, I was pretty sure I had just walked into a room the size of Texas. Ivory columns spanned from floor to ceiling (which seemed to be about forty feet high).

     Then I saw the people walking around in the palace. These people were not like the villagers. These people were dressed in much fancier clothes and glittering with wealth. Jewels sparkled from the ladies' throats and ears. Hair was piled on top of their heads with small ornaments placed here and there. They walked with their heads high. They were beautiful and they knew it. The whole place (including the people) sparkled. It was amazing. If only I wanted to be there.

     But I didn't. This was not my home.

     On with the mission.

Rali led me and the bodyguards up a small flight of stairs off of this main entry room. At the top of the stairs were three sets of doors with lights above them.

"Are these elevators?" I asked Rali.

"They are much like your elevators on Earth, yes. Only ours do not run on wires and cables. It is called a lyptra. You will find many things similar to Earth here, and even more things that are not," he answered.

We got on one of the lyptras (well, Rali and I and only a few of the guards...there was only so much space) and Rali punched a button. I never felt the thing move and was about to complain to Rali about the importance of hustle when suddenly the doors to the lyptra opened and we were on a different floor.

"How did that happen? I didn't even feel it start moving," I said.

"As I said, there are many things here that are not as they are on your planet," he said. A little too smugly for my taste.

I followed Rali out of the lyptra and we walked down a long hallway that curved consistently to the left. As if reading my mind, Rali told me "Everything in the palace is placed around an inner column. The hallways twist around it. You could take a stroll from the first floor, all the way to the top without ever climbing a step."

"That sounds exhausting." I didn't want him to think for a second that I thought this place was the most beautiful and interesting place I had ever been. I didn't want to give my kidnapper any satisfaction, whatsoever. "So, are we almost there? Are we going to the king's room? Will he be with other people? How should I approach him?"

I kept asking Rali these questions as we walked and I noticed that all the beautiful people we were passing would stop and bow just like the villagers. They must have heard about me, too. Then I heard one of these people say, "Good day, Your Highness," as we passed.

Wow. They were already calling me "Your Highness"? That was a little presumptive, I thought.

And then it hit me. I stopped walking. I slammed on my brakes. "Oh...oh no. No no no." I turned slowly and looked Rali right in the eyes.

"Rali, I asked you earlier about what to call the king and you said 'King Valiar', right?" *I have to be wrong. I just have to be wrong.*

"Yes, I did," he said.

"Then you said something about what his friends call him, right?" *No, it could not be true.*

"Yes, I did," he repeated.

"So… What do the king's friends call him?" *Please don't be true, please don't be true. Please let me be wrong.*

"Well, Annie. My friends call me Rali."

Chapter 4

"You liar!" I screamed at Rali. "How dare you lie to me like this?"

As if that wasn't enough to cause a scene, I shoved him in the chest – which had no effect - and kicked at his shins with my aforementioned Blahniks. My arms were grabbed from behind and I was held back by one of the Royal Bodyguards. But he only had my arms. I continued kicking in Rali's direction even though I was about five feet away from him at that point.

"I did not lie to you," he said calmly. "Why are you angry with me? I thought you might be pleased."

"'Pleased'? Really? 'Pleased'? You must think very highly of yourself. Ha! I'm not 'pleased' at all. Send me back! I want to see my family." And that is when I finally stopped kicking. I was getting quite tired and I was too mad to keep kicking the air anyway. If he would just move a few feet closer...

"Guards, we will take her to her room. Please keep a good hold on her, Ivarr. She's feisty." He flashed that mischievous grin and I hated him at that moment.

I was led (or dragged, really) to my new room in the palace. Rali opened the door when we got to the room and I was tossed inside. Rali came in after me and the guards stayed in the hallway. He walked towards me.

"Don't you dare come near me. After all, I am 'feisty'. You never know what I might do," I threatened.

"You mean like slap me in the chest? Or kick at my knees? Really, Annie. Threatening violence is not your best option here," he laughed.

"It doesn't seem that I have any options, Your Royal Highness."

"Oh, Annie. We are close now. Please call me Rali as you have been."

"We are not close. We will never be close. You have taken me from my home. Away from everything and everyone I know and love. You made me think the king might let me go back home. You gave me that hope knowing the whole time that it wasn't true. You knew I would not be given that chance. That is cruel, Rali," I said.

"Ah, so you will still call me Rali after all. I am glad." He smiled.

I grabbed the closest thing I could find, which turned out to be a statuette of some type of bird, and threw it at him as hard as I could. It headed straight for his forehead but he dodged it easily. It shattered into pieces as it hit the wall behind him.

It was quiet for a moment. The only sound was my heavy breathing. I needed to calm down. I had to continue fighting or else I knew I would break down and cry. I couldn't show him weakness. I saw a short bench to my right and sat down. I just needed to catch my breath before I ran at him full speed and knocked him down. That was my next plan. It was brilliant, I know. I didn't have a chance to try it, though, before he started toward the door.

"I will leave you for now. You need to rest. You have had a bit of a shock, I am sure. I hope you will find that what I am offering you is everything you have ever wanted." He walked through the door and turned back to face me. "You were right, Annie. There is more to life. This is it. Here, on Idonea."

Then he closed the door behind him. I waited only a minute before going to see if it was locked. It wasn't. But it might as well have been. There were two bodyguards stationed right outside.

I wasn't going anywhere.

I spent the next ten minutes pacing in front of the door, muttering curse words under my breath. And I do not use curse words on a regular basis. The best I can do is the word 'dam'. And even then, if I ever I say it, I have to picture it in my mind spelled without an 'n' to make it not an actual bad word. My father had told me when I was a little girl that any time he heard someone curse, they just sounded a little less intelligent to him. I only ever wanted my daddy to think the best of me so I made it a point never to curse. Even after he died. So the fact that I was, at this time, using actual curse words, indicates just how mad I was.

This man, Rali, had taken me from my home, he had given me hope and then crushed it. And then he sat back while I made a fool of myself asking about the king, and the whole time, it was him. Rali was the king of Idonea. And he had brought me here to marry him - excuse me - to maybe marry him. Well, surely he could choose one of the women from his own planet who adored him. I would just have to be as unappealing as I possibly could.

It would be hard, but I was up for the challenge.

But what then? What if he did choose someone else? Would he let me go home at that point? Why would he need to keep me around then? I pondered these thoughts when I looked out the room's only window. Both of the suns had set. The indigo tapestry of sky was dotted with thousands of brilliant white diamonds. I had never seen so many stars at once. As I stood there I counted six shooting stars. Nearer than any of the glittering stars was a small glowing red orb. I wondered what it could be. Behind me I saw the gigantic bed near the open balcony doors and I went over to lie down and rest. I didn't even make it under the covers before I fell into a deep sleep.

I dreamed of my father. I often did. He was carrying me on his shoulders. I must've been about five years old. We were at the pond near our house and we were going to feed the ducks. He put me down on the grass and gave me a slice of bread for the ducks. As we threw our pieces of bread, my father was telling me stories. He always told me great stories. He had such an imagination. While my father was talking, one of the ducks began running towards me and flapping its wings. I was scared and ran into my father's arms. He picked me up and rubbed my back saying "It's okay, Annie. I've got you. I will never let anything hurt you, ever." I grabbed my daddy's face in my little five - year old hands and said "Daddy, I will never let anything hurt you, either, okay?" Then he smiled and hugged me tight.

And then I woke up.

The sun was shining into the room and lighting up everything it touched. I must've slept all night...however long that was. I sat up in my bed and looked around. No, it hadn't been a nightmare. I was still here, on Idonea.

The door to my room was still closed. To my right was the large balcony with long sheer sky blue drapes hanging down at the entry. I sat in a spacious room with a couch, two overstuffed chairs with ottomans, a small table, the bench I had rested on when I first arrived, and the end of the massive bed. There were two doors besides the one I had entered through. I got up and opened one of them to find a luxurious bathroom with a spacious bathtub and a shower the size of my bedroom back home. There was also a large vanity mirror with lights all around it and a bench in front of it. I walked out of the bathroom and headed for the other door, but when I put my hand on the doorknob, I realized it was being turned from the other side.

I jumped back, grabbed a lamp off a table next to the wall and prepared to strike. Maybe it was Rali and I could knock him out and run past him. Run to where, exactly? No time to think about that, the door was opening. I held the lamp up high ready to swing, when a petite woman walked through.

She saw me with the lamp and screamed. Then we both just stood there, me holding the lamp, she with her mouth open and eyes wide. She held both hands up in front of her in a sign of surrender. We stared at each other for a long moment before she finally spoke.

"You are Annie, yes? I am Freya. Please, will you put down the lamp? I mean you no harm. I have come to help," she said.

"Help? Yes, I could use your help." I put down the lamp. "Freya, I need you to help me get out. Can you help me get back home?"

She stared at me blankly, so I started to repeat what I had said.

"Freya, listen, I need you to tell me how to get back home. How do I --"

She interrupted, "No, My Lady. I am not here to help you leave. The king will not allow it. I am your lady-in-waiting. I am here to help you get accustomed to our kingdom. Shall we get dressed?"

"What? But that's not..." I trailed off.

I don't know why it had taken this long for me to break down. Maybe I had been too mad to cry earlier, or maybe I had been in shock. But at that moment, having that little woman tell me so matter-of-factly that I couldn't leave was the last straw. I crumpled to the floor as if the bones in my legs had been melted. I put my hands over my face, curled up into a ball and sobbed.

I was alone, on a strange planet, far from home and everyone I loved. There seemed to be no way for me to escape, and Rali, the man I had once fantasized about taking me to his far off land, had done just that. Only it turned out, that wasn't what I wanted. I wanted my boring life back. I wanted my mom, my sister, Erika, and Jake. I wanted to be back at the bookstore, back in my apartment, back in my own bed. But I would never see any of those things again. I knew it.

And I sobbed.

Chapter 5

    Freya let me cry. She didn't try to talk to me or comfort me with lies like, it will be all right. Everything will be okay. I think maybe she was too smart to try that. Maybe she knew I needed to cry and get it all out.
    I cried for the loss of my mom. I cried for the loss of my best friend. I cried for the loss of my boyfriend. And I cried simply out of the loneliness I felt in this new land. I laid on the floor for a long time. An hour? Maybe more? And finally when I had no more tears to cry, I got to my feet, looked around the room, and thought to myself, *this is my room. This is where I live. This is my new life.*

"Are you better now, My Lady?" asked Freya. She sat in a chair in the corner while I wept.

"Yes," I answered. I knew it wasn't true, but I was too numb to say anything else.

"Perhaps I shall draw you a warm bath. That always helps me when I am feeling down. Would you like that?" she asked.

"Yes."

I followed Freya into the large bathroom and sat down on the bench while she prepared the bath. I watched as she added some salts and flower petals to the running water. She did it so tenderly, so carefully. She smiled and hummed to herself the whole time she was preparing the bath. I studied her while she worked. She looked like she was maybe in her late fifties. She had dark, tanned skin, long dark hair that probably fell below her waist, but I couldn't tell since she had wrapped it up into a neat knot right above her neck. She was very thin and small. I would have been surprised if she even made five feet. It was calming to watch her work.

While I listened to her soft humming, I looked around the bathroom and thought to myself, *this is my bathroom. This is my lady-in-waiting. This is my new life.*

Freya turned off the bathwater after the tub was filled. Steam came off the top of the water, and the whole room smelled like lavender and vanilla. I rose from the bench and began to undress. Freya politely turned her head away until I was completely in the water. She stayed in the bathroom with me the whole time. I'm sure she had been ordered to watch me at all times to make sure I didn't try to off myself. She didn't need to worry about that, though. I was too dazed to try anything that drastic.

I laid in the warm, fragrant water and thought, *this is my new life. This is my new life.* Maybe if I repeated it enough in my head, I would learn to be okay with that fact, though I knew it wouldn't work that way.

    I sighed loudly, too loudly, I guess. Freya looked at me and said, "I hope you do not mind me saying, My Lady, but I really do hope you give your new home a chance. It is a beautiful place to live. And you get to live in the palace and possibly be the queen. I think that is something to be happy about. Do you not agree?"

    I didn't reply. I knew she was trying to help, but I didn't care. I didn't care about anything.

    "When you are finished with your bath, we will get you dressed. Then I can show you around your new home a bit. Would you like that?" she asked.

    I wished people would stop calling this place my home. It wasn't. My home was far away, and I would never see it again. I stayed silent and hoped she would stop talking. She didn't.

    "My Lady, we do not know each other well, yet. I know this must all be strange and foreign to you. Please, let me help you in any way I can."

    I still did not reply. I was empty. I had nothing to say, nothing I could say to make her or myself feel better. So why waste my breath?

    Freya seemed to get the hint and stayed quiet after that.

    I soaked in the warm water until my toes and fingers were nice and pruny. Then Freya handed me a robe and I wrapped myself in it. It was so soft. So luxurious. I stayed in the robe and walked out of the bathroom and into the bedroom. I went straight back to the bed, climbed in and pulled the covers up to my chin. I planned to stay there all day, all night...maybe all week. I didn't want to get dressed, or even move for that matter. I just wanted to lay there and not think about where I was, or where I would never be again. I wanted to not think about my mom and how much she loved me. I wanted to not think about my friends...or about Jake. Oh, Jake. He had loved me even when I made it hard for him. And I wanted to not think about my future bookstore, having coffee with Erika, calling my little sister on the phone at least three times a week...

It turned out I hadn't been out of tears. They came back in full force. I couldn't stop them. I was no longer numb to what was happening to me. I felt sad. I felt angry. I felt hopeless. I lay under the covers in my bathrobe and sobbed for a second time. Freya took her seat on the chair in the corner and waited for me to run out of tears again. I was sorry that she had been given the job of being my lady-in-waiting. How depressing...and boring. All I could do was lay around and cry.

Yes, I was pitiful. But I couldn't help it. My life had been stolen. How many times had I been at home, lying awake in bed, dreaming about a life somewhere else? Hundreds of times. How many times had I felt sorry for myself because of the boring life I led? Thousands of times. How many times had I searched the skies hoping that a different life awaited me out there? Too many to count. And yet when it actually happened, all I wanted was to go back to how it had been before.

As I laid there crying, I heard the door to my room open and close. I was hoping Freya had finally left me alone, but I wasn't that lucky. As soon as I heard his voice, my tears stopped, and my anger began to build.

"Hello, Freya. How is our new tenant?" asked Rali.

"Well, Your Highness, she is tired from her journey. And I think she is a bit unhappy. But I am sure she will feel better after she rests," she answered.

"Unhappy? Why should she feel unhappy? I have given her the greatest opportunity. Does she not see that?"

I knew he was addressing Freya, but I was too angry to keep my mouth shut.

"No, Sir, I don't see this great opportunity." I sat up in the bed. He looked surprised, and a bit concerned by my tear-streaked face. "I see only that I have been kidnapped by you. Yes, you have kidnapped me. I was not given a choice in the matter. So don't act surprised if I don't fall to the ground, kiss your feet, and thank you every time I see you. Now, get out and leave me alone." I turned away and lay back down. I hoped to hear his hasty retreat. Instead he spoke.

"I only did what you wanted, whether you will admit it or not. You were not happy on Earth. Yes, you have family there, but you can also have a family here. You think you had love there, but that was not love. Admit it, Annie. You do not love Jake. You never did. Why have you hesitated to give him the marriage he has wanted? Would you do that if you really loved him? Be honest with yourself and you will see--"

"I said, get out!" I didn't turn to look at him this time. I couldn't. I didn't want him to see any acknowledgement of truth in my face. I didn't want him to see that what he had said about Jake was...

No, it wasn't true. I did love Jake. And I wouldn't let Rali tell me otherwise. I wouldn't let him tell me anything, ever again. I didn't want to see him, or talk to him again. I wanted him to walk out of the room, and never come back. I listened for his footsteps and after a minute or so, I finally heard him leave the room. My teeth were clenched and my hands balled into tight fists. That man infuriated me. My life had been stolen. It had been taken from me without even asking. And who did I have to blame for it?

Rali. The mighty king himself—that man who had infiltrated my dreams now infiltrated my life. He had taken it upon himself to make life-changing decisions for me. What made him think he had the right to do that? Just because he was king on this planet did not mean he could rule my life. And then for him to tell me how I felt about Jake? Unacceptable. No, I was no longer numb. Not at all. I was no longer sad. Not one bit. I was furious at Rali. I was not going to let him make any more decisions for me. I was going to get out of here. I wasn't yet sure how exactly, but I was going to get back home. I had gone from Earth to Idonea, there had to be a way to make the return trip.

    I didn't know how long it might take me, but I was going to find out how Rali got me here, and I was going to go back—without his consent, without his help, and without his knowledge. I had work to do. And I couldn't very well do it wearing a bathrobe. It was time to get dressed.

Chapter 6

"Freya," I sat up in the bed and looked for my lady-in-waiting, "Freya? I'm ready to get dressed," I told her.

"Oh good, My Lady. Let me help you. I will show you to your wardrobe."

Freya practically jumped out of her chair and was across the room in seconds. She must have been excited for something to do rather than listen to my sobs. I watched as she walked to what looked like an ordinary wall. But she placed her hand carefully on one spot and the wall lit up around her hand. Then I heard a soft beep and the wall slid open. I had to admit, that was pretty cool. I got out of bed and walked to the secret opening. Freya must have read my thoughts as I approached. "The women here at court are very protective of their dresses and special outfits," she said. "Every room has a secret panel just for the purpose of holding those items. You and I are the only two people who can open this panel in your room. See here on the wall where there is a slight indentation? When you place the palm of your hand there, it will read it, and the door will open."

"Wow. All of this just because the women don't want their clothes taken?" I asked.

"Well, not so much taken as being copied. Every lady here at court has their own lady-in-waiting who also designs and makes their outfits. It is like a contest every day to see who is the best dressed." She had started to smile and then quickly stopped herself. "Now, I speak a little forwardly, forgive me. Not everyone here feels that way about their appearance, please do not think that. But sadly, most of the women care only about how they appear to the men. Especially..." she trailed off.

"Especially to the king," I finished for her. "Sure. Makes sense."

Great. So not only was I stuck in a place I didn't want to be, but I was surrounded by women who were shallow, and would be judging me by my appearance every time they saw me. Good thing I didn't care. All I cared about was getting home.

"So does that mean you made all of the clothes that are in here?" I asked Freya.

"Yes, My Lady, I did. And I would like you to know that I took care in choosing just the right fabrics and designs for you. I was given only a little information about you before you came, but I tried to make outfits that would suit you." She smiled at me nervously and then waved her hand towards the hanging clothes, inviting me to peruse them.

I glanced at the amazing array of clothing I saw inside the wardrobe, in categories both familiar to me, and unfamiliar. There were dresses of sparkling white, royal purple, deep red, bright yellow, light pink, coal grey, and more. Next to each dress were garments that looked like cardigans, only they were much more delicate...some made entirely of lace. There were also some folded items that looked more my speed. They were mostly black or grey and included some plain cotton shirts and pants. I really appreciated that Freya had included some comfortable items.

"Freya, these are beautiful. I'm sure I will be the envy of every woman here when I wear these." I thought a kind word for Freya wouldn't hurt. I needed a friend or two. I needed friends who could provide me with information on how to get back home. Not that I intended to use Freya. But I needed any kind of help I could get.

"Thank you, My Lady. I worked very hard to make them beautiful for you. I am glad you like them. Now, which would you like to wear today?" she asked me.

I wanted to grab a pair of the black pants and a black shirt, but I knew she wouldn't approve. Also, I needed to make an effort to fit in here. I couldn't give anyone, especially Rali, any indication that I was trying to get home. If I did, I was afraid he might go to extremes to be sure I didn't go anywhere. So, I inspected some of the less glamorous dresses and chose a simple...well, relatively simple, cobalt blue dress. It was strapless, made of a soft cotton blend and flowed straight down to the floor. There was one of those fancy cardigans hanging next to it and Freya gently removed it from the hanger. I slipped the blue dress on over my head. It fit perfectly...so perfectly. Then Freya slipped the lacy silver cardigan on...backwards? No, I was wrong, this wasn't a simple cardigan.

"This is called a feela," said Freya. "Every woman at court wears these over their dresses. It is considered improper to show too much...um...skin."

"Then why aren't the dresses made to be more conservative to begin with?" I asked.

"Well, some women do wear higher necks and longer sleeves, but that has gone out of fashion with the younger ladies. They prefer the much more showy feela. It is sort of like an accessory to the dress," she answered.

"So you weren't kidding when you said it's a contest every day," I joked.

She laughed. "No, I was quite serious. But please do not tell anyone I said anything like that. I am already not..."

Freya trailed off and then stopped talking completely. She walked around behind me to fasten the feela in the back. I couldn't see her face anymore, but I had heard a sadness in her voice while she talked.

"Freya? Are you okay? What were you saying? You are 'already not' what?" I asked. Freya did not answer at first. She just finished fastening my garment and then stood in front of me to inspect her work.

"What's wrong, Freya? I won't tell anyone what you said. I promise. Why would anyone care anyway?"

Freya sighed, and then spoke. "My Lady, I will tell you. You should know the truth about your lady-in-waiting."

She paused for a long while and I started to think she had actually decided not to tell me anything when she finally started to speak.

"I have worked in the palace as a lady-in-waiting for twenty-five years all together now. When I first came here, I was one of seven ladies for the queen herself."

"Do you mean Rali's mother?" I asked.

"Yes. Her name was Emla. She was so beautiful, and so kind. His Highness has her eyes, you know." Freya smiled as she spoke of the past queen. "Emla was admired by everyone in the kingdom, but especially by her husband. Oh, it would've melted anyone's heart to see them together. Theirs was a rare union. They were inseparable. It just broke her heart when he died."

Freya looked down and was quiet for a moment before she continued.

"Well, after her husband, the king, died, many women at court began to groom their daughters --if they had one about the right age--for his highness, King Valiar. As it happened, most of the other ladies-in-waiting did have a daughter or two that were around the young king's age...myself included."

"Freya, you have a daughter?" I asked.

"I had a daughter, yes. Her name was Katrin." Freya beamed. "I had her when I was very young. She had dark hair, like myself, and dark eyes. She was a happy girl. She was not like the others. I did not raise her to care about what was on the outside of a person, but on the inside. She did not have great ambitions to be queen, though I wouldn't have minded it. She loved being with the people. Most of her friends were not courtiers, but people in the village. She spent most of her time in the village, with the children. She was a teacher to some of them. They loved her as I did."

Freya's smile began to fade as she continued.

"The other ladies of the queen did not like that my daughter was different from theirs. They didn't want anything to set her apart--cause her to be more noticed by the young king than their own daughters. They would never have admitted it, but they were jealous. Jealous of her joy, her life, her happiness...

The King

"Well, they decided I had to go. In shaming me, they thought my daughter would also be shamed, and therefore, not attractive to the king. So they put one of the queen's most treasured necklaces in a drawer in my room. It was one of her favorites that her husband had given to her. Then they went to the queen and told her that they had seen me take it. The guards were sent to search my room and there they found it. I knew I hadn't taken it, my daughter knew I hadn't taken it...and I suspect the queen knew it as well. But she had no choice. It was either make me leave my position as her lady-in-waiting, or keep me and lose support from most of the courtiers."

"Why would that be such a big deal? She was the queen. Why did she need support from them?" I asked.

"Here in Idonea, while we do have a monarchy, it is almost always the people at court who run the kingdom. If a king or queen goes against the majority of the courtiers, well, they lose their support in many ways, but most importantly, they lose financial support. Every kingdom and country needs money to make itself function. No king or queen wants to be responsible for such a great loss. Or even a rebellion. This place has seen enough of that. It would be troubling for the kingdom, but also for them. They could be overturned. A new king and queen could be chosen. But that has not happened for a very long time." She paused for a moment and had me sit at the vanity in the bathroom while she fixed my hair.

"So what happened after the necklace was found in your room?"

"I was asked politely to gather my things and leave the palace, so I took a few belongings, and Katrin and I moved into a small cottage in the village. She did not mind in the least. She was sad for me that I had to leave my queen, but she always told me we were better off with the people in the village. I did miss the queen, but enjoyed being with my daughter. I only wish I had had more time to be with her."

Freya's voice became a little softer as she continued. "Katrin became ill quite suddenly. She was here and then a week later, she was gone. They couldn't save her." Freya stopped brushing my hair and stood still for a moment.

"I'm very sorry, Freya. It must be horrible to lose a child," I said.

"Thank you, My Lady. I weep for her still, though it was almost four years ago." She continued brushing my hair and we were both quiet for a few minutes.

"Freya, the queen made you leave, but you are back now. How did that happen?" I asked.

She smiled. "After my daughter died, King Valiar found a place for me here as a seamstress. He had remembered my service to his mother. She had spoken of me fondly to her son. She had told him many times how she missed me and was sad about how things had worked out. My new job as seamstress did not involve making clothes for the courtiers or anything like that. There are still many here who do not like me even though the threat of my daughter no longer exists..." she paused. "Anyway, a few weeks ago, the king found a new position for me. A new visitor, you My Lady, would be coming to our kingdom and would need the utmost care in getting accustomed to our ways. So I accepted. I did miss being a lady-in-waiting. The excitement, the beautiful clothes... I was ready to welcome you to our kingdom."

I smiled at her in the mirror. This poor woman had been through so much. Betrayed by the other ladies, banished from court, and then…to lose her daughter! It was tragic. And then she managed to pull herself together and come back to court to serve me. And she was happy to do it. I couldn't help but feel a little special.

"I'm glad you came back," I said.

"Oh yes, so am I." She smiled at me. "I would not have been able to refuse King Valiar, whatever his request. He has been such a good king these past years. King Valiar is very just, very brave...and very handsome."

I didn't like the grin she aimed at me.

"He is handsome...a very handsome liar." *Oops.* I hadn't meant to say that last part out loud.

"My Lady, please," said Freya. "You must try to look past that."

What? Look past the fact that he had, in fact, stolen me from my home? My family and friends? Wasn't gonna happen.

"Sorry, Freya. You're right. I'll try." I was going to have to do a better job of hiding my bitterness toward Rali. He was king here. While I didn't plan to go overboard with praises for him, I couldn't let anyone know my real feelings. My real intentions.

"Well, My Lady, what do you think?" Freya motioned towards my reflection in the mirror. She had dressed my hair simply, thank goodness. But it was appealing as she had made one small braid on one side and draped it in and out of a loose knot at the nape of my neck.

"Perfect, Freya. Thank you."

I walked back to the bedroom and found the full length mirror. My blue dress fit snugly along my torso and fell loose to the floor. The lacy silver feela was also fitted right to me. It had a high neckline and the sleeves went just to my elbow. The bottom of it came just above my waistline. I looked...good. I mean, wow! I looked really good.

"You are a miracle worker, Freya." I said.

She laughed. "I am no miracle worker. You gave me a very good foundation to start with."

"So, where are we off to today?" I asked her.

"Let's start with the courtyard, shall we?"

I draped my arm through hers, and she led the way out of the bedroom. It was time to begin my research.

Chapter 7

As we walked through palace hallways and rode down to the courtyards on the lyptra, I began making a mental list of what I needed to do while I was here. The main objective was, of course, getting back home. But in order to do that, I needed to accomplish other tasks.

1. Learn all I could about how I physically got to Idonea.
2. Find out if I could get home by myself, and if not, find out who I needed to help me.
3. Figure out how to get past any guards.
4. Keep my plan to myself.

Having Freya show me around would definitely help me find out where guards were stationed and how observant they were. The problem was, since I was the new visitor, I was pretty much going to be watched wherever I went. Just going to the courtyards outside the palace was quite an ordeal. People stared at me as if I had fireworks shooting out of the top of my head. I just liked thinking it was because of how spectacular I looked, not because I was new and strange. Maybe it was a bit of both.

I had noticed guards at every entrance to the palace, and some walking in pairs down the hallways. There were no guards at the entrances to the lyptras, and very few in the courtyards, and those guards stayed near the palace doors.

"Isn't it beautiful, My Lady?"

I turned towards Freya and pretended I had been admiring the palace grounds the whole time. Instead of assessing the best escape route.

"Oh, yes," I said. "Just lovely." Once I actually looked around, I really did agree with what she had said. The courtyards extended about fifty yards in front of the palace; and as we made our way around to the back, I noticed they were even larger there. The flowers that were growing there all had very large blooms with bold colors. Bright reds, yellows, and oranges seemed to flow off the stems at all different heights, creating a cascading effect. There were many pathways formed by short hedges leading in between the bright flowers and there were benches placed here and there. It would have been a great place to sit and read a book...if there had been any shade. Having two suns in the sky must've made it harder to create much shade. I followed one of the pathways and looked around me as I strolled. A small creek ran through the courtyard, and some gold and white fish were swimming in the clear water. Their fins sparkled along the edges as if dipped in gold flakes. Tall hedges obstructed my view, and I couldn't see down to the village. I would have to find a reason to visit the village sometime. It had seemed like such a charming and happy place when I passed through it the day before. And perhaps Freya would show me where she used to live.

I wandered the gardens surrounding the palace. Freya gave me some distance, but stayed within sight. I did not see many courtiers in the gardens, and the few that I did see did not try to approach me--and I was fine with that. I had just discovered a pretty bubbling little waterfall in the creek when Freya called me over to where she was examining one of the flowers, so I headed towards her. She was standing near the palace wall and gently holding a group of white flowers in her hand.

"This one has fallen off but still is pretty. Here, let me put it in your hair, My Lady."

As she delicately placed the petals in my hair, she continued talking. "This was my queen's favorite flower. It is called syringa. There are many blossoms on one stem. She found that very intriguing. She would say that just as this flower wears many blooms, so can a person wear many faces."

That's interesting, I thought to myself.

"There you go, My Lady," said Freya as she finished fastening the flower in my hair.

"Thank you, Freya. And please, you can call me Annie."

"If that is what you wish," she said.

"It is," I said with a smile.

"Alright then...Annie. Where shall we go next?" she asked.

"Honestly, Freya, I have no idea. You know this place, what would you like to show me?"

"Well, My La...I mean, Annie," she smiled at me and continued, "What is something you normally enjoy doing? What kinds of things did you do when you were..." She grew silent. She knew she shouldn't bring up the subject of my home. But she didn't do it on purpose, she was trying to help, so I was not offended.

"Freya, it's okay. At home, I liked to read. I liked to sit outside on a nice day with a good book and read for hours...with a cup of coffee." Just thinking about that made me smile. And also miss my home.

"Coffee? Oh, yes, coffee...we do not have that here," she informed me.

"No coffee? I may not survive," I joked…kind of.

She laughed. "But I can show you something I think you might like. Come with me."

She reached for my arm and led me through one of the rear entrances to the palace. One guard on each side of the door...got it. Freya and I got back on one of the lyptras and she punched a button. I decided I was going to have to learn to work one of these things. I added it to my mental list.

5. Learn to run the lyptras.

When the doors opened, Freya led me out and to the right. There were a few courtiers headed our way so we stepped aside to let them pass. As they brushed past us, I saw my beautiful flower petals get swept out of my hair and land on the floor near my feet. I bent down to pick them up as a man reached them first.

"Such a shame. These flowers no longer get to frame such a beautiful face," he said. He straightened up at the same time I did.

"Hello," he said.

"Hello," I said back.

Geez, was everybody on this planet gorgeous? The man in front of me was lean, muscular, and tall. He had short, dark blond hair that was combed away from his face. A few strands, however, had come free and were resting just above his eyes. His eyes...they were dark blue, like sapphires and, well…dreamy. He had a square jaw covered by just a bit of stubble, like he had forgotten to shave that morning. I stared at him like a giddy school girl.

"My name is Durin," he said. "And you are...?"

He had full lips and I could see his straight white teeth when he talked. Oh! Did he just ask me a question? What did he say?

"Um...what?" Ugh, I was so awkward.

He laughed and then repeated, "I am Durin. Who might you be?"

"Oh, me…I'm Annie."

"It's nice to meet you, Annie. So, are you *the* Annie I've heard so much about?" he asked.

"That depends, I guess. Have you heard good things or bad things?"

He laughed again. I was glad he thought I was joking. It was a little less awkward that way.

"Well, Annie, I have heard that you came here from Earth and that you are quite beautiful. I can only assume the first is true until you confirm the fact, but I can see very plainly that the second is quite accurate." He smiled again and my knees just about gave out.

"Thank you, Durin. I am from Earth, though I didn't come here as much as I was brought here," I tried to hide the bitterness in my voice. I don't think I did a very good job.

"Well, even if it was not your idea, I do hope you find things that bring you joy while you are here. Perhaps you might even make some good friends among us."

"I, uh...hope I do. Thank you," I replied.

Freya walked over to us. "Yes, we all hope she likes it here. Come on, My Lady, we must go. I have ordered lunch to be served in your room. We don't want it to get cold." She took my arm and led me away from my new acquaintance... though I left a bit reluctantly.

As we walked away I heard Durin say, "I will see you again soon, I hope."

I tried to reply but he was walking in the opposite direction. I turned my eyes back towards the direction I was heading.

"Don't you think you were a bit short with him, Freya?"

"My Lady, I...I didn't mean to be rude. I just think that...well, maybe you should..."

"What, Freya?"

"Lunch will be getting cold." That was all she said and I could tell she didn't want to say more. I tried to figure out why she seemed upset about my talking to Durin. The only thing I could figure was that she expected and wanted me to marry Rali. So I shouldn't be fraternizing with any other men. Made sense. Didn't mean I had to agree with her, though.

As we made our way back to my room, I went back over my 'to do' list. I had made a little bit of progress on number three, finding out about where guards were stationed, so I made a note of that. And then I added another thing to my list.

6. Find out more about Durin...for research purposes, of course.

The King

We made it back to my room without any further incidents. I walked in, expecting lunch waiting for me, but saw no trays or any food.

"Freya? I thought you said my lunch was getting cold."

She shrugged. "Well, maybe they are late in bringing it to you. That can happen sometimes."

She didn't look me in the eye when she spoke.

"Freya, you said you had something to show me that I might like. Where were we going? And then why did you say we needed to get back to my room for a lunch that is not here?" I was getting suspicious. Freya stayed silent. My suspicions were confirmed that she had made up a story to get me away from anyone who might distract me from the king. That just frustrated me to no end. Not only was Rali keeping me here against my will, but my maid was in on this whole scheme with him. I shook my head. I had to get out of here.

"Fine, Freya. You don't have to explain why you lied to me. It's no big deal, really. I get it. However, I am getting hungry and wouldn't mind having that lunch that you claimed would be here."

"Yes, My Lady," she said and walked out the door without saying another word.

I wandered over to the balcony that I had yet to set foot on since I had gotten there. It was a large balcony off one side of the palace. From it I could see out to the village. It was a much larger village than I had originally thought. Apparently the palace was situated on the edge of the kingdom. From my balcony I could see the gates where I had come in, but I could also see the kingdom spreading out in the other direction. It really was a magnificent view. Lots of little cottages and shops were all crammed together next to winding pathways, but as the kingdom went further out the houses grew bigger and were set on larger pieces of land. And were those crops I saw growing? Were those cows I saw grazing? There were farms here! Well, it made sense, I guess. The Idoneans had to eat.

As I stood there staring out into this new world, I heard the bedroom door open and in came my lunch on a silver platter. I walked over, realizing just how hungry I was, and was so happy to see a roasted chicken with potatoes and carrots. Normal food. I admit I had been a little worried that since I was on a strange planet I would be eating strange food. Like a slimy fish with four eyes or something. But this lunch looked delicious. And I ate it in about three minutes.

When I was done I walked over to the bed and laid down. I hadn't intended to fall asleep, but I did. It was a dreamless sleep. It was a restful sleep. Something I had needed badly.

When Freya came through the door a couple of hours later, it woke me up. I opened my eyes and watched her walk in softly and head towards the secret closet. I sat up in bed and watched as she opened the closet and inspected a few of the fancier dresses.

"What's up, Freya?" I asked.

She looked at me and said, "Up? What do you mean what is up?" She looked up at the ceiling.

"No, I didn't mean..." I sighed. I was going to have to be careful about using Earth expressions. "I meant to ask what you were doing."

"Oh, I am deciding which dress will be best for the ball tomorrow night," she said.

"The ball? What ball?"

"Oh, the ball. The one that is held to introduce the eligible ladies to the king and courtiers. It is the event that begins the whole thing. Yes, after the king is formally introduced to the young maidens that wish to marry him, then begins the courting period."

"...I'm sorry, what?" I was dumbfounded.

"Yes, the courting period. When the king and the eligible ladies spend time getting to know one another. It can seem a bit unnecessary since the king has known most of the ladies for years. Anyway, during this period, the king will meet with the ladies all together at times; but if he wishes, he can single one out to get to know...a little better."

You could have knocked me over with a feather.

"You mean Rali is going to 'meet'...how many women are we talking about?"

"Around thirty or so."

"Thirty? Wow. Okay. So he is going to meet all these women, that he already knows, and then spend some 'getting to know you' time with a few special ones, and then he will decide who he will marry?"

"Yes. Usually there are only three or four that are seriously considered, but the king will do his best to show attention to as many as he can. You know, to keep the courtiers happy," said Freya.

As she was describing this royal procedure, I was thinking about all the nights I sat watching a certain "reality" television show that sounded like pretty much the same thing. Erika and I constantly made fun of the people on that show and what fools they made of themselves to win the heart of the man who must have been so very desperate for a girlfriend.

Imagine if they were also competing to be a queen...

"You've got to be kidding me," was all I could say. "Is this how things have always been done here?"

"Oh, yes. This has always been deemed to be the best way by both the kings of Idonea, and the people," she answered.

"Well, geez. So, tomorrow night, I have to stand up in front of all these courtiers and 'meet' the king? Show myself as an 'eligible lady' who desires only to be his wife and the next queen? Seriously?"

"Yes." She nodded her head and didn't seem to understand why I couldn't grasp this information.

"Oh, dear Lord." I fell back onto the bed and thought about what the next night held for me. Getting all dolled up, being formally introduced to the man who had brought me here against my will, having the whole kingdom scrutinize me, and the whole time, having to pretend I'm not trying to figure out the best way to get out of here and get back home. It was going to be hard, it was going to be exhausting...but apparently, it had to be done.

Freya walked over to the bed, and smiled. "Do not worry, Annie. I will be there with you. And you never know. You might just have a good time."

I highly doubted that.

Chapter 8

The rest of the afternoon was spent with Freya instructing me on some Idonean traditions, rules, and manners in order to prepare me for the ball the next evening. The more things she told me, the less I wanted to go...which was hard to believe since I hadn't wanted to go at all in the first place.

"And you must remember that when the king asks you to dance, you will accept...with a smile on your face." Freya looked up at me from her chair where she was adding a few finishing touches to the dress she had chosen for me to wear to the ball.

"Yes, ma'am," I sighed. I walked over to the balcony so I could look over the kingdom while Freya continued her instructions. I looked down at the village and wondered about the people who lived there. Were they happy? They had looked that way when I had seen them the day before. Did they envy the beautiful, glamorous courtiers? *I wonder...*

I thought about Freya's daughter, Katrin, who had preferred the village to the palace. I wondered if Katrin and I would have been friends. If she had still been alive, would she have been where I was? Preparing for the ball the next evening? Preparing to be courted by the king and competing to become his queen? Would she have hated the prospect as much as I did?

I must have been completely lost in my own thoughts. I hadn't even heard him come in.

"This is a pretty nice place I have here, wouldn't you say?" he asked as he walked up behind me. "Oh, that is right, you already did say that."

I turned to face Rali. "Should I bow when you grace me with your presence, Your Highness? I'm afraid I don't know all your customs, yet."

He stopped where he was, only a few feet from me, and seemed to be inspecting my face. "Most people would hear what you just said and appreciate your show of respect and your desire to learn more about the kingdom," he said and then paused.

"I am guessing you are not 'most people'?" I ventured.

"No, I am not. I can recognize sarcasm. You are dripping with it." He walked up to where I was, put both hands on the balcony railing and looked out over his kingdom. I returned to my previous spot and did the same. We stood there in silence for a few minutes, admiring the beautiful scene before us. I sneaked a few sideways glances at this man, at my abductor. Standing right next to him I could tell he was about a foot taller than me. I was about five foot four, so that would put him well over six feet. His black hair reached almost to his shoulders and was gently blowing in the breeze. His lips, while not as...voluminous as Durin's, were still quite ample. His eyes...well, I still tried not to look into those eyes. I didn't want to feel any sort of attraction to this man. Not anymore. Not ever. I looked away from him and back out to the land. I tried to figure out which direction I would need to go once I got out of the palace. I was just making out the small pathway we had taken from that first building when he spoke.

"There's something I would like to show you. If you would let me."

"What is it?" I asked Rali.

"Something that I think will help you feel more at home here." He smiled at me, but it was not his usual mischievous grin. This time there was no joking behind it.

I walked back inside the room, away from Rali. "I think I should stay in my room. Freya has been teaching me about your customs, and I'm sure we have a lot more to go over." I did not want to be alone with this man. He was a liar, he was a thief, and I wouldn't let him try to win me over the way I was sure he had done with all the other women he knew. Not that he could. I was not like them.

"Freya," he asked, "would it be all right with you if I stole your lady from you for a little while?"

"Ha!" I laughed. "Not the best choice of words. You already stole me once, why not again, huh?"

He sighed, closed his eyes and rubbed his temples. Annie Watts, trying peoples' patience all over the universe!

"Very well then. Freya, may I borrow your lady for a little while? I promise to bring her back." He looked at me while he was addressing Freya and then cocked his head as if to ask me if I approved of the word change. I avoided his gaze.

Freya answered him, "Your Highness has my permission." Then she turned to me, "My Lady...remember your manners."

Everyone was against me.

I sighed. "Fine. Let's go."

"Please do try to contain your excitement. Your enthusiasm makes you seem needy," said Rali as we headed towards the door.

"Oh, I would just die if the king were to find me unattractive in any way. I live for his acceptance." I walked past him, opened the door and stepped into the hallway. There were the guards, assigned to watch my every move I was sure. I waited for Rali to catch up and said, "Where to?"

"This way, please." He held out his arm to the left and began walking in that direction. I starting following behind him and then decided to quicken my pace and walk next to him instead. I was not his servant. I was not one of his admiring courtiers who longed for his attention. No, I was Anne Watts, and I would be subservient to no one.

The problem was, he knew where we were going. I didn't. Whenever we turned left, I had to speed up a bit to keep pace, but if we turned right, we bumped into each other.

Walking on principle isn't always easy.

After a few hallways, a ride down on the lyptra, another hallway, a few turns, and a few bumps, we stopped in front of a relatively plain-looking door. It was not as large as most of the doors I had seen in the palace, and not nearly as ornate. But when Rali opened the door, I stepped in and gasped. It was a library. One enormous room full of thousands of books. Hundreds of thousands. I walked in a little further and spun in a slow circle in order to see the whole room. The walls had shelves full of books, from the floor to the ceiling, which was about fifty feet high. There were also some shelves in the middle of the room, that rose about twenty feet in the air, and they were also crammed with books. I just stared at this place, mouth open, eyes wide, and said nothing.

"What do you think of my library?" Rali asked.

"I think...it's amazing."

"Good. I hoped you would feel that way. I am very proud of the Royal Library. Though it is not as grand as it once was, I am working on restoring it to its former glory." He walked over to where I was standing and continued. "There used to be many more books. The Royal Library was not only housed in this room, but the two on either side, as well. There were glorious murals painted on the walls and on the ceilings. One of the rooms had long tables and benches where people could sit and read." He looked around as if remembering what it used to look like. "Yes, it was grand."

"What happened?" I was immediately mad at myself for caring.

"Unfortunately, the palace was attacked over twenty-five years ago. Most of the rooms on this floor were burned and badly damaged, including the library. It was a great loss. No one was hurt in the fire, but we lost much of our recorded history. What we have left is now kept in a much...safer place."

This raised so many questions in my head, but I was determined not to care. "Who would attack the palace? Is it not just your kingdom here on this planet?" ...okay, not that determined.

"It is only my kingdom here on *this* planet--"

"What? You mean there are other inhabited planets I don't know about?" Of course. Why not? I hadn't known about this one.

"There is a smaller planet that is close—too close, really--to Idonea. It is called Helgrind. It means 'gates of hell'."

"Sounds lovely," I quipped.

He laughed. "It is quite horrible...and hot."

Made sense.

"Is Helgrind that glowing red ball in the sky I can see from my balcony?"

He nodded. "The planet of Helgrind is inhabited by the Hyrokkin. They are the people of fire. They eat, breathe, and speak fire. They have only to touch you and you will burn. They know nothing but hatred and destruction. Their world is a place of suffering, a place of despair. They are an angry, vengeful people...and they hate all of us on Idonea."

"Why?" I asked.

"Well...we sent them there in the first place. They used to be just like us. They were Idoneans."

"Ah. Well, I would probably be mad then, too."

He chuckled.

"Why were they sent to that awful place?"

"They were criminals. A long time ago, about a hundred years after the beginning of Idonea, fights broke out in the village constantly, murders were an everyday occurrence, and theft was rampant. There were not enough prisons to hold them; not enough guards to protect the people. A decision was made by the king that the criminals must be sent away from Idonea. The king and his council knew there was a neighboring planet that was reachable by ship, so those who had committed crimes against fellow Idoneans were rounded up one by one and shipped away. After living there for so long, the people began to change. They no longer resembled the people they had once been. Living on the planet of fire...transformed them."

"Did the king know what that planet was like when he sent them there?" I asked.

He sighed. "Yes. He did. But what I do not know is if his intention was for them to survive there...or to die. And I do not know which is worse."

We stood silently for a moment. I didn't like thinking about those people living on a planet that seemed so hot, hopeless and miserable. Rali must have noticed the downward direction our conversation had taken and changed the subject.

"Anyway, Annie, I just wanted to bring you here, to a place I thought you might enjoy. I want you to feel free to come here at any time and read whatever you like." He smiled at me.

I looked around at the walls full of books and wondered how they had all gotten there. I walked towards one of the bookshelves and took a book in my hands. *Jane Eyre*. I smiled and tears welled up in my eyes. I had read this book many times at home. My mother had given it to me when I was fifteen years old. I had her to thank for my love of reading.

Rali walked over to see which book I was holding.

"This is a good one," I told him. "In fact it is my mother's second favorite book of all time. She loved it so much that she named my little sister 'Jane'."

"Ah. Her second favorite? What is her favorite?"

I looked up at him, smiled and said, "Anne of Green Gables."

He looked at me then, but he didn't smile. He just looked at me as if he was considering what he should say next. But instead of saying anything, he turned and walked towards a different bookshelf. I put *Jane Eyre* back on the shelf and looked to see what else was there.

"Is there any sort of catalogue for this library? What kind of order are the books in?" I asked him.

"There is no catalogue except what is in my head. There is still a lot of work to be done to restore this place. What are you looking for and I will tell you if we have it."

Again, I didn't want to seem too interested or even look like I was happy that he had shown me this place. But since I would be spending some time there, I wanted to know which books I could read while I endured my stay in Idonea... however short it would be.

"I like all the books by Jane Austen. I read *Pride and Prejudice* at least once every year. Do you have any of those?"

He walked to the end of one of the bookshelves in the middle of the room, stopped, scanned the row for a moment, and then came back carrying three books by Ms. Austen. I took them from him eagerly....but I did not thank him, because I didn't care and was not grateful. Then I asked him about *Anne of Green Gables* and he said he was sorry but he did not have that one. I told him it didn't matter. I really only enjoyed reading the copy my mother had given me, anyway. She had written on the inside cover of it, "To my Annie. May you love this book as I do. And may you find your 'kindred spirit'. I love you. Mom."

"'Kindred spirit'?" he asked.

"You'd have to read the book, I guess."

"I see."

I walked past him with my nose high in the air and continued looking through the books on the shelves. I saw a lot of familiar authors and titles, and many that were unfamiliar. Most of the books were in English, or some form of it, and there were some in French, German, and even some in Chinese. I was marveling at the large collection and variety of books held here when something occurred to me. And then I wondered why I hadn't thought to ask him this earlier.

"Rali?"

"Yes?"

"Where did all these books come from? I mean, most of them are in English, some in other languages, but all languages from Earth."

"Most of these books are from Earth, so, yes, they would be in those languages," Rali answered.

"Yes, but why aren't there any in some strange alien words? And on that same note, why does everyone here speak English?"

"Well, most speak English, some speak German, and some speak a kind of mixture of both."

"No, I mean...you're not getting me, here. I'm on a different planet, with people not from Earth. Shouldn't you all be speaking in beeps and squawks and unintelligible noises or something?"

He stared at me, obviously not following what I was saying...like I was speaking in beeps and squawks. And then understanding fell over his face and he began to laugh. He laughed quietly at first, and then his laugh grew a little louder and a little louder until it became almost uncontrollable. I was trying to figure out what was so funny when he finally calmed himself down. Had he just wiped a tear from his eye?

"Annie, you are priceless," he said. "Now that I understand your question, I will give you an answer. The reason we speak 'Earth' language, is because we are from Earth. That is the original home of the first people of Idonea."

Okay...what?

"Explain," I said - or more accurately - demanded.

"Yes, Annie, the first people to come to this planet came here from Earth. That was about a thousand years ago."

"But how did they get here?" I asked.

"The same way you did. Pretty much. You see, while many people on Earth were just beginning their civilizations, my people-my ancestors-had begun theirs long before and were quite advanced. They had discovered a way to travel through space while most others on Earth were still struggling to travel over water. When this far away planet was discovered here by my ancestors, they decided to begin a new world."

He stopped talking then and leaned back against a table as if what he had said had just explained everything I could ever want to know.

It hadn't.

"Okay, but why? Why leave Earth? And how many people came? And why did my history books in school not mention any of this? Didn't anyone notice they had disappeared?"

"Well, I think they had done all they could do on Earth. I think they were looking for something...something more, you know?"

I did know. I had also been looking for something more. And here it was. I sighed. But they had chosen to come here. I hadn't.

I was about to continue my line of questioning when a guard came rushing in the room.

"Your Highness, you are needed in the council chambers immediately."

"What is wrong?" he asked the guard.

"There has been another sighting, much closer to the palace than last time."

"Yes, tell them I am on my way," he said to the guard. Then he turned to me and said, "I am sorry, Annie, I must go. Please stay here as long as you like. I will have one of the

Royal Guards stay and take you back to your room when you are ready."

And then he hurried out with the guard.

I was left standing alone in the spacious library with many unanswered questions.

I grabbed a few books, walked into the hallway where the Royal Guard was waiting, and was led back to my room.

The rest of the evening was spent in my room with Freya. I ate my dinner there (lamb with rice and asparagus) and read from one of the books I had borrowed from the Royal Library. I also went over my mental checklist and realized that, even though I had learned some about the history of Idonea, I was not any closer to getting back home. I needed to focus. I told myself that the next morning, I would do more research. Maybe Freya would have some information about how people got to and from this planet. But would she figure out why I was asking? I would have to be clever about how I asked. Maybe there would be a book in the library about it. I would have to find my way back there and dig through some of those shelves on my own. I couldn't very well ask Rali to show me the books that described how I could get back home...if such a book existed. I had a lot to do and I was going to have to do it while being "courted" by the man I needed to get away from.

But in the meantime, I was going to put on some comfortable clothes, and crawl into bed with a book. There wasn't anything I could do at that very moment to escape so I was going to enjoy myself for that one moment.

"But only this once," I told myself.

Chapter 9

When I got out of bed the next morning, I made a plan. I would go back to the library and search for books that could give me information about how to get home. Then I would go from there and get any more information I could from Freya. I also thought I might meet some useful people at the ball I was being forced to attend. I tried to look at that event as an opportunity for intelligence gathering, rather than as a parade of desperate women.

Freya was already in my room when I got up. She was folding towels to be put back into the bathroom. I saw a silver tray on a table near the door and walked over to it, assuming my breakfast was on it. My stomach started growling as I approached the tray. But there was not any food on it. Instead there was a book. *Anne of Green Gables*. It looked like the same version of the book I had had at home. I picked it up. Yes, it was so similar, even looked as though it had been read hundreds of times. Before I even opened it to look at the inside of the front cover, I already knew what I would see. There it was, my mother's handwriting. This wasn't just like my book, it *was* my book. But how did it get here?

"The king brought you a present this morning, but you were still sleeping. I told him to leave it on the table...oh, I see you have found it," said Freya.

"Umm...yes. I did. Rali brought this? Here? Where did he get it? How did he get it?"

"Oh, I do not know. I did not ask him. Why? What is it, may I ask?"

"It's a book from my home. I told him about it yesterday. But how did he get it here?"

"Ah, so that is who left on the Bridge last night," she said. Then she smiled as she went back to her work.

The Bridge? Was that how I had gotten here? Had Rali gone to Earth just to get my book for me? I was hoping I could ask Freya these things without making her too suspicious.

"Freya, what is the Bridge?"

"The Bridge is the transportation used between Idonea and Earth. It is how you came here with the king," she told me.

"Ah. And Rali can just...hitch a ride on it whenever he wants to? How does he do that?"

She looked at me for a long moment before she continued. "He is the king and he knows how to use the Bridge. There are only a few who know how. It is a powerful thing, I know that much. I am sure I will never understand it. Nor would I ever want to. There is no need for people like us to know how it works. For we will never need to use it."

That was about as much information as I would get from Freya. She didn't know how to run the Bridge, and even if she had, I was sure she would never tell me.

"Was it just the book that the king brought for you? I was sure he had left something else, as well." She walked over to where I was standing near the door. "Ah, yes. Here we are." She bent down and picked up a box off the floor that was sitting next to the table. She handed it to me. There was a note on the top that said,

> *Annie, I hope these things will help you feel more at home here.*
> *I will see you tonight. Enjoy.*
> *Rali*

I opened up the box - I could smell it before I even got the box completely opened - coffee. And a coffee maker. He had brought me the book that held so much meaning for me, and some coffee to enjoy with it. Wow, he was really putting in some effort here.

"You know, Annie, if it is in fact true that the king went to Earth to bring these things back for you, well, he must care for you very much, indeed," said Freya.

"Why do you say that? If he can easily pop in and out of worlds just by using the Bridge, it's not that big a gesture, is it?" I asked.

"Well, maybe not before...but don't you think that since he took you from Earth, people there might be watching for him? Did anyone see him take you?"

I thought back to that day. "Yes. I was with my friend, and we were on a pretty busy sidewalk. I'm sure many people saw him, and my friend knew exactly what he looked like. She saw him up close that day."

"Do you not see? It would be very risky for him to go back there now. Where was the book? In your home?"

I nodded.

"So, not only did he have to get onto the planet without being spotted, but he had to get into your home," she pointed out.

Normally, I would have thought that seemed like such a huge invasion of privacy. But after being in the situation I was in, here on another planet, I was able to look past that. And she was right. People would have been looking for him. He had kidnapped me in the middle of the day, in front of multitudes of people, including my best friend. I bet she had called the police, my mom, and Jake. Maybe descriptions of him had even been on the news. And Rali was not a hard man to spot.

"Well, if it was, in fact, that risky, I'm sure he sent someone else for these things. After all, he is the king here. I'm sure he wouldn't do something that dangerous just for me." Did I really believe that? Or did I just not want to believe he would do something like that for me?

"I doubt he sent someone else. He would never trust anyone else to do something he considers so important. He would have to do it himself."

That sounded about right, judging from what I knew about Rali. He had come himself to find me, to watch me, to bring me to Idonea. Maybe he had done this for me. Maybe he had risked getting caught just so I could have my book and my coffee. Could he really be that thoughtful? That considerate?

I refused to entertain the possibility. There was no way. If he really cared, he would've taken me back home rather than go all the way to Earth just to grab a few presents. This would not change my opinion of him. Not in the least.

"If I were you," said Freya, "I would try to find a nice way to thank the king. Would you like me to help you get a note to him?"

"No, thank you. I will be sure to thank him when I see him tonight. That should be fine," I replied.

Freya was disappointed in my answer. She sighed. "As you wish, My Lady. I will go and get your breakfast now."

She walked out of the room and closed the door behind her. I was sorry she was upset with me, but I was not going to go out of my way to be gracious to Rali. What did I owe him? The way I saw it, absolutely nothing.

I walked over to the balcony and went over the information I had learned from Freya.

1. The king could use the Bridge whenever he wanted.
2. There were others that knew how to use it.

My next step was to search the library, and to find out who, besides the king, knew how to use the Bridge. Okay, so how was I going to get Freya to let me wander around by myself? I didn't have much time to figure it out before she returned with my food.

"Here we are, My Lady. Eggs, sausage, and fresh strawberries. Enjoy." She wheeled a cart over to the table and placed my breakfast there. I walked over and sat down, hoping that while I ate I might get a chance to ask for some alone time.

"Well, My Lady --" she began.

"I asked you to call me Annie," I reminded her.

"Oh, yes. I am sorry. Well, Annie, what shall we do this morning? We could go to the village if you like. Or perhaps you would like to see where the ball will be held?"

"Umm...well, maybe. But I was kind of hoping to just rest this morning. I have a big night ahead of me and should probably take it easy. In fact, you could probably take the morning off." I gave her a big smile and tried to seem as genuine as I possibly could. But it didn't work.

"Of course we can stay in this morning if that is what you desire. But I will stay with you. There is always work to be done when you are a lady-in-waiting. If you want to read your book, or take a long bath, I will busy myself with something, do not worry about that. But please let me know if you would like for me to take you anywhere."

My shoulders slumped. She wasn't being very cooperative. How was I supposed to get back home if she wouldn't leave me alone for more than fifteen minutes? Well, if she was here to stay, at least I could try to pump her for more information.

I thought I would try out my new coffee maker, and as my coffee brewed (the smell brought back memories), I sat down on the end of the bed and began my oh-so subtle questioning.

"So, Freya, yesterday when I was in the library with the king, he had to leave suddenly. One of the guards came in and said something about a sighting? That 'they' were close to the palace? What did that mean? Is it something bad?"

Freya had been cleaning up my breakfast dishes and putting them back on the cart. She stopped and turned to me. "Has the king told you about the Hyrokkin?"

"Yes," I told her.

"That is who the guard was talking about, I am sure. Do not worry, they could never get into the palace, there are many guards here. But it is still a frightening thought that they are getting on our planet at all." She finished clearing the table and pushed the cart to the door. Then she returned to where I was and sat next to me on the bed.

I asked her, "If the Hyrokkin can get close to the palace, how do we know they can't get in? From what Rali has told me about them, I know I don't want them anywhere near me."

She put one arm around my shoulders. "Do not fret. The palace is heavily guarded: two guards for each entrance, and there are guards on every floor that are constantly watching the halls. You even have your own two guards right outside your door. That should make you feel secure."

"Yes, I guess it should. But if the guards are just standing out there, don't they get tired? Or bored? Wouldn't that make them less alert?" I asked.

"Well, your guards are changed every three hours. That keeps them fresh and on alert," she smiled at me. "So do not worry. And anyway, as I said, the Hyrokkin would never be allowed to get that far."

"Thanks, Freya." I got up from the bed and poured myself some coffee. Then I continued my questioning.

"Does anyone know how the Hyrokkin are getting here? Are they using the Bridge to get on the planet?"

"Oh no, their planet is close enough that they can get here by ship, though I am not sure how any ships got into their hands. And anyway, they do not have an entrance to the Bridge on their planet and I do not think they would know how to use it even if they did."

And there was my opening.

"Well, who does know how to use it? What if something happened to the king? Who could run the Bridge?"

Thankfully, she took the bait. "There are two men stationed at the Bridge at all times. It is their duty to guard and run the Bridge. You probably saw them when you came here."

I thought back to that day and did remember two faces looking down at me when I had woken up there.

"So then, they would know if the Hyrokkin were using the Bridge," I said.

"Yes. And they most definitely are not."

"Well, is there an entrance to the Bridge on Earth?"

"Not that I know of," said Freya.

"Then how did Rali get me here?" I wondered out loud.

"Well, the two men who run the Bridge can use it to bring him back from particular points. It takes a bit of planning and timing, but he can be brought back from just about anywhere."

"All right then." I got my coffee cup and grabbed my book (my present from the king) and sat down on the couch to read for a while. Freya decided to use this time to prepare my dress and accessories for the ball.

I had learned from her that the guards outside my room rotated every three hours. How did that work? Would that be a good time for me to try to escape? Or make it even harder for me to get past them? But if I could get past them, I knew now that there were two men at the Bridge that could run it. Maybe I could convince them to send me home. I wondered if they took bribes. Not that I had anything to offer them.

I opened up the book that Rali had brought...my book, and read the words my mother had written. I said to myself, "I'm coming home, Mom. I'm not sure how yet, but I will get home to you."

The rest of the morning passed peacefully; and, after lunch, Freya insisted that I lie down to take a nap. I wasn't tired, but I did get some rest. Mostly I spent the time trying to mentally prepare myself for the ball. I was going to have to be on my best behavior. No show of bitterness towards Rali allowed, I told myself. However, I also did not plan to drool over him or bat my eyelashes at him. I was going to have to dance with some of the men at court, Freya had told me. I was not looking forward to that, but hoped that I could learn more about this place from some of those men. I must have dozed off for a short time because I awoke to Freya's voice telling me it was time to get ready.

I got up and went into the bathroom where Freya had already prepared a hot bath for me. I soaked for as long as I could. But Freya finally made me get out and dry off. I sat on the bench in front of the large mirror while she dried and then styled my hair. This time she left it down and put loose curls in it. My hair fell just to the middle of my back, and the curls made it look very beautiful. She put only a little bit of makeup on me, which suited me. Some mascara and a bit of lip gloss was the daily norm for me.

When we were finished in the bathroom, we moved into the bedroom to put on my dress. Freya had chosen a dress for me that was made of ivory-colored silk. It was a strapless A-line dress and hugged my waist perfectly. The back of the dress was just a little longer than the front which caused a small train to form as I walked. The feela that Freya had made to go over it was fabulous. It was made of gold lace and gold ribbon edging. It fit right over the dress, and the neckline of it went just below my collarbone and to the edge of my shoulders. The sleeves were three-quarter length. Freya had matched the dress and feela with gold shoes that had a moderately high heel and open toe.

As I looked at the gorgeous woman in the mirror -yes, I said it, I looked gorgeous - Freya told me, "Now I will warn you, the other ladies will have very grand dresses on tonight."

"Nicer than this? I don't think so," I said.

"Oh, Annie, you just wait. I made this dress just for you. If I had been attending any of the other ladies, they would have thought this dress much too simple for them. But I knew if I made a typical Idonean dress for you, that you would not like it. No, I want you to be happy and to feel beautiful. Do you feel beautiful, Annie?" she asked me.

"Yes, Freya. I do."

"All right then. It is time to go." We walked to the ballroom, arm in arm. She spent the travel time giving me last minute reminders on what to do and, more importantly, what not to do.

"Do not walk too fast when you enter with one of the royal guards. And do not speak to them while you are being presented. Just smile. We are arriving after the other women, for you are the last to be presented this evening. The others will have arrived a few minutes apart from each other, and will already be inside. Now when you are formally introduced to the king, do not roll your eyes or say anything mean, or rude or...well, just don't say anything. And remember to--"

"I've got this, Freya. I'll just remember to think of what I would normally do, and then do the opposite. Don't worry, I'm on it." I smiled at her and she sighed.

When we got to the doors of the ballroom, Freya handed me off to a very tall and muscular royal guard. When I put my hand around his forearm it felt like I was holding on to solid rock. I was just wondering if he had been one of the guards that greeted me so warmly that first day, when the doors to the ballroom opened and I heard my name being announced.

"Ladies and Gentlemen of Idonea, I present to you, Miss Anne Watts."

Chapter 10

    The ballroom was enormous. The ceiling was high with crystal chandeliers hanging from it. There must have been dozens of them. The walls had tall gold and silver panels that went from the floor to the ceiling. There were tables off to the sides covered with trays and trays of food, and at the front of the room was a platform with steps leading up to what I could only assume was the king's throne. The courtiers stood all around the room, leaving an aisle for the eligible women to walk down in order to be officially presented to the king. The aisle led from the doors, straight up to the throne. There, the other women stood, all waiting for me to get there before the king would arrive and meet us.

The King

So, I began my walk down the aisle. All eyes were on me. I was the stranger, the foreigner, the unknown variable in this whole competition. The courtiers looked me up and down and whispered to each other. I was sure they were placing bets as to how long I would last, or how soon the king would make it clear that he prefers women of his own "kind." I was just certain they were judging what I was wearing and deciding it wasn't good enough for their court. I didn't care. I didn't want their favor or their support. I didn't need them to like me. I just needed to find out if any of them could help me.

"Geez, they are staring at me as if I had six arms," I whispered to the guard.

No reply.

"Or maybe more like ten arms..."

Silence.

I looked up at him - way up - and whispered, "So, are you not allowed to talk? Like the guards at Buckingham Palace? How about smiling? Would you get fired if I made you smile?"

Still no reply. He didn't even act like I had said anything to him. So I did the only thing I could think of. I tried again. I needed some entertainment.

"I actually thought it would be exciting for the courtiers if I came in naked and riding bareback on a white horse. You know, something different. But Freya said 'no'. I was pretty upset," I said.

Victory! A tiny smile from the big serious guard. It happened quickly, but it happened. I was very proud of myself.

"I saw that," I whispered. "And for my next trick, I will make you laugh out loud--"

But I didn't get a chance to work on that trick. We had walked all the way to the front where the other women vying for Rali's attention were standing. And Freya hadn't been kidding about their dresses. They all had on bright, flowery ball gowns, with big full skirts. Each one had a fantastic hairdo; either piled high on their heads or down like mine but with feathers and flowers intertwined in braids. I was definitely the one thing that was not like the others. And judging by the scowls on some of the faces, these girls didn't seem to approve. However, I was pretty sure they wouldn't have liked me any better if I had shown up dressed up just like they were. I was new. I had been brought here by the king himself. I was competition.

No, these women were not going to be my friends.

"Ladies and Gentleman of the Court, please welcome King Valiar's Hopefuls," said a booming voice.

I started laughing. I couldn't help it. 'Hopefuls'? Really? They couldn't think of anything else? I found that pretty ridiculous so I laughed. Oops. My hands flew to my mouth. I was not behaving myself. I was hoping I would be saved from Freya's wrath by the fact that I probably wasn't heard over the roaring applause and cheers that followed the announcement. But, unfortunately, I had spotted Freya standing behind one of the tables and she was shaking her head at me. Better try harder. I cleared my throat, straightened myself up and held my chin high. I looked around while the applause began to die down and realized that we, um... Hopefuls, were standing in a kind of semi-circle, with the king's throne in the middle. It was just the perfect arrangement for all of us to be able to really get a good look at the competition. Of course, they were all looking at me, so it felt wrong for me to look at any of them. So I just stared straight ahead and waited for this whole thing to get underway. As soon as all was quiet in the ballroom, the announcer--who I could not see anywhere--proclaimed the entrance of the king.

The King

"Ladies and Gentlemen of the Court, Hopefuls, please rise for your king."

Rise? I looked around. No one was sitting.

"Please welcome King Ralnnulf Aerick Valiar."

Ralnnulf? Yes, 'Rali' was definitely easier to say...and, most likely, to spell.

The room erupted in applause and cheers again. And in walked the king.

Dam.

He was wearing black fitted pants with tall black boots. He had on a grey tunic with gold edging, and over that was a black sleeveless leather jacket that hung all the way down to his knees. Would it be considered a jacket? Or a vest? I couldn't be sure, but whatever it was, it was striking. It had gold edging, like the tunic, and gold embroidery on the front. His smile was big and his eyes were sparkling. He looked really good.

And that made me really frustrated.

He had entered from a door near the front of the room, and waved to the courtiers on the way to his throne. Once the king had reached his throne and was seated, the crowd was silenced. It was time to introduce the ladies.

Let the games begin.

"Your Highness," said the elusive announcer, "may I introduce you to your first Hopeful."

The king stood up and smiled at the first girl who began to approach him.

"Miss Luta Arrud," said the voice.

Luta almost tripped over her dress in her obvious nervousness to meet the king. However, she made it the whole way without embarrassing herself too much. When she reached Rali, he took her hand and lightly kissed the back of it. Then they said a few words (which I couldn't hear - not that I was trying), and she walked off the platform and over to a row of cushioned chairs to one side of the ballroom. I hadn't noticed those before. I was happy to see that I wouldn't have to stand throughout this entire ordeal.

The voice boomed again.

"Miss Helinn Hummel."

Aw, that was a cute name. And Helinn was just as cute as her name. She was very petite and seemed to float to the platform in her light blue puffy dress. She smiled sweetly at Rali, received her kiss, and floated to her seat.

"Geira Landvik."

Well that name wasn't quite as cute...and neither was she. Geira lumbered up to the platform and, oh my, I was pretty sure she weighed more than the king. And the throne. Put together. But she received her kiss as the others did, and then the poor platform creaked and groaned under the weight of hefty Geira as she made her way to her seat.

I watched as about twenty more ladies met Rali and received their kiss. Most of them were very beautiful and elegant. They had definitely been trained for this sort of thing. After standing in line for what seemed like an eternity, I realized there were only two more women ahead of me. Let's hurry this up, I thought to myself.

The voice announced the next Hopeful.

"Miss Sindri Lange."

A hush fell over the crowd. Quite literally, people began to 'hush' those around them. They didn't want to miss this one, apparently. I figured maybe I should pay attention as well.

I watched Sindri Lange walk across the platform -- and she was exquisite. She had long dark hair that fell almost to her waist. Some of it had been braided with red feathers intertwined. Her dress was covered in crimson sequins. It sparkled from every angle. She was very slender and tall. Her skin was tanned and flawless. Wow, even I couldn't take my eyes off of her. As she approached the king, her smile grew bigger...as did his. She held out her hand and he held it for a moment before giving it his royal kiss. I couldn't be certain, but I was pretty sure his lips had lingered on her hand longer than on anyone else's. Not that I cared...I didn't. It was just an observation.

They spoke a few words to each other and then they both laughed. He still hadn't let go of her hand. Finally, after what seemed like half an hour, Sindri made her way off of the platform and went to her seat.

The next girl to meet the king was Margret Lange. I assumed she must be Sindri's sister. Margret was not quite as remarkable as her sister, but she was still very lovely, and she carried herself very well. She did not take as long with the king as her sister had; and, before I knew it, I heard my name.

"Miss Anne Watts."

I reminded myself not to look bitter. I put on my best fake smile, and walked over to the king. He was smiling at me the way he had when I first met him. He knew I hated this. He knew I was dying a little inside and he seemed to be relishing every moment.

"Hello, Annie," he said. "You look absolutely stunning this evening."

"Thank you," I replied.

"Most women usually offer their hand to me at this point," he said.

I held up my hand to him and he kissed it. I wish I could say it was disgusting to feel his lips on me. But it wasn't...at all.

Dam.

I kept my fake smile on my face and said, "Thank you, Your Highness. May I go to my seat now?"

He chuckled softly and said, "Yes, Annie. Please do as you wish. I will see you again later."

I walked to the other side of the platform and then headed for the only empty cushioned chair. I sat down as lady-like as I could and let out a huge sigh of relief.

"Ladies and Gentlemen of the Court, thank you for coming, and please enjoy your evening." Rali had addressed everyone in the room-and with that announcement, the musicians in the back began to play, and some palace workers began mingling among the guests with trays of hor d'oeurves. The courtiers began milling about and talking to one another.

I looked over to the place I had seen Freya standing earlier but she was not there. I searched the crowd for her but could not find her.

"So you are *the* Anne. I have been dying to meet you ever since I heard you were here." Margret, the girl who had been presented just before me, was seated next to me and seemed genuinely happy to meet me.

"Yes, I am the Anne. In the flesh. But most people call me Annie."

"I'm Margret, but you can just call me Maggie if you want. Isn't this all so exciting? Here we are, all dressed up in our finest, and one of us will be the queen! And even though I know it will not be me, it is still thrilling to meet and dance with the other men who are here to find a wife. They are all so handsome, and powerful, and--"

"Wait, what? I'm sorry, did you say the 'other men who are here to find a wife'?" I asked Maggie.

"Well, yes. You know. The Hopefuls who are not chosen by the king are given --"

"Margret!" Maggie's sentence was not interrupted by me this time, but by her sister, Sindri, the exquisite one herself. Sindri was seated on the other side of Maggie.

"What?" Maggie asked her sister.

"We are not here to make friends. Stop gossiping and sit up straight," ordered Sindri.

Maggie sat up straight, but risked a sideways glance over to me and smiled. "We will talk more later," she whispered to me.

"Quiet, Margret," snapped her sister.

Wow, I was really starting to dislike Sindri. But her sister, Maggie, seemed nice enough. I would have to find her later, away from her bossy sister, and see what I could learn from her.

When the musicians ended their first song and began the next, a few couples began to dance. The music was enchanting and romantic. The strings were melodic and fluid while the flutes and other woodwinds were light and colorful. The song they were playing at this time was a waltz. The dancing couples looked beautiful moving across the dance floor. The men all wore dark tunics or coats, and the women-- though a bit poofy for my taste-- all looked so bright and colorful and pretty. I felt like I had been transported to eighteenth century Europe and placed in the middle of a crowded ballroom.

Suddenly I noticed that all the Hopefuls seated near me had straightened up, nice and tall, and were all eagerly smiling. Then I saw why. Rali was walking toward us. It was time for him to get to know us, I guess. He was not headed toward me, so that was good. I could sit and people watch for a while longer. Rali had asked cute little Helinn Hummel to dance first. It was kind of hard not to giggle at the incongruity of their heights as he led her to the dance floor. But no one else giggled. So neither did I. After all, I was on my best behavior.

I watched as many of the other Hopefuls, including Maggie, were asked to dance by some of the male courtiers. Only a few of us were left sitting out the first dance. I was probably the only one who was glad to be left out. I looked around for Freya again, and finally saw her on the other side of the room. She was looking at me and when she finally caught my eye, she quickly put her hand under her chin and tapped it. What did that mean? Oh, she was reminding me to hold my chin up. So I did. Then she shook her shoulders back and forth a bit. What was that one? Oh, yes, sit up straight and don't slouch. Got it.

I sighed. This was going to be a long night.

I sat through the next dance, and the next. Maggie had also sat out the last dance, but hadn't tried talking to me anymore. She must've been afraid her sister might see. But then, as the previous dance was ending, I heard Maggie gasp and say, "Oh my goodness. He is here."

I was intrigued. I had to ask her.

"Who is here?"

"The general," she whispered to me. "He is the most handsome man in the kingdom -- after the king, of course -- and one of the most powerful men as well. None of the Hopefuls would mind losing the king so much if they knew they could have General Durin."

"What?" I shouted more than whispered. I looked in the direction Maggie had been staring, and yep, there he was. The man who had made my knees turn to jelly the day before. And he was coming straight toward me. I sat up straight, held my chin up, and smiled.

"We meet again," he said as he approached.

"So we do," I said.

"May I have this dance?" he asked me.

I was silent for a moment, as if I had to actually consider his proposition.

"Yes, you may." I offered him my hand and he took it. As we walked, I forced myself to think of Jake, so as not to be tempted, and began repeating in my head *I have a boyfriend, I have a boyfriend.* Durin led me out to the dance floor and I could feel many pairs of eyes on us. We passed Sindri as she returned to her seat, and her eyes widened. That made me smile. We stopped in the middle of the dance floor and turned to face each other. He was even more gorgeous than I had remembered. I prayed that my knees stayed solid while we danced. He put one hand on my waist and held my right hand with the other. I put my left hand on his shoulder, and when the music began, we danced.

He moved so easily to the music...and somehow I did, too. It must've been because of my graceful partner.

"Are you enjoying yourself tonight?" he asked as we glided across the dance floor.

"I am a little bit...now," I said.

He laughed. "Good, I am glad. To be honest, I don't usually come to these gatherings. They are not my favorite way to spend an evening. But, I just had to see you again."

What? He came here to see me? Hold it together, knees.

"Thank you. That is very thoughtful of you to say," I told him.

"Oh, I am not thoughtful at all. In fact, I am a very selfish man. I am here because I want to know you better. You are quite fascinating, you know."

Yes, I do.

"Well, thank you, again. What do you want to know?" I asked him.

"Everything. But first, you do not seem to be like the other Hopefuls. Would I be wrong to assume that you are not here to impress the king?"

"I guess you could say that I am not quite as...enthusiastic as the others about being paraded around in front of the kingdom."

"So I am not wrong," he smiled at me.

I laughed, "No, I guess you aren't."

"That is good. All this ceremony just for him is ridiculous. Anyway, I think you could do better."

I raised my eyebrows as he continued.

"You know, I never liked the way these things have been done. The choosing of the queen has been done this way for hundreds of years, but I detest it."

"Why is that?" I asked.

"Well, there must be hundreds of women in this kingdom that are the king's age. Yet, he only can choose from a small percentage. What if the perfect woman for him lives in the village? What if the only woman who could truly make him happy is on the other side of the planet?"

"Or universe," I said quietly. He hadn't heard me and continued talking.

"It just seems to me that the king might be missing out."

"So, you are saying that there is not one among us 'Hopefuls' that will make Rali happy?" I joked.

"Well, maybe one. But if there is one that special among the Hopefuls, someone else might want a chance to grab her for himself." He looked down at me and grinned.

"Ah, so that is your real argument with this whole method. You don't like that Rali gets first choice. He might scoop up the best one."

"He is the king. What could be more desirable to a woman than that?" he asked.

I laughed. "Many things could be more desirable. It would take a lot more than an impressive title to win me over."

"Well, then, I guess that means I have a chance."

I looked up at him, surprised at how forward he was being. I wasn't sure if I should be upset or excited. One thing I was sure of-- my inner-monologue had changed from *I have a boyfriend* to *I had a boyfriend.*

"So, Durin, excuse me, General Durin --" I began.

"Just Durin, please."

"All right. Tell me, how are you already a general? Most of the time when I see an Army General in the movies they are about sixty years old. Do you just look really young for your age? Or are you some sort of Phenom?"

"Well, I am thirty-five, and usually one here does not make the position of general until at least their late forties. But I am very good at what I do, and it doesn't hurt that my family had a very high standing here at court. I have been in the King's Army since the age of sixteen. I have fought in many battles and helped make decisions that led to great victories against the Hyrokkin. My family name was definitely in my favor, but I believe I have earned my position mainly through my own efforts and achievements."

"I am impressed," I said.

"Am I winning you over yet?" he asked slyly.

"Oh, you've got to do even better than that. Remember? It takes more than a title."

"All right then, I'll have to try harder."

Durin and I continued dancing and talking and laughing. Toward the end of the song, I glanced over Durin's shoulder and saw Rali. He stared right at us.

And he did not look pleased.

Chapter 11

When the song came to an end, I was very sorry to be led back to my seat by Durin. But I did enjoy seeing the faces on some of the other Hopefuls as we walked together. Oh, they did not like that one bit. The foreigner had been chosen to dance by the General Durin. The best part was that, after he left me in my cushioned chair, he turned around and walked off towards the table of food instead of asking another woman to dance.

I wished I'd had that option. But I had to stay in my seat in case any other eligible bachelor wanted to dance. I was hoping I would have my previous luck of being a wallflower, but seeing that I was good enough to dance with the general seemed to raise my desirability level among the other men.

I sighed.

I didn't get much rest after that. I danced with men as young as eighteen, and as old as sixty two. Some were handsome, some were...not so handsome. A few of them were actually quite charming, but they had the unfortunate luck of being subconsciously compared to Durin. One of the men, however, was very helpful to me by filling me in on what I thought Maggie might have been starting to tell me earlier. This man's name was Leif. He was in his forties, and very nice to talk to while we danced.

"I have to admit, Annie, when I heard that King Valiar had brought someone here from Earth to be a Hopeful, I was a little concerned about how you would fit in here. But you seem to be doing quite well," said Leif.

"Thank you, yes. I am still getting used to this new place and getting to know people, but I am trying to do my best to fit in," I lied through my fake smile.

"I hope that you do enjoy yourself here, and please let me know if there is anything I can help you with."

Perfect.

"Actually, Leif, I am a bit confused about one thing I heard tonight and I might need some clarification," I began.

"Of course, tell me what it is and I will try to help you."

"Well, one of the other Hopefuls mentioned something about what happens to the girls who are not chosen by the king in the end--"

"Oh? And why should you worry about that? Do you not believe the king will choose you? That is what most of the Hopefuls believe, anyway," he said.

"Sure, well...just in case, what is it, exactly, that happens to the, um...rejects?"

"Well, that is a harsh word," he laughed. "But to answer your question, any Hopeful who is not chosen to be queen, then becomes available to the other eligible men in the kingdom. That is another purpose for this ball, you know? For us, the eligible men, to meet you, our potential wives."

I almost threw up right there on the dance floor.

"Oh, all right. I see. That sounds...so romantic. Do you mind if we stop now? I have been dancing a lot this evening and I think I need to rest for a bit."

He looked disappointed but agreed to take me back to my chair.

I thanked him for the dance and then dropped into my chair. So, I was not only being considered as a wife for the man I hated, but also for men I didn't even know or care to know? This was getting worse by the minute. Now I knew the answer to the question of what happened to me if Rali chose someone else. I wouldn't be going home, I would be married off to a stranger and stuck, forever, on this planet.

I needed some water and some fresh air. I figured I could get at least one of those things. I found Freya standing nearby and motioned for her to bring me a drink. She quickly brought me some water and I gulped down the entire glass.

"Freya, why didn't you tell me?" I asked her.

"Tell you what?"

"That I will be married off to some stranger if I'm not chosen by the king?"

She looked guilty.

"Well, Annie, I...I just, I know how hard this has been for you and I did not want to worry your heart with things that do not matter."

"Things that do not matter? What is that supposed to mean?"

"I do not think you need to concern yourself with what happens to the women that are not chosen by the king, because you *will* be chosen. And do not worry about what everyone is saying about Sindri, either. She may think she has already won, but she has not," Freya said bitterly, narrowing her eyes.

Well, that made me feel so much better. I reminded myself then that, if all went well, I would be home in a week, so really, none of this mattered. I also made a mental note to ask Freya at some point what she meant about Sindri thinking she had already won. Without letting her suspect that I cared. Because I didn't.

"Sure, Freya. Thanks for the water."

She nodded and then left me alone to think. I needed to get through this petty "courting" stuff, and put all of my efforts into getting home. I needed to find out more about the two guardians of the Bridge that Freya had mentioned and how I could get them to help me. I sat in my chair with my head in one hand and my eyes closed for what seemed like an hour. I was deep in thought when I heard the words, "May I have this dance?"

His was the last voice I wanted to hear. I opened my eyes and looked up at Rali. He stood in front of me, hand reaching for mine, with a smile on his face. A genuine smile this time.

"Fine. I mean...yes." I tried to collect myself and gave him my hand. He led me out to the dance floor where everyone watched. I was getting used to that by now. The music began, and we danced in silence before he finally spoke.

"You are upset with me again," he said.

"Again? The word 'again' would imply that at some point I was not upset with you. You should have said, 'You are upset with me still.' That would have been more accurate."

"I do not understand why you are holding on to this anger towards me. Are you not happy with what I have given you? Is this not what you wanted?"

"Rali, I was bored on earth. That happens. It doesn't mean I wanted to be flown to another planet and be forced to marry someone I don't love," I answered.

"You do not love me?"

"Oh my gosh, are you kidding me right now? First of all, I barely even know you, and what I do know does not work in your favor. Secondly, if--no...when--you don't choose me, I'm supposed to marry one of these other guys? Seriously? What's that about? Women here can't be trusted to make their own decisions?"

"Well, you seemed happy enough with one of 'these other guys'," he said.

"I don't even know what you're talking about," I fibbed.

Rali laughed. "You are a terrible liar. Though I would rather have you desiring me above any other, I do see why you would be attracted to General Durin. Many of the ladies are. He can seem very appealing, I am sure."

"He can 'seem' very appealing? But he's really not? Are you trying to change my opinion of him?"

"So, you do think well of him. And a minute ago you had no idea what I was talking about."

"I never said... Listen, it was just nice dancing and talking with Durin. That's all. He's a nice guy and he has the advantage because he's never kidnapped me." *Good one, Annie.*

"If you knew him a little better you may not say that. However, I will leave the topic of General Durin alone for now. I would like to move on to something else you said. Why did you say 'when' I don't choose you? What makes you think I wouldn't?"

"Well, for starters, I don't even want to be here. Then there's the fact that I just don't belong here with you. And then there's Sindri..." I stopped. *What did I just say?*

"What did you just say?" asked Rali.

"Um...nothing. I said I don't belong here and then I just stopped talking. Yeah, I'm pretty sure that's the last thing I said." I cringed. What was wrong with me?

He smiled. And this was a new smile. I hadn't seen this one before. It was a sweet smile. It was endearing.

I immediately looked away.

"Well, if that is where you stopped talking, then I will address only the things you mentioned...and not the thing you did not mention. I know you do not want to be here now, but if you let me show you what your life can be like, you might change your mind. You might start to realize that you do, in fact, belong here."

"But, Rali, I don't belong here. This is not my home. What makes you think I could just forget about my home and my family? And I still don't even know why you brought me here. Why me? Of all people?"

"Annie, I do not expect you to forget about your home and family. I ask that you open your mind to a new home. And concerning your family, maybe...maybe you could actually learn more. You could become closer by..." He looked as if he were struggling to find the words.

"Learn more about what? How would I get closer to my family by being on another planet far away from them?"

He looked like he wanted to say more, but didn't quite know how to say it. Then the music ended, and he lost his chance. Rali led me back to my seat. I glanced at him as I sat down in my chair and he looked a bit troubled.

"Is everything okay?" I asked him.

He forced a smile. "Yes, everything is...quite all right. Enjoy the rest of your evening."

And then he walked away.

I was left wondering what I had done to make him upset. What had he been trying to say to me earlier? And why was I wasting my time worrying about Rali's feelings when I had more important things to worry about?

"When can I get out of here?" I said quietly to myself...but not quietly enough. Maggie had heard and her sister was not around, so I guess she felt it was okay to talk to me then.

"You cannot leave yet. There are still a few more required dances before we can dance with whomever we want. Or leave if that is what you really want. I do not know why you would want to, though," she said.

"Oh, I'm just tired is all. Are you having a nice time?" I asked her.

"Oh, yes. King Valiar danced with me once, and I have danced with two colonels, a captain and a lieutenant. But that doesn't even compare to you. You have danced with the king *and* General Durin. He hasn't danced with anyone else tonight. Only you. I am sure many of the other Hopefuls envy you."

"Or hate me," I said.

"Well, I do not hate you," she said.

I looked at her and smiled. "Thank you, Maggie. That's actually pretty nice to hear."

She smiled back and then looked out to the dance floor.

"Annie, I think the general is coming back to dance with you again," said Maggie.

She was right. He was coming across the room and smiling at me. But he was beaten to me by a short and squatty lieutenant named Olaf.

"May I have this dance?" asked Olaf as he held out his hand.

I wanted to say Absolutely not ever, but there were rules. I figured I could just grit my teeth and survive this unwanted dance partner and then reward myself with a follow up dance with Durin.

So I gave Olaf my hand, and glanced over his shoulder at Durin. We shared a knowing look that we would dance together soon.

I headed for the middle of the dance floor where I was usually led, but Olaf guided me closer to the outskirts of the group of dancers. Fine. I wanted as few people to see me dancing with him as possible. I was sure it would not be pretty.

"Well, Lieutenant, are you having a nice time?" I asked. I thought maybe we could hold a decent conversation to make this go a little faster.

"Yes. The ladies here tonight are very beautiful to look at. But none so much as you," he answered.

"Well, that is very kind. So, do you live near the palace?" I was asking him the questions but looking around the room for Durin. Durin being so much nicer to look at.

"Yes," he said simply.

"That's nice. It is a beautiful planet to live on."

"Yes."

He was not helping this go any faster. I gave up on my search for Durin and looked at Olaf's face before I asked my next question and realized that he was not looking back at my face, but in a bit more southerly direction. Great.

"Excuse me, Lieutenant, but I am up here," I said sharply.

He looked up at my eyes quickly...but as his eyes moved up, his hand, which had been on my waist, went in the opposite direction.

"Hey, let's try to keep our hands a little higher, if you please."

He moved his hand back up to my waist...but then it kept on going up.

"Woah, okay. I'm done. I'm going back to my seat."

I stepped back from his grip but he grabbed me and slammed me into his body before I could get far enough away from him.

"You do not get it, woman. You are here for my benefit. You do not walk away from me until I say you can."

I put both hands against his chest and pushed as hard as I could. I got myself far enough from his body that I was able to smack him across the face pretty hard. He let go of me and put his hand up to his face.

"You pervert!" I yelled. I turned to storm off but ran right into Rali's solid chest.

"Can someone explain to me what is going on here?" His hands were balled into fists by his sides. I saw Durin running up behind him and realized that half of the room stopped and stared at me and the lieutenant, who was still holding his face in one hand.

"I would be glad to," I began. "This...this jerk was trying to feel me up. His hands were everywhere."

Rali looked at me and then at the red-faced lieutenant. "Lieutenant Olaf? Can you explain what happened?" he asked.

"What?" I screamed at Rali. "Why are you asking him? I just told you what happened. This guy's hands were all over me!"

"Annie, let me handle this the way I--"

As he was talking, he got pushed out of the way by Durin, who went straight for Olaf and punched him right in the nose. Olaf went stumbling backwards into an ivory column and fell forward onto his beaten up face.

Wow.

"General!" Rali looked furious.

"I am sorry, Sir, but I felt like taking care of this a little more…efficiently than you." Durin straightened his jacket, glanced at me, and then turned and walked away.

I looked at Rali to see what his next move was, and at the same time he seemed to be doing the same to me. Finally, while still looking at me, he called for his guards. When they got to us, he took his eyes away from me.

"Ivarr, take the lieutenant to the infirmary. I will check on him soon."

"Yes, Your Highness," Ivarr said. Then he and another guard lifted Olaf off the floor and carried him out a side door.

Rali looked back at me, and the rest of the people in the room returned to their previous activity. Though many of them still threw some sideways glances in our direction.

"What?" I asked Rali. "Are you upset that I've caused your evening to not run according to plan? Have I ruined your little 'coming out' party? So sorry. Guess I shouldn't have been so appealing to that creep. My bad." I realized I was breathing heavily and tried to calm myself down.

Rali just continued to look at me. The corners of his mouth turned down and his eyes were stormy.

I stood there until my breathing returned to normal. "Rali, look, I--"

Before I could finish, he turned and walked away.

I was left bewildered, standing alone at the edge of the dance floor, while couples spun carelessly around me, as if I wasn't even there. I slowly made my way back to my seat-- because I had no idea what else to do--and ran into Freya on the way.

"Annie," she said, "Are you all right? What happened?"

I sighed. "I don't know, Freya. I've made him mad, somehow. I don't know what I did. It wasn't my fault. What else was I supposed to do? Let that guy grab me wherever he wanted?" I felt like crying. "Why is he so upset with me?"

"I am not following you. Let who grab you?"

"That jerk Lieutenant."

"Lieutenant Olaf tried to grab you? And you are sad that he is upset with you?" Freya looked confused.

"No. I mean, yes-the lieutenant did that. But I'm not sad about him."

"Why are you sad? Who is upset with you?" she asked.

"Rali."

She paused, looked at me kinda funny, and then smiled.

"Why are you smiling? This isn't funny."

"I am smiling because you are sad," she said matter-of-factly.

"What? Well, I'm sorry, Freya, but you're kind of mean."

She laughed. "Do you not see? You are sad that you have upset the king. You do care for him. If even just a little bit."

"Freya...no. That's not what I said. I'm not sad. I don't...ugh...it's not like that."

"Then what is it like?" She looked too triumphant for my taste.

"I'm just sad that I caused a scene. I was trying to be good and behave myself, but I couldn't, not when that guy couldn't behave himself."

"All right, I believe you. We will go back and sit down. The required dances are almost over and then we can go back to your room if you would like."

"Yes, I would like that very much."

We got back to my seat and I fell into my chair. Luckily, most of the other Hopefuls were out dancing, so I could enjoy a quiet moment to myself.

I sat and thought about why I had been so upset. Was Freya getting at something? Was I sad that I had upset Rali? No, I told myself. I was mad because Rali hadn't done anything to defend me. He was supposed to care about me, right? Why wasn't he the one who had punched Olaf?

And why did I want him to have been the one to punch Olaf?

"Annie. Are you all right?" Durin had appeared out of nowhere and was right in front of me looking very concerned.

"Huh? Oh, hi. Yes, I'm fine. Just a bit shaken, I guess."

"Come on," he said.

"Huh?" Couldn't I think of a better reply?

"Come on, let's go."

"Go where? I can't leave yet."

"Why not? You are not from here. You do not have to follow the rules of this place."

"Yes, but, I have already caused enough problems. I really don't want to be any more trouble. Please, I need to stay here just a little longer." I really and truly did not want to be the talk of all the kingdom the next day. And leaving the ball early arm in arm with Durin would have pretty much guaranteed that I would be.

He looked annoyed for a minute, but then said, "Okay. We will do it your way. Can we at least dance together?"

"Am I allowed to dance with the same person twice?" I asked him. He gave me a look that told me I was really starting to aggravate him, so I quickly said, "Sounds great. Let's dance."

His look softened and we headed back to the dance floor.

Chapter 12

The general and I danced and talked quite easily for two straight songs. I was sure we were breaking some kind of rule, but I just told myself not to care. I enjoyed being with Durin, so that was where I was going to stay until I was allowed to leave. I happened to notice that while I danced two songs with Durin, Rali had been dancing those same two songs with beautiful Sindri. Well, then, I guess I wasn't breaking any rules. And I was happy where I was...and so was Rali, it seemed. And that was fine with me. Just fine.

When the song ended, we stopped and applauded the musicians, as all the other courtiers did. When the musicians announced the next song as the last, I breathed a sigh of relief.

The music started and I stepped towards Durin to resume our dancing positions. But we were interrupted.

"May I cut in?" asked Rali through clenched teeth. His eyes still reflected anger.

Durin looked at him for a long intense moment, as if he considered actually refusing the king, then finally said, "Of course, Your Highness." Durin flashed me a rueful look and handed me over to Rali.

Rali took my hand in his, and put his other hand on the small of my back. When the music started, we moved, but stayed silent. I didn't even look at him. We must've danced through half of the song, when to my surprise, I spoke first.

"Why are you mad at me? What did I do wrong?" I asked.

Rali let out a breath. "You did not do anything wrong, Annie."

"Then why are you mad at me?"

"I am not mad at you. I am mad at...at this situation."

"What situation, exactly? The situation where I was harassed and you didn't do anything about it? Or the situation where you had to leave your lovely dance partner to come scold me for my inappropriate behavior?"

He looked at me but said nothing. So I kept going.

"I know, you're mad at the situation where you were outdone by your general." I winced. *Oooh...shouldn't have said that, Annie.*

"Outdone? Is that how you see it?" he asked. "You know, I suspected as much. I was hoping I was wrong."

"What do you mean?"

"You think that Durin handled that situation well, that he was justified. You think that I came off as weak. You think that Durin is your hero," Rali said.

"Well...I think that, given the circumstances, what Durin did was more...assertive, more gallant. I was obviously upset. In distress, even..." I put on my best pitiful face.

"And you wanted your 'knight in shining armor' to ride in and save the day. Well, I am sorry I could not be that for you, but I have a kingdom to run, and a responsibility to everyone in it. I cannot walk around striking every person that wrongs me or those I care about."

"But you didn't do anything. Nothing. You stood there and acted like I was a tattling child."

"I did not do anything? Annie, let me explain something. I am the king of this land. I handle things the way I see fit. And I did not think the best way to handle this was to hurt the lieutenant physically for just a moment when I, as king, could hurt him in a way that he will feel much longer than Durin's punch to the nose. Do you think I was happy about what you said he had done? Do you think I did not believe you? Of course I did. I was furious. Believe me, I wanted to do what Durin did. But I have more authority and power than Durin. And more self-control. If Durin had not taken matters into his own hands and made a mess of the whole thing, I might have taken you with me when I visited the lieutenant in the infirmary immediately after. You could have been there to watch the humiliation on Olaf's face when I told him he has been stripped from his position as lieutenant, and has been ordered to leave his home on the palace grounds by tomorrow morning. You could have seen the actions I take when someone I care about has been hurt. But instead, I told him on my own, while you were here, thinking about how Durin came to your rescue, and the feeble king stood to the side, powerless." He looked away from me for a moment, like he was trying to hide the hurt showing on his face.

I was stunned. I was speechless...for once.

The King

Rali turned his eyes back to me and waited for my response. It didn't come. There wasn't one. I could only stare straight ahead at his chest and try to get through the rest of the dance without thinking about the mistake I had made in my judgment.

"Annie, I just--" he said softly but was interrupted by the voice.

"Ladies and Gentlemen of the court, thank you for coming this evening. King Valiar's Hopefuls, thank you, as well. You may now leave your seats, and please, enjoy the rest of your night."

I stepped back from Rali, quietly thanked him for the dance, and walked away.

I felt lost. I was in the middle of a ballroom, swimming through a sea of bright sparkling fish and dark hungry sharks. I had to get out of there. I headed straight for the exit when someone grabbed my arm. It was Durin.

"I am sorry, Annie. I did not want to give you up to him, but I could not refuse the king." He looked a bit wounded. But not defeated.

"It's not your fault, Durin. Anyway, if you don't mind, I really need to--"

Before I could finish my sentence, his arms were around me, and his lips were on mine. He kissed me. He kissed me passionately, hungrily. As if he had been starving for my kiss all night long. We were so close; we were so alone in that very moment, we were so...not alone. We weren't alone at all. We were in the middle of a very populated ballroom full of gossiping courtiers. I pulled away as quickly as I could.

"Durin I...I'm sorry. I have to go."

I hurried past him hoping that somehow, just maybe, nobody had seen that.

I rushed out through the same doors I had come in. I pretty much ran to the lyptras, stopped in front of one and then remembered that I still hadn't learned how to use these things.

I turned and was about to make my way up the winding hallway when I saw the royal guard that escorted me into the ballroom earlier that night. It seemed like so long ago.

"Hey! Hi, remember me? Can you help me? Please. I need to get back to my room, but I don't know how this works."

He stopped and looked at me, and then quickly made his way over to where I stood.

"Oh, thank you so much! I am really not up to walking all the way to my room."

The guard pressed a button (I tried to pay attention) and the doors to the lyptra opened. I stepped in, but the guard stayed where he was.

"Aren't you coming? I don't know how to run this thing."

He hesitated, looked around, and then stepped in with me. The doors closed and he pushed the button just below the highest one and then the blue one at the bottom. I took careful notice of that so I wouldn't need to find a guard next time.

We rode silently on the lyptra, and soon, the doors had opened on my floor. Before stepping out, I turned to him and said, "Thank you so much. Can I ask your name?"

He was quiet.

"No one is around; you won't get in trouble. What is your name?"

"Arthur," he said in a very deep voice.

"Well, Arthur, thank you again."

"You are welcome, My Lady." He bowed and then the doors closed. I turned and walked to my room.

The King

As soon as I walked into my room and closed the doors behind me, I went straight to the open balcony. I wanted to feel the fresh air on my face. I wanted to stare out into the endless sky. I breathed deeply and finally felt a moment of calm. This evening had been exhausting. And perplexing. I had felt nervousness, excitement, joy, anger, betrayal...and, above all, confusion. I couldn't understand why I had been upset that Durin had hit the grabby Lieutenant, and that Rali had not. Why had I been concerned that Rali seemed mad at me? I hated him...didn't I?

Yes, he had brought me to a place he thought I would want to be. Yes, he had risked his own safety to bring me treasures from home in order to make me more comfortable. Yes, he had ended up taking much more extreme measures towards the awful Olaf who had gone too far with me. But that didn't matter. I didn't care about any of that. After all, I hated this man. I really and truly...disliked him. Mostly, sometimes.

I closed my eyes and shook my head. The truth was, I knew I didn't hate him. I didn't even dislike him. The reason I had been so upset was because I was fighting feelings that I knew were there. They had been there all along. But I didn't want them to come to the surface. That would take the focus off getting home, and getting home was what I wanted.

Right?

I sighed. I leaned both elbows on the railing and closed my eyes. I tried to clear my mind and relax. I focused on the sound of the wind, the calming breeze, I breathed in and out deeply.

Ah, silence...

BANG! The door to my room slammed shut and I whirled around in time to see Rali storming towards me. I stepped down into my room to grab something-anything-to protect myself with...not that I thought he was going to hit me, but he looked pretty mad.

"You-after all I have done-have you no respect?" he growled.

"What? What are you...?"

He was in front of me so quickly that I had no time to react. His hands gripped both of my shoulders and he pushed me back against the wall. His face was right in front of mine. It was so close...so close I could see deep into those sea-green eyes. Those eyes that had once hypnotized me were now staring daggers at me. And I was scared.

"I have offered you a kingdom. I have risked my life to make you happy. I have changed the way things are done here, just to offer you the life you have been seeking. And you spit on it."

I take it all back. He wasn't mad, he was furious.

"Wha...what? I don't understand. Rali, I--"

"Do not call me that. You were right, we are not close. I had hoped..." He trailed off and his grip on my shoulders started to ease up.

"Ral...Your Highness, I don't know what happened, but you have to let me go," I told him.

Wrong move. I had apparently forgotten the advice he gave me earlier about not demanding things of the king. He returned his grip on my shoulders, and this time he got even closer to my face. "You know exactly what happened, Annie. I saw it. Everyone saw it."

Oh. No. The kiss. I looked into Rali's eyes trying to figure out what to say. When I looked, I noticed tiny specks of gold in his eyes. Why hadn't I noticed that before? Maybe because I had never been in the same proximity to them as I was now, only inches away. I was brought back to the present situation when he squeezed my shoulders even tighter.

"Ow! Listen, I know what you saw, but it was not what you think," I began.

"So, you accidentally tripped and landed on Durin's lips? Is that what happened?" he said sarcastically.

"No, that's not what I meant. I meant that it wasn't me-- I mean it was, but he kissed me."

"You did not look too desperate to get away from him."

"Well, I didn't... Can you please let go? I can explain. We can talk. But honestly, you're scaring me right now," I pleaded.

It didn't seem to work at first, but after a long moment, he slowly loosened his grip entirely and stepped back from me. I breathed a little easier and relaxed my poor shoulders.

"Well?" he said coldly. "Explain."

I racked my brain trying to think of the best way to say anything.

"Okay, yes, Durin kissed me. But I wasn't expecting it, or asking for it. I was trying to get back to my room."

"You expect me to believe that you did not want him to kiss you? You had been fawning over him all evening."

"I was not fawning--"

"You know, Annie. I am disappointed in you, really. To chase after someone like General Durin. I thought you were much too intelligent to do something like that."

"Wha...How dare you judge me on my...my smartness." I flinched. "And anyway, why do you care? I am not 'chasing after' anyone here. I am trying to go home. I don't want to be here. I don't want to compete for the heart of someone that I...someone I..."

"Someone you hate?" he snapped. "Well, I have been trying to make you see beyond the opinion you have of me as your cruel 'abductor'. I have been going against Idonean tradition to convince you that I am someone that could make you happy--"

"Then let me go home. That would make me happy. Just send me back to my home." The tears started rolling down my cheeks and I couldn't stop them.

He stood there and watched as the tears poured down my face. He seemed to soften a bit, and I felt some hope that his anger was passing.

"Rali, please. I thank you for trying to make me happy here. But I don't belong here. You have to see that. You have to let me go back home now."

I just couldn't get this whole *don't tell the king what to do* thing down. I saw the anger come rushing back.

"I do not have to do anything that you tell me to do. I am the king, and--"

"You are not my king. I am not one of your people to be ruled," I said through the tears.

He was in my face again, quickly.

"Listen to what I say, Annie Watts," he put one hand on each side of my face and brought us within inches of each other. My hands went to his waist to steady myself. "I am never sending you back to Earth. I have brought you here to stay. And that is exactly what you will do."

We stood that way for what seemed like centuries, close enough to see into each other's souls if we dared to look. Close enough to breathe the same air. Close enough to...to...

He suddenly removed his hands, began to back away from me and said, "I cannot let you go, Annie. I will not let you go."

And then he turned and walked out of the room, closing the door behind him.

The King

I was still for a while, trying to understand what had happened. He had been so angry. He frightened me. And he made it clear that I was never going home.

I continued to cry. I walked to the balcony, looked out into the sky and let the tears fall. I looked at the stars, out into the black abyss of space and thought about my home and my family that was out there somewhere. Then I looked into the bedroom where the king had just left. The king, who was determined to keep me on his planet. The king, who had laid out my whole life for me without even asking. The king who I, only moments before, had admitted growing feelings for...

No.

There were no feelings now except my growing determination to get home. He could not and would not rule my life. I was going home, that very night.

With new purpose, I went to my wardrobe and pulled out some black stretch pants, and a black, long-sleeved cotton shirt. I pulled my long blonde hair back into a ponytail. There were guards outside my door...

But none outside my window.

I took off my shoes, got dressed in my dark clothes and walked onto the balcony. I put my hands on the railing and looked over the edge. It was a long way down to the courtyard. I looked at the palace wall to my left at the gold and silver trellis. It went all the way from the top of the palace, to the bottom. I could climb it. Maybe not all the way down, but at least down to another window where there wouldn't be any guards. Then I would make my way to the Bridge. I didn't know yet how I would get the guardians of the Bridge to send me back home, but I didn't care about the details at the moment. I had to leave. I had to get away from Rali immediately.

I slowly swung one leg over the side of the balcony and reached for the lattice. It was pretty easy to reach, and I quickly got both legs and both arms in good climbing positions. I said a silent Thank you to Jake for making me take those two rock climbing classes. Even if all I learned from them was Don't look down. It was good advice.

I began my descent carefully. Step by step, hand over hand. I prayed no one would be out and see the lady from Earth trying to climb her way down the palace wall to freedom. I stayed focused, took my time, and I did not look down.

While I was slowly making my way down, I stopped suddenly when I noticed a man standing on his balcony. I held my breath and hoped he wouldn't look my way. Luckily, he turned and walked in his room as I inched my way past. I muttered a curse word to myself when I almost made him turn back as my foot slipped from its perch and made a slight squeak. He paused for a moment but then went back in his room. I realized then that I had probably 'cursed' more in one day than I had in my entire life. I needed to get a handle on my language.

After making it down about eight floors, I saw a window within reach; and, when I got close enough to look in, I found an empty hallway. I climbed in through the window, and crept silently down the hall. I peeked around corners and watched for guards. There were a few times I had to dive into an alcove or hide behind a piece of furniture when I heard someone coming; but, miraculously, I made it to the second floor. I would have to find a way to get into the courtyard without using one of the entrances. There were guards at every one of them. So I decided to climb out another window, back onto the trellis, and then climb down to an empty part of the courtyard. And it worked.

The King

I silently dropped down onto the courtyard's soft grass. My bare feet didn't make much sound. It was very dark and I blended in well with my choice of outfit. I could see an opening in the tall hedges and decided to get as close as I could before I headed to the kingdom's gates, and then to the Bridge. I crept a few feet forward and stopped behind a bush. No guards. I crept a little further to a low bench and stopped. No guards. No one else was in the courtyard. I got a little braver and began to run towards the hedge. I was almost there. I just had to pass the cascading flower bushes and I would make it to the hedges. Almost there, a few more yards, closer...closer...

Running at full speed, I was suddenly 'clotheslined' by someone's arm jutting out of the darkness. The force of the collision sent me straight onto my back. My neck felt like it was on fire and my head and back throbbed. I finally caught my breath.

"Ow," I groaned and reached for my aching back.

An unnatural, low, tormented voice laughed and said, "Where are you going, princess? The fun is just about to begin."

His laugh was joined by two others. Someone rolled me onto my belly and wrapped a burning chain around my wrists.

There I was, having just climbed out of my balcony and made my way stealthily through the palace, and now I was sprawled on the courtyard in the dark and in a lot of pain...and I was pretty sure I had just been captured by the Hyrokkin.

Dam.

Chapter 13

"This worked out much better than we had planned," said one of the horrible voices. "We thought it must be our lucky day when we saw you creeping through the courtyard. Sneaking out to meet your lover? King Valiar not man enough for you?" he snickered. "We could've told you that."

The one who was talking then ordered the other two to pick me up off the ground. That was a very painful ordeal. I was still having trouble breathing after running into, what I assumed, was one of their arms. And not only was my neck sore from hitting the arm at full speed, but it felt like it was on fire. Plus, falling that hard onto my back had knocked the wind out of me. My head was still throbbing from that impact, as well.

The King

I was in bad shape.

I was lifted off the ground by my arms and set onto my feet. I tried wriggling myself out of the wrist chains. Bad idea. The more I moved, the more they burned. And two of the Hyrokkin had a very strong hold on me, anyway. I wasn't getting away from them.

They were all three taller than me, though one was much taller than all of us. They had two arms and two legs like the rest of us, but their skin was rough and dry and almost looked like red tree bark. They wore hardly any clothes. I remembered Rali telling me that anything they touched just burned. I looked down to where they were gripping my arms and I realized they were wearing some sort of heavy gloves. They were rubbery, black, and had tiny bumps all over them. They felt like gardening gloves, only thicker. It must've been what enabled them to hold onto me without setting me on fire. The two shorter ones took position on either side of me and the tall one stood in front, facing me. I looked around to see if there were any guards or anyone at all that I could call to. No one. I was alone. No one would be looking for me for hours. These monsters would take me to their planet of Helgrind as a prisoner, I guessed. And no one would ever know.

"All right," the tall one addressed the other two. "You do not let go of her no matter what the king says. Even when he says he agrees to our deal, we let go of her only when we have the Sidas Array in our hands. Do you understand?"

"Yes, Aldro," the other two answered.

I tried to say something but my voice barely cracked. When the tall one--Aldro--noticed I was trying to speak, he cocked his head and grinned.

"Having trouble, my dear? Is there something you wanted? Maybe you want to beg for your life? Try some flattery, maybe? As much as I would like that, we really must be getting on with our plans."

I coughed a little and tried again. "No...no, I'm not..." Ouch. It really hurt to talk. "I'm not begging. But what deal are you talking about?" My voice was almost a whisper.

"Well, princess, your king has something we want. Now we have something he wants. So we will propose a trade. It is very simple."

Trade me?

"What are you trying to trade for me?" I kinda wondered how much I was worth.

The tall one glanced around, perhaps checking to be sure we were still alone before he continued.

"We will trade you for the Sidas Array."

The Sidas Array? Where had I heard that before?

"What is that?" I asked.

The three monsters began to chuckle quietly.

"The Sidas Array? You do not know?" asked the tall one.

"I wouldn't have asked if I already knew, now would I?"

The short ones tightened their grip on my arms. Maybe I should watch my tongue.

Aldro sneered at me and then said, "The Sidas Array is a power source. It is what runs the Bridge. It can also be used for other purposes. The king has it and we want it. So now we shall have it."

"Wait, you think the king is going to trade something that important...for me?" If I wasn't afraid of completely tearing up the inside of my burning throat, I would've laughed hysterically.

"King Valiar cherishes human life. He works very hard to protect everyone in his kingdom. We are, at this moment, in possession of his most treasured human. Yes, he will trade."

"Um...do you have me confused with someone else? The king won't trade anything for me. He hates the sight of me." I pictured the angry and hurt face that Rali had shown me earlier that night. "So, if you don't mind, I was kind of in the middle of something. Sorry your plan is not as awesome as you thought it was-and it's really not-but I gotta get going. So if you could just undo these really hot chain things on my wrists, that would be stupendous."

Aldro laughed. "Your annoying chatter will not distract me from my goal."

Hey, I'm not annoying.

"You are one of the king's favorites. You are the one he brought here himself from Earth. He will trade for you." He looked at the two others holding onto my arms, motioned us forward and said, "Let's go."

"I'm telling you, this won't work. He won't trade me for something so powerful. He wouldn't even trade me for a sock, actually."

"Be quiet," ordered Aldro.

"Why? So you can continue going over your amazing plan in your head? Keep praising yourself for your brilliant idea? Listen, I've got better things I could be doing."

"Silence," he said.

He obviously didn't know me very well.

"Gotta think about all the wonderful things you're gonna do when you get the Sidas...whatever it's called? You shouldn't waste your time or mine, cuz you're not going to get it."

I should've shut my mouth.

Aldro whipped around with a dagger in his hand (where on Earth...I mean, Idonea had he been carrying that thing?) and sliced it down the left side of my face, from my temple, to the middle of my cheek. It happened quickly, and the pain was sharp. I staggered backwards and almost fell, but the short Hyrokkin held me up.

"You will learn to obey my commands, princess," he said while holding the bloody dagger in front of me so I could get a good look at it.

I gritted my teeth. I seriously considered spitting in his face, but the pain in the side of my cheek and neck reminded me why that probably wasn't the best idea.

He turned around and our little foursome walked towards the palace entrance. I didn't know how they planned to get in there, but I didn't care either. I just couldn't believe that, after all the trouble of getting away from the palace, I was now being marched right back in.

As we approached the front entrance, we were quickly spotted by the guards. They unsheathed their swords and called to the other guards for help. They must've had some sort of radios in their helmets because, almost immediately, there appeared a dozen guards in front of us, blocking the doors. They all stood, with their swords out, ready to strike the tall fiend, when he stepped aside and motioned towards me, their hostage. The guards froze, swords poised in mid-air.

"Now, we wouldn't want to make the king angry, would we? You strike me, my friends kill her, the king banishes you. I am sure you see why it is in your best interest to let me speak to His Royal Highness."

The guards still did not move. Finally the guard on the end lowered his sword, spoke quietly on this secret radio device that I decided I needed to learn more about, and then ordered the other guards to stand down. Immediately, they all lowered their swords and put them away. They cleared a path to the door to the palace (I was kinda shocked) and I was led inside by the two Hyrokkin, the three of us following Aldro. We walked to the lyptra, got on, and went all the way to the top. There were no courtiers to be seen anywhere. They must have all been back in their rooms sleeping and dreaming about the wonderful time they had spent at the ball. I envied them.

When we exited the lyptra, there were four guards there. They, like the guards at the entrance, made a path for us, as if we were honored guests. We turned left and the guards followed. After a short walk down the hallway, we followed Aldro through a doorway on the right side of the hall. I wondered how he knew where we were going. He knew exactly where he was going, as if he had been there before. We walked up a broad set of stairs and stepped into a long room with a single door on the opposite end. To our right, windows stretched from the ceiling, almost all the way down to the floor. The moonlight spilled across the floor in horizontal lines. A fire burned in a fireplace on the left wall crackling and filling the room with a woodsy fragrance. I stared at the door on the opposite end, wondering where it led, when it opened and Rali strode through it. He walked with a grin and a sword at his belt. I wished I could get a better view of him, but the tall one shifted to stand in front of me. I couldn't be sure if Rali had even seen me.

"Good evening, gentlemen," Rali said to the monsters. "To what do I owe the pleasure of your visit?"

Aldro laughed. "Pleasure? The pleasure is all ours. We have found something that belongs to you and have decided to return it to its rightful owner."

"Ah. I am intrigued. You have found something of mine all the way over in Helgrind? Surely you are not admitting to trespassing on my kingdom."

The Hyrokkin were silent and Rali laughed.

"Tell me, what is it that you have found?" he asked them.

Aldro stepped aside and there I was...in all my glory. Blood was streaming down the left side of my face, and I was just sure my neck must've looked horrible.

Rali looked at me as I came into view and I thought I saw a look of dismay pass over his face, but it was so quick I couldn't be sure it had happened.

What was he thinking? *How has Annie gotten herself into this mess?* was probably a good guess.

Rali looked back at the tall one. "I thank you for returning my dear Hopeful. Please, hand her to the guards and be on your way. I will be sure they stand down as you leave the palace. You have my word."

Aldro laughed. "Oh no, we are not giving her back that easily. A treasure like this?" He motioned towards me and I made eye contact with Rali. His expression remained cool and calm. The two shorter Hyrokkin tightened their grip on my arms. Aldro's dagger appeared in his hand again and he held it to my throat.

"We offer you a trade," Aldro said. "We will return her to you, when you give us the Sidas Array."

Rali looked at him quizzically. "I am sorry. I must not have heard you correctly. You want me to give you the Sidas Array in exchange for...her?"

"Yes, that is our offer," answered Aldro.

My big mouth decided it had been quiet too long, I guess. I jumped in.

"Rali, I tried to tell them it was ridiculous. I told them you wouldn't--"

"Shut up, princess," snapped Aldro. He turned to Rali and said, "If you refuse, we will be taking her back to Helgrind with us. We are in need of good women there. The men outnumber the women nearly five to one. Our Leader would appreciate this gift, I am sure. She would be...very welcome there." He grinned at me lasciviously and I wanted to puke.

Rali seemed to mull it over, "That does not sound like much fun for her, does it?" He smiled at the tall one but then quickly his smile vanished. He continued more seriously. "The problem here is that the Sidas Array is such a powerful tool. It can be used for many purposes, as you well know." Rali looked at Aldro and began walking towards us. "And then there is the woman..." he motioned towards me. He shook his head. "No, I do not think that this could be considered an even trade."

"See, that's what I said," I began, "but these guys--"

The dagger Aldro plunged into my upper thigh shut me up pretty quickly...and made it hard to stand up. I groaned and started to fall to the side, but the two shorter Hyrokkin held me up by my arms as Aldro returned the dagger to where he had been holding it in front of my throat.

And I thought I had been in pain in the courtyard.

Aldro looked back at Rali after stabbing my leg and waited for a response. Maybe he was hoping that Rali would feel sorry for me and make a sympathy trade or something. But I knew he wouldn't. I knew the whole time that I was about to be taken to Helgrind. And I was terrified.

Rali said to the tall one, "Like I told you, gentlemen, this is not an even trade, especially when you keep damaging your goods. I am sorry you wasted your time. You can let yourselves out. My guards will stand down."

And with that, Rali turned and walked away.

He walked away from me. I had known that he wouldn't trade me, but knowing that didn't make it any less painful when it actually happened. He had abandoned me. He knew that I was about to be exposed to all sorts of horrors and tortures...and he walked away.

Rali went through the door on the other side of the room and closed it behind him. Aldro stood there for a moment, let out a heavy sigh, and then turned to walk back out the door we had come through. The two shorter ones turned me around and we followed behind him. It was hard for me to move with a wound in my left thigh, so I limped along down the stairs trying to decide what my next move should be. But the reality swept over me that it would be a waste of my time. There were no more moves. I wasn't going home, and Rali was letting these monsters take me away from him. I was kind of surprised that I didn't know which one upset me more.

There was no more hope. No more planning and no one to help me.

Aldro glanced back at me. "We will let the Leader decide what to do with you."

Fabulous.

We made it down the stairs and walked through the doorway. The guards, as commanded, were all standing to the side, watching me be led to my doom. I looked up at one of them who caught my eye...it was Arthur. He was the only guard who dared make eye contact with me as I passed.

"Arthur. Arthur, please help me. Please!" I begged as we walked by. Arthur made no move to rescue me, but I noticed his eyes flash to the right down the hallway. It was barely noticeable.

I peeked back at Arthur who was behind me, when I heard a rush of wind to my right and suddenly, Aldro was down on the ground, with a sword protruding from his stomach. He groaned as the life left his wide eyes. Rali pulled the sword out of the monster's stomach.

"Rali?" I was shocked, yet relieved.

He grabbed his sword and eyed the short Hyrokkin on my left. The Hyrokkin let go of me and lunged toward Rali. But Rali was too quick. He spun and as the Hyrokkin flew by, his head was neatly removed from his body by Rali's sword. Rali turned back to face us. There was one fiend left...and he had removed one of his gloves and was holding the bare hand straight at my side. His ungloved hand was now a lethal weapon. It would burn on contact, and right now, it was preparing to burn its way deep into my torso.

Rali stood prepared to strike, sword in hand and dagger in his belt. The monster stood prepared to kill. I stood...very still. I looked at Rali and saw no anger in his face. Just pure and steady determination. I didn't know who would strike first, who would make the first move. But I was hoping it would be Rali. I tried to think of a way I could help, but I was just having trouble standing at that time. Finally, Rali spoke up.

"Give her to me, and I will be sure you leave here unharmed."

"Oh no, you promised we would be unharmed a minute ago. I cannot trust you," answered the monster.

"I promised you that my guards would stand down. And they have. No trust has been broken. Now, your choice is either to hand her over and walk free, or hold on to her and die. Which one will it be?"

The remaining Hyrokkin monster laughed eerily and said, "Your sword will do you no good here. I can burn a hole through her before you even reach me."

Rali furrowed his brow. "You make a very good point." He dropped his sword and it clattered on the ground next to his feet. He then pulled his dagger from his belt and said, "Yes. This will work much better."

The monster growled at Rali.

Rali's dagger shot through the air straight for the monster's throat when the monster plunged his fiery hand into my side, right below my ribcage. Then he let go of me and I was falling to the floor in slow motion. I was falling, falling...

And then I was in his arms. We were on the floor in the hallway. I could hear guards running towards us and Rali yelling out orders. Everything seemed to be moving so slowly, and everything was slightly out of focus, as if I were dreaming. My eyes wanted to close, but I kept hearing a voice. A lovely voice telling me to stay with him. It said, "Look at me, Annie. Look at me. You are going to be all right. The doctor is coming, Annie. Do not close your eyes. Annie? Look at me. Stay with me."

I wanted to stay. I tried to stay...but it was too hard. My eyes closed, and I drifted into a deep, dark sleep.

Chapter 14

    I was back in my bed at home, on earth. I must've been about nine years old. My father had come into my room to tuck me in and tell me one of his amazing bedtime stories. He had done that ever since I could remember. I loved his stories.
    "What story are you going to tell me tonight, Daddy?" I asked him.
    "I think I will tell the story about the magic star."
    "Oooh, that sounds great. Tell it," I squealed.
    "All right. Long ago, there was a star that burned hundreds of thousands of miles away from Earth. And it had magical powers."
    "What could it do?" I asked eagerly.
    He laughed. "Well, it could cause things to happen that no one ever thought possible."

"Like what?"

"Well, for example, you know how you and I love to look at the night sky and dream of what could be out there?"

"Yes, Daddy."

"Imagine if you could actually go out there and look for yourself? This magic star could make that happen. It had the power to zoom anyone off to wherever they wanted to go."

"Wow," I whispered to myself. "What else could the magic star do?" I asked him.

"That's not impressive enough?" he laughed.

"Yeah, I guess. But you said the star helps us go and look out into space. What if we wanted to stay there? Could the magic star make that happen?"

"Why would you want to stay there?" my daddy asked me. "Wouldn't you miss me and your mom and sister?"

"I'd bring you all with me. And we could start our own new world, called...Annieland!"

"Ah, that sounds like a marvelous plan. I would love to go to Annieland with you someday. But for now, it's time for bed."

"Aw, no more stories?"

"Not tonight. But go to sleep and you will dream of new worlds, new adventures, and maybe even of Annieland." He smiled at me.

I smiled back at him and yawned. "Okay, Daddy. Goodnight. I love you."

"I love you, too, Annie."

Then my father turned out the light, stepped into the hallway, and closed the door.

I laid in the bedroom of my childhood, and drifted off to sleep, hoping that in my dreams I could fly away on the magic star to a bright new place, and live a spectacularly exciting and wondrous life.

The King

I woke up, and I was no longer nine-years old, nor was I in my childhood home. I opened my eyes and I was lying on my left side, on a huge, ivory and gold bed with cool, silky sheets that smelled of lavender. Everything was a little blurry, but I could make out a very large room, with luxurious furniture placed throughout. Long sheer drapes hung over a large balcony. My vision was beginning to clear and when I looked out the view from the balcony, I could see...two small suns.

Oh yeah.

I started to turn onto my back... Ow! Bad idea. I groaned and immediately someone was at my side.

"Annie? Can you hear me?" said a voice that I knew.

I looked up into familiar eyes. "Rali?"

He smiled. "Yes, it is me. Are you in much pain?"

"Umm...yeah. Very much."

Rali, who had been sitting on the bed next to me, stood and motioned someone over to my side. I assumed it was a doctor. He carried a few small tools with him and shined a light in my eyes. He checked heartbeat, pulse, and all the other doctor stuff. He asked me where I felt the most pain and I told him it was mainly my side, but also some in my leg. The doctor said a few words to Rali and then left. Rali resumed his place next to me.

"The doctor said he will give you some medicine for the pain. Your wounds have already begun to heal quickly, thanks to him. The doctors and medical practices in Idonea are very advanced. He gave you a special tonic that the doctors and healers have used here for years. It is made from minerals found in our waters. There is nothing like it on Earth. Nothing as accelerated. You will be as good as new in a few days," he said encouragingly. He smiled at me, but I wasn't buying that he was happy at all.

"Where am I?"

"You are in my room. It was the closest place to bring you after the incident." He looked away from me.

So that was it. He was upset. Well, of course. I had tried to escape, which allowed the Hyrokkin to grab me and use me as a bargaining tool. I helped them gain entrance into the palace and then Rali had had to fight them...though it wasn't much of a fight. Rali had pretty much dominated the three of them...but not before one of them had managed to stab me in the side. I had caused a lot of trouble for Rali, and now I was imposing on his private chambers in the palace.

I placed my hand on top of his. "Rali, thank you."

He looked down at my hand for a moment and said nothing. Then he got up, called Freya over, who I realized had been standing in the corner, and told her to stay with me.

He looked back and said, "I have places I need to be. I will check in on you later. Get some rest."

Then he spoke to one of the guards, and walked out of the room. When he walked through the door, I could see through to the other side and I saw the foyer where we had been just the night before when all of this had happened. We had been right outside of Rali's bedroom.

I asked Freya to help me sit up.

"I do not think that is a good idea, Annie. It might be very painful," she said.

"Freya, I am thirsty, and I want to sit up. Please just help me. We'll do it slowly."

"Yes, ma'am," she said with a huff.

I held out my hand and she grabbed it and pulled while I pushed up on the bed with the other hand. Oh, it did not feel good.

"Ow, ow, slower, slower…" I made it into a sitting position, leaning back against the headboard. I was puffing and panting and in more pain. My own fault, I guess.

"Water, please, Freya."

She hustled over to bring me some water. I gulped it down and asked for more. I gulped down the next glass she brought me, too. Then I set down the glass and decided to examine the damage done by the Hyrokkin.

I moved the sheet away and noticed I was wearing a long, ivory colored tunic. I blended right in with the sheets. I looked up at Freya and she read my thoughts.

"It is the king's. Do not worry, the doctor and I were the ones to change your clothing."

Ah, add that to the list of things that Rali could be upset about. I had not only taken his bed, but his shirt, too.

The wound in my thigh had only a few stitches and did not look too scary. I lifted the tunic up enough to peek at my side where I knew the Hyrokkin had gouged me. I was expecting to see half of my torso burned into ashes, or maybe a big bloody wound too disgusting to ever look at again. I flinched when I got the shirt high enough…but then relaxed. It wasn't so bad. It was definitely a big wound, but the doctor had stitched up most of it, and some of it was just bandaged. It was pretty painful, but it didn't look nearly as bad as I thought. The Hyrokkin must not have had time to make too deep of a hole in my body. Maybe I would survive this after all.

"Okay, Freya, now help me get up," I told her.

"What? Oh, no ma'am. You are staying right here. Doctor's and king's orders."

"Well, I never heard the doctor say that, and Rali does not control me. Now help me up, let's go."

She didn't move.

"Freya, please," I worked up some tears. "I have to get out of this room. It's...it's just so close to where this all happened. I hate being reminded of it. I can't heal if I am so close to it all. Please, Freya, please. You have to help me escape from the scene of the attack that almost killed me!"

I'd like to thank the Academy...

She hesitated, sighed, and then gave in.

"All right, Annie. But this is going to hurt. And if the king gets angry at me, I am putting full blame on you."

That's just fine with me, I thought. He probably couldn't be any angrier at me than he already was.

I slowly moved my legs over the edge of the bed and braced myself for the worst. I edged forward and, bit by bit, began to put some weight on my legs. Oh, dear Lord! That didn't feel good. Freya put one of my arms over her shoulders, and told me to lean as much weight as I could on her. I think I pretty much put all of my weight on her. Poor Freya.

We walked that way out the door, and down the hallway to the lyptra, and then to my room. It took quite a while. Once we got to my room, I sat down as gently as possible on the bed and laid down. Freya had brought the pain medicine with her and gave some to me. It took only a few minutes to start working. I asked Freya why she hadn't thought to give me the pain meds before we took the trek from Rali's room to mine. She answered that if I had not felt much pain on our walk, I might have moved more than I should have and caused damage to my healing wounds. Made sense. Painful sense.

The pain meds made me sleepy, so I pulled the covers up around me and decided to take a nap. Rali said I needed rest, so that was what I was going to do. See? I followed the king's commands. But only the ones I liked.

I fell into a restless sleep. I had visions of Hyrokkin, visions of Rali walking away. I tossed and turned, and felt a little pain in my side each time. Every once in a while I heard voices in my room. Freya's, Rali's and a voice I didn't know as well...probably the doctor. I heard bits and pieces of conversations about me, but none of them really registered in my partially drugged, mostly sleepy state.

"How did she survive this?" I heard Freya ask.

Rali answered, "The doctor said the heat from his hand helped stop the bleeding."

"So, she should have bled out?"

"Yes. But her wound was actually cauterized..."

Then I drifted back out.

Later I heard Rali again. He was asking Freya if she knew how the Hyrokkin had gotten to me.

"I don't know. I didn't even know she had come back to her room. I thought she was with..."

"You thought she was with Durin. Yes. Freya, do you think she...?"

"No, Your Highness. I think she enjoys his company, but that is all. It is in his favor that he is not the one who brought her here. I think that is foremost in her mind right now," answered Freya.

"Do you think he has told her anything?"

"I cannot be sure, yet, Your Highness."

I was out again after that, for a while, I think. When I woke up, no one was in my room except Freya.

"Freya?" I said.

"Yes, Annie. I am here." She came quickly to my side with a glass of water. I slowly sat up and drank the whole thing.

"Freya...I'm so sorry," I said. And then I started to cry. Maybe it was the pain medication, maybe it was just the exhaustion I felt after the whole nightmare. But I couldn't keep from crying. She held me in her arms and stroked my hair.

"Ssh. Annie, do not be sorry. This is not your fault."

"But it is. I am the one who tried to run away. That's how they got me. And because of that they were able to get into the palace, and cause a bloody mess."

"You tried to escape? How? There are guards outside your door."

I was about to answer her when Rali walked in. He saw that I was awake and rushed over to my bedside. He pulled a chair up close and sat down.

"How are you feeling?" he asked me. "Why are you crying? Is the pain that bad?"

Freya got up from the bed and walked over to the couch to sit down. I guess she thought Rali and I needed a moment.

"Well, yes, I am still in some pain...but that is not why I'm crying. I'm just...I'm so sorry, Rali. I mean, Your Highness."

"Please, it is still Rali to you. And why are you sorry? What wrong have you done here?" he asked.

"Well, the Hyrokkin. They got into your palace because of me. I tried to run away and that is when they got me. I just wanted to go home. I feel horrible that I've messed things up and endangered your people."

"You tried to what? How? How were you not seen by the guards posted outside your room?"

"Uh...well, I didn't go out the door."

Rali looked around the room as if trying to figure out how I had escaped. He looked over to the balcony, got up from his chair, and walked out into the fresh air. I slowly got out of bed and followed him. Freya began to get up and help me, but I motioned her away.

Rali bent over the railing and looked down. Then he turned around to look at me. "Get back in bed, Annie," he ordered. I ignored him, of course, and kept walking to where he was on the balcony.

"I will feel better if I can get some fresh air."

Rali shook his head but then came and took my arm and helped me the rest of the way. He stared out over the railing and looked puzzled.

I pointed to the palace wall. "I climbed down the trellis." He looked at the trellis and then back at me.

"What? You climbed down that? The whole way?"

"Well, no. Just eight floors. Then I climbed in a window and snuck past your guards," I admitted.

He looked at me in shock. "Wow, Annie. You must really hate me to have risked your life to get away." His eyes looked sad and angry. And I felt ashamed.

"I don't hate you. I didn't hate you. I just wanted to get home. I'm sorry. I know I've messed up. I know I've caused trouble for your kingdom. I'm so sorry."

Rali came closer to me and held my shoulders in his hands...gently this time. "Do not be sorry. This is not your fault. I was cruel. I was the one who made you come here against your will. If it is anyone's fault, it is mine."

Then he let go of me and walked back into my room.

I thought he was going to leave, but he turned back around to face me and said, "I have given this some thought. Annie, this is not what I had planned for you…for us. If I had left well enough alone, you would be at home, saving up for your bookstore, having coffee with your friends. But I brought you here, and you were almost killed." He took a step closer to me. "I will let you go home."

"What?" I was shocked.

"Yes, but please, give me some time. Give me some time to show you how much I...how much I want you to stay. The day I choose my bride, we call it Kostera, is in six days. If at the end of six days you still want to go home, I will take you myself."

I didn't know what to say. All that planning I was doing, climbing out the window and risking my life to get home...and here Rali was, telling me I could leave. He would take me himself. I had no words. So I limped the few steps separating us and wrapped my arms around him.

"Thank you, Rali," I said as the tears fell. "Thank you."

He put his arms around me, too, and we stood that way for a few quiet minutes.

He withdrew his grasp first and we stepped away from each other. He had a smile on his face, but it was forced, I could tell.

"I am glad you are happy. I will leave you in Freya's care for now. The doctor will be in shortly to see how your healing has progressed."

Then he turned and walked towards the door. Before he went out of the room, though, he turned and said, "Annie, I meant what I said to the Hyrokkin. Trading you for the Sidas Array would not have been an even trade. I would've been giving them something of lesser value."

And then he left.

Chapter 15

I was so happy. So relieved. I no longer worried about getting home to my friends and family. In six days it would happen. I wondered about the people at home. Were they searching for me? They probably thought I was somewhere on Earth. Even though Erika had watched as I was launched into the sky, surely no one would have thought that I had actually been taken to a different planet. I imagined what must have been taking place back on Earth while I was gone. Erika had probably called the police and told them her story. The police probably then called my mom, maybe Jake. They would have posted signs or reported to the news about my abduction while Erika gave them a description of my abductor. He was tall, with raven black hair. He was lean and muscular, strong and brave. His eyes were mesmerizing and hypnotic, sea green with little specks of gold. And lips that...oh, wait. They probably wouldn't have described him quite like that.

Ahem, anyway…

After Rali left my room, I asked Freya to draw a bath for me. I wanted to soak for a while and try to enjoy my six days as a captive before going back home. Ah, home. I would be there before I knew it.

Freya helped me into the bath, where I stayed as long as she would let me. Then I got out, and Freya wrapped me in the same luxurious robe that I'd worn on my first day in Idonea. I thought back to that night, before all of this had happened, and remembered how dazed and numb I had been towards everything. It was all so unbelievable; it had been too much. Now things were different. There was a light at the end of the tunnel. I could now put a positive spin on anything. I had been brought to a beautiful planet. Yes, I had been close to death, but because of that, I could now enjoy six days here, like a vacation really, and know that I would soon be going back home, where I knew what to do. Where everything was comfortable and expected.

Comfortable and expected. Once I had found that boring, but things had changed. After what I had experienced, I needed some boredom in my life.

I went into my room and Freya had picked out a simple pale yellow outfit for me. It included a fitted long-sleeved shirt which fell mid-thigh, and matching leggings. This will do nicely, I thought. I got dressed and then Freya put my hair into a low ponytail. She curled the ends to fancy me up a bit. I didn't care. I was in a great mood. I was still in some pain, but Rali's decision to let me go home helped eased much of the pain I had previously felt.

After Freya finished doing my hair, she said, "Annie, you are still healing. I do hope you plan to stay in and rest today."

"Freya, I think that is a good idea. If you will start the coffee pot, I will sit on the couch and read all afternoon if you would like," I said.

"Yes ma'am. That sounds wonderful." Freya went directly to the coffee pot (brought to me by Rali) and started the coffee. I had shown her how to work it the day before. I watched Freya as she worked and thought about how I would miss her when I left. She had been so good to me. I was determined to be as sweet as possible to her while I was still on Idonea. While I waited for my coffee, I walked over to my bedside table and picked up the copy *of Anne of Green Gables* that Rali had brought for me. I opened up the front cover and read the words my mother had written there. I had expected to smile over those words...but I couldn't. All I could think about was how that book had gotten to me here on Idonea. *Rali.* He traveled to Earth and back just so I would feel some comfort here. He could've been caught...and then what? What would've happened to him? Would he have been arrested? Charged with my kidnapping? When they couldn't find my body, could he have been sentenced to death?

No. Surely he had known he wouldn't get caught. Otherwise he would never have done it, right? Of course not. Why would he risk his life--his kingdom--for me?

Then his last words came rushing back. *I would've been giving them something of lesser value.*

I sighed. He cared for me. Why he cared, I couldn't figure out. I had been nothing but trouble since I arrived. I hadn't followed the rules. I climbed out the window to get away. I brought the Hyrokkin closer to him than he had ever wanted, I was sure.

Well, I didn't want to think about that now. My coffee was ready, and I was going to relax and enjoy my vacation. I took my book over to the couch where Freya met me with a steaming mug, and I curled up to read.

"Enjoy, My Lady," said Freya as she handed me my coffee.

"Freya..."

"Sorry...Enjoy, Annie," she said with a smile.

Yes, I was going to miss her.

That evening, after I ate some dinner, I walked out onto the balcony to enjoy the view and some fresh air. I looked out over the village and decided I would go there the next day to see it closely for once. Looking down to the courtyard below, I saw the exact spot where I had been captured. I glanced away quickly and instead focused on the palace entrance. There, as I watched, I saw a lady in a purple-sequined gown walking down the lane away from the palace doors and to the end of the courtyard. Even from far away I could see that she was beautiful. Her long dark hair flowed freely behind her as she glided down the path. She seemed to be in a hurry to get where she was going. I looked toward the end of the path where she was headed and saw a man waiting.

It was Rali. There was no mistaking it. It was him. The beautiful woman approached Rali and held out her hand. He kissed it. Then the couple walked over to a waiting carriage where he helped her climb into one seat, and then he went around to the other side and climbed in next to her. Rali grabbed the reins and the carriage began to move. The carriage left the palace and went down into the village. I was pretty sure I had just watched Rali and the exquisite Sindri beginning their beautiful evening together.

Well, it's a good thing I didn't care. Because if I had cared, I would've been pretty upset, maybe jealous, even...but I wasn't. Not in the slightest. Nope, not Annie Watts. I was fine. Just fine. I was super happy. I was going home soon. What did I care about Rali taking Sindri out on a date? What did I care if they had a wonderful time? What did I care if he married her and they lived happily ever...

Ugh.

I walked away from the balcony and sat on my bed. I focused on being happy about going home. I tried to imagine being back with Jake, my boyfriend. I would go home to him, home to our future. We would get married and buy my bookstore, and we would be happy.

"Are you all right, Annie?"

Freya had been in her room (adjacent to mine) but had come in to check on me. She walked over and sat next to me on my bed.

"Yes, I'm fine. I just saw...I mean, I am hurting a little bit because of my wounds." Yes, I was hurting because I had barely survived an awful attack. That was it. "Are there any more pain meds, Freya? I think I need to sleep for a while."

"Yes, the doctor left some for me to give you. I will get them."

She left the bed, went to her room, and returned with a pill and glass of water. I took the pill eagerly and laid down in my bed. Freya came over to my bedside and sat in the chair that Rali had pulled up earlier.

"Freya?"

"Yes, Annie."

"Do you think it will be different when I go home?"

"What do you mean?" she asked.

"Well, I mean… My whole life, I've wondered what else was out there. My father and I both would always look up to the sky and think about the possibilities. It always seemed that I was missing something. So do you think that now--now that I know what is out there--out here, will I feel more content? Will it be different?"

Freya sighed. "I do not know."

We sat in silence for a moment while I thought about going back home.

"Annie, I want you to know that I am happy for you. I am happy that you are being given the chance to go back home." She smiled at me and then looked down.

"What is it Freya? You say you are happy but I don't believe you. What's wrong?" I asked her.

"Well, it's just that..." she started to tear up. "It's just that I will...I will miss you, Annie." And then she started to cry.

I sat up and put my arms around her little body.

"Freya, I will miss you, too. You have been wonderful to me. You have put up with me even when I'm difficult. Which is most of the time."

She laughed a little, and I sat back so we could face each other.

"Yes, you have been difficult at times, but that is what makes you special. It makes you different. You are yourself. You are always Annie. You are not trying to please anyone or impress anyone. You do what you feel is right. And I think that is why the king likes you so."

"Well, he may say things like that, but I don't think he means them. He is sending me home. He knows I don't belong here, Freya, and I'm sure he will be happy choosing another woman to spend the rest of his life with." I laid back down in my bed and pulled the covers up to my chin.

"Why do you say that? Of course he means the things he says. He would never be dishonest. He is not that kind of man. His mother did not raise him that way. He says what he means. What he said to you about your value, he meant. Do not think otherwise," Freya said. She stopped crying and now actually seemed a little upset at what I said. She rose from the chair and walked back to her room to let me sleep. I could feel the medicine's effect starting to kick in and I yawned.

"Freya," I called after her. "I didn't mean to upset you. I am just...just saying what I think...like you said I do. I wouldn't be me if I didn't, right?"

She stopped before closing her door and turned to look at me while I spoke.

"If Rali really cared, he wouldn't be...I wouldn't have seen..." I yawned.

"Wouldn't have seen what?" Freya asked.

"Well, I saw him...and Sindri...and they...they were..."

"What? You saw the king and Sindri? Together? What were they doing?"

"Going somewhere I think...yes...they...he kissed her hand...and they...they...they left."

I yawned again. And then I was asleep. I slept all night long.

"Annie. Annie, wake up. It is time for breakfast," called Freya.

Mmmm...food. That sounded wonderful. I roused myself from my peaceful sleep and slowly sat up in bed. I still felt some discomfort in my side and thigh, but was able to gently get myself up and out of bed. I would do almost anything for food.

"Freya, breakfast sounds great. What are we having?" I asked as I limped to the table my food was usually served on.

"Oh, I do not know. You will find out when you get there." She walked to my closet.

"Huh? Get where?"

"To the breakfast," she said casually. She pulled out a charcoal grey dress and sparkly turquoise feela.

"To the breakfast? Not just a breakfast? Is this a special breakfast? Where is it? Where are we going?"

"*We* are not going anywhere. You are going to the dining hall to have breakfast with the king and some of the Hopefuls."

"Um...nope. Sorry. As lovely as that sounds, I am an invalid and should stay close to my room." I walked back towards my bed and was stopped in my tracks when I was hit from behind by a small couch pillow.

"Hey! What was that for?" I turned around and saw Freya standing by the couch and scowling at me.

"Listen, My Lady. You are going to this breakfast. You are going to meet with the ladies and the king." She walked closer to me and continued. "You are going to have fun." She turned around and walked back to the dress she had picked out. "Come, come, Annie. Time is passing and you are not even dressed yet."

I sighed. "When am I supposed to be there?"

"Oh...in about ten minutes."

"Ten minutes? Come on, Freya. Let's get dressed and you need to do my hair. I need help here, I'm crippled." I hurried as fast as my broken body would let me. The dress was simple yet elegant and, of course, fit me perfectly. Freya left my hair down but added a few crisscrossing braids down the back. Then she brought me some sparkly turquoise shoes that just looked painful.

"Oh, I don't think I can pull that off. Remember, I was stabbed in the thigh and then burned a bit in the middle. Walking is not my best thing right now," I told her.

"But the other Hopefuls will be looking at everything you are wearing. They will be judging your dress, your whole outfit, and I want them to...to like it." She looked at me expectantly.

Then I understood what she was trying to get at. The other women would be judging her on the ensembles she was creating for me. And the shoes were a part of that. Freya had something to prove to the courtiers who had had her banished from court, who made her leave her beloved queen.

"All right, Freya. Let's compromise. I really don't think I can walk in those shoes...but I'll carry them. How about that?"

She hesitated for a moment but then smiled. "Yes. That is fine. Thank you, Annie." She handed me the jeweled shoes and I took a quick glimpse of myself in the mirror (gorgeous, even though there was a long thin scar on my face), and off I went to the breakfast.

Freya walked me to the dining room since I didn't know where it was, and it would've taken me a lot longer limping there on my own. The dining room was on the main floor just to the east of the ballroom. Freya walked me to the door, gave me a quick hug, handed me my shoes and then gently (but firmly) pushed me into the room.

There were about seven Hopefuls already seated at a round, beautifully set table. When I came in, or more accurately, limped in, they all stopped their chatter and looked at me. I smiled and began the slow walk to an empty seat at the table. It didn't look like Rali had arrived yet. It was just us girls. The room was silent as I limped to my chair, found an empty seat beside Maggie, and sat down.

"Good morning," I said to the quiet ladies. Most of them just ignored me, but Maggie said, "Good morning, Annie." I felt a bit of relief then.

"I'm glad you're here," I whispered to Maggie. "I don't think the others want to see me right now."

"I think they are wondering about your, um...entrance. Are you all right? What happened?" She looked at the left side of my face. Oh, right. My scar from that first dagger strike.

One of the other Hopefuls echoed Maggie's question. "Yes, what happened to you? You look absolutely horrible." It was cute little Helinn Hummel who asked. Suddenly she didn't seem so cute to me anymore.

I realized everyone was waiting for me to answer. "Oh, well..." I quickly debated in my head if I should tell them the truth or make something up. I was pretty sure I might cause some sort of panic if I told them what had really happened. But then, they probably wouldn't believe it if I told them. What had I to lose?

"You know, it's a funny story, really. I climbed out my balcony and down to the courtyard the other night. And wouldn't you know? I ran into some nasty Hyrokkin. They cut me up pretty badly. Guess I won't be climbing out my balcony again anytime soon, am I right?"

No reply from any of them. They all sat and stared.
"Pretty crazy, huh?"
Nothing.
Then Sindri said to me, "If you are not going to tell the truth, just do not say anything to us at all."

Then they all turned away from me and got back to their conversations. Fine with me. *Where is the food?*

"Did that really happen?" Maggie whispered to me.

"Um...more or less. So, Maggie, how are things?"

"What things?" she asked.

"Oh, any things. What have you been up to? Any progress on, um...meeting eligible bachelors?" I figured that was what most of the female courtiers were working on these days.

Maggie smiled. "Well, there is this one man. He is a captain in the King's Army. He is very handsome."

"That sounds nice. Do you all...hang out?" I had no idea what the courting rituals were on Idonea.

"Hang out?"

"Yeah, um...go on dates?"

"Oh, yes, dates. Well, we have been on one. It was very nice." Maggie smiled, but then she looked away.

"I'm glad for you. When will you see him again?" I asked.

"I do not know if I will see him again. At least not anytime soon."

"Why not?"

"Well, I am pretty busy right now. My sister needs my help a lot. Her lady-in-waiting cannot always handle all the tasks that Sindri gives her. I am often asked to help mend her dresses or fix her hair."

"That doesn't seem fair to you."

"It's all right. After all, Sindri will most likely be the next queen. It is kind of...an honor for me to be serving her, or so she tells me. I can pursue my goals after she has attained hers."

I sat back in my chair. So, Sindri considered herself the next queen already. Fine. Just fine. I looked across the table where she chatted with the other Hopefuls. She did look like a queen, already seated regally amongst her ladies-in-waiting.

And her ladies were hanging on every word she said. I decided to listen in to their conversation.

"So, Sindri," said one of the Hopefuls. I think her name was Rota, "Do tell. How was your evening with the king?"

I so did not want to hear this.

Sindri spoke to the whole table as if she were holding a press conference. "Oh, Rota, it was so wonderful. It was just the two of us out together. His Highness was such a gentleman. He took me to the best place in the village for dinner. It was beautiful. And he looked beautiful...almost as beautiful as me." And then she giggled. And then the others giggled.

Then 'not so cute anymore' Helinn jumped into the conversation. "Tell us all the details, Sindri. When the king brought you back to your room, was there...a goodnight kiss?"

The whole table went completely silent. It was like middle school again. Oh, the suspense!

Sindri smiled and said, "Well, Helinn. A lady doesn't kiss and tell," she lowered her voice, "but the king is a wonderful kisser."

The table erupted in whispers and soft giggles.

Except for me. I started laughing.

Everyone stopped and stared wide-eyed at me.

I didn't realize this for a minute and just kept laughing to myself. Then I heard Sindri address me...a bit rudely, I might add.

"Excuse me, Anne, but what is so funny?"

"Well," I cleared my throat before continuing, "It's just that, well you said 'A lady doesn't kiss and tell', but you did. I...just found it rather humorous that you would prove to us that you are not a 'lady'. That's all."

"Of course I am a lady. How dare you suggest otherwise?"

"I didn't. You did."

"I did no such thing."

"But you just said--"

"I know what I said. I do not need it repeated back to me. And I do not need to prove to anyone that I am, in fact, a lady!" She emphasized that last word by banging one fist on the table. A very lady-like fist, of course.

Rali walked up behind her and said, "No one can argue the fact that you are a lady, Sindri."

We all turned our attention to him, and Sindri seemed a bit embarrassed. She defended herself by informing Rali that I had, in fact, argued that point.

He chuckled, then glanced at me. "Why am I not surprised that Annie is the source of your frustration?"

I didn't know how to take that comment exactly. So I ignored it. Seriously, where was the food?

Rali sat down in the chair between Sindri (of course) and Helinn. As soon as he sat down, all the girls put on their sweetest smiles and gazed longingly at Rali.

"How are you all doing this morning?" he asked us.

There was an assortment of Fine and Wonderfully and one girl just giggled. Sindri waited for the other Hopefuls to quiet down before she answered.

"I am fine, Your Highness, though a bit tired after our rendezvous last night." She smiled and batted her eyelashes. She really and truly batted her eyelashes. I didn't know people really did that.

I rolled my eyes.

"Ah, yes. I am glad you enjoyed yourself," Rali told her. He glanced at me quickly and then, just as quickly, away again. Then he turned to the rest of the table and announced that our breakfast was about to be served.

Dear God, finally!

The servants carried in trays of eggs, sausage, fruits, and many different kinds of breads, jams, and some honey. We were all served water and juice, but I was served a special treat, just for me. One servant put a mug of coffee in front of me. It smelled rich and strong. I looked up at Rali and he was smiling.

"I hope you do not mind. I had Freya break into your stash so you could have some this morning."

I smiled back at him and thanked him.

Sindri watched us as we exchanged glances and quickly asked Rali if he had a busy day ahead of him. I took that opportunity to focus on the reason I had come.

The food. I put some of everything on my plate. It all smelled delicious. It took me about five minutes to eat it all and then I went in for seconds. I was reaching for a crusty croissant when I noticed it had gotten silent and all eyes were on me...again.

"What?" I asked.

"Oh, nothing," answered Sindri. "It is just that you are attacking your food like you have not eaten in years. It is quite repulsive."

I answered, "Probably not how a lady would eat, huh Sindri?"

She scowled at me. Rali laughed and said, "Actually, I like to see a woman with a healthy appetite. It is quite rare around here."

Almost immediately the other Hopefuls (Sindri included) grabbed their forks and began to gobble down their food.

"Wow. This is unbelievable," I said quietly to myself. I looked across the table at Rali and we seemed to be sharing the same thought. While the other girls ate, Rali and I did our best not to laugh.

The King

Chapter 16

When I left the dining room after breakfast, I made a new mental checklist.

1. Try to enjoy my 'vacation' in Idonea
2. Go out of my way to annoy Sindri whenever possible
3. Be nice to Freya and Maggie
4. Enjoy Rali's company...but don't get attached

I pursued the third one first. I waited for Maggie outside of the dining room and, luckily, she wasn't with her sister. I figured Sindri had stayed behind to get some more 'alone time' with Rali. And that was fine. Just fine.

"Hey, Maggie," I called to her. She saw me and smiled.

"Hi. Do you need me for something?" Poor thing. She had probably been so used to her sister making demands of her that whenever someone called her name she assumed they needed her help.

"I just wanted to walk with you. Where are you off to?" I asked her.

"I thought I might go to my room and relax for a little while. Sindri is, um...busy elsewhere and will not need me for a while. Would you like to join me?"

"I'd love to." We headed off towards the lyptra and I tried not to think about where else Sindri was being 'busy'.

"So, Maggie, what do you do to relax?"

"Well, sometimes I take a walk, sometimes I knit, or if I have time, I watch television."

What? That was a surprise. I stopped walking and she looked at me kinda funny.

"What is it?" she asked me.

"You have television here?"

"Of course, silly. You think we can transport people through space but cannot figure out radio waves?" she smiled.

"Well...I just... How come I've never seen one here? Where are they?"

"There are not a lot, really. Some of the courtiers have one. I think there is one in the Council Chambers, and I would assume there is one in the king's room."

I tried to remember if I had seen one during my short stay there. "No, I don't think he has one."

...oops.

This time it was Maggie's turn to stop walking and look surprised. I knew what was coming. I could be so stupid sometimes.

"Um...and how do you know this?"

"Oh, well..." Think, Annie, think. "I was just assuming, like you." I cringed. Really, Annie? Was that the best you could do?

She grinned at me and said, "No, you were not assuming. You know. When were you in his room? Even Sindri has not been there."

I will admit, that made me happy.

"It's not what you think, Maggie. I didn't plan for me to be there. Neither did he. It's totally not worth talking about, seriously."

As we got on a lyptra, the smile on her face told me she didn't really believe my answer, though she should have. I sighed. I hoped she wouldn't tell her sister...actually, maybe I kinda hoped she did. That would help complete task number two on my list for sure.

"I think there is more to you and the king than you are willing to tell me, Miss Annie Watts from Earth. I saw how you looked at each other today," Maggie said.

"What? No. I told you, I did not mean to be in his room. Nothing has happened. Nothing will happen," I told her. We stood in silence for a moment. "What did you mean? How did we…look at each other?"

Maggie laughed and said, "Oh, it was not anything worth talking about, seriously."

Touché, Maggie.

We got off the lyptra and made a right turn towards her room. I had learned from her that almost all of the courtiers lived in or near the palace. Many of them had larger estates farther out, but preferred to stay close to the palace most of the time. It was the courtiers and their families that owned the farms, the mills, the shops, and the homes in the kingdom. The people who lived in the village did the work, earned the money, and then paid the money back to the courtiers in the form of rent.

I asked Maggie, "Do the people in the village ever feel upset about that? Would they ever like the chance to own their own homes and shops? Or even their own farms?"

"Oh, I think they are happy with how things are. It is a good system."

I wondered to myself if Maggie really believed that, or if that was just what she was raised to think.

We were almost to her door when I heard Durin call my name.

"Annie, dear God, there you are. I went to your room and Freya said you were at breakfast with the king. I have been so worried about you after I heard what happened."

I shot a quick look at Maggie.

"After what happened?" she asked.

"Nothing, Maggie. Just me being stupid and getting myself hurt." I turned to Durin, "But I'm just fine. No big deal." I winked at him hoping he would get the hint. He looked at me, then at Maggie, and then back at me.

"Right, well, still. I wanted to check on you. Are you all right?" He looked genuinely concerned...and really gorgeous.

"Yes. Thank you."

Then we all kind of stood there in an awkward silence. Was he going to leave? Was he going to stay? Was Maggie going to ask any more questions about my injuries? Finally Maggie spoke.

"Well, Annie, thank you for walking with me to my room. I appreciate your company. We should get together soon and talk more, all right?"

"Of course, Maggie. Anytime."

Maggie walked into her room and closed the door behind her. I looked up at Durin and said, "You can't just go around announcing to everyone what happened. It might cause a panic and Rali would be mad." I did realize that what I had just told him not to do, I had just done at breakfast. But I knew those girls wouldn't believe a word I said. Especially since it was such a fantastic story. But still, I made a mental note not to do stuff like that anymore.

"So sorry, my dear," he said. "So, are we in a fight now?" he said through a grin.

I laughed. "No, we are not in a fight."

We began walking in no particular direction.

"How are you really, Annie? I can see that you are limping. How badly were you hurt?"

"Oh, stabbed in the leg, sliced up face," I turned my scarred side to him, "and then a nice burning puncture in my side. You know--the usual."

"Oh Annie, I cannot believe it. If I had been there, none of this would have happened."

I laughed to myself when I thought about how he had actually (though indirectly) been the cause of this. Normally, I wouldn't have found that so funny. But my attitude had changed. I had been through so much lately. Abduction, escape, almost killed by fire monsters… But now I knew I would be leaving this place soon, so I was able to laugh a lot of things off. I'm sure that helped my blood pressure.

"It's okay. I'm fine now."

We walked a few steps before a thought occurred to me. "So, Durin, how did you hear about what happened?" I asked him. I was pretty sure Rali wouldn't have spread the news to anyone who hadn't been there.

Durin shrugged his shoulders and said, "I am the general. I know everything that happens here."

"Okay, but who told you? Rali?"

He laughed and said, "No. One of the guards who was there."

"Oh. So, when did you find out?"

"I do not remember exactly. Some time yesterday. Why? What is it with all these questions?"

"Well, if you found out yesterday, why are you just now coming to find me?"

He seemed to be getting frustrated and it took him a minute to answer. "Listen, I have a lot I have to do here. I cannot just…just run to your side whenever I want. I was busy with matters concerning the kingdom."

"Oh. Okay. I guess it doesn't really matter. You know, Rali has many things to do, too, but he was able to be by my side," I teased.

Durin stopped walking, grabbed my arm and turned me to face him. "What do you mean by that? Do you think Rali cares more for you than I do? Because if that is what you think, I can--"

"No. No, I'm sorry. I was just joking. You can let go now."

He held on for a moment longer and I made a mental note not to try to make Durin jealous anymore. While I was standing that close to him, I was able to look deep into his eyes. I was close enough that I could see the same gold specks in his eyes that I had seen in Rali's. He let go of me and I stepped back.

"Your eyes. They have gold in them just like Rali's. Does everyone have that?" I asked him.

He frowned and said, "You have to be pretty close to someone to notice it. I am saddened that you have been close enough to him to see it."

"Well, it wasn't really my choice. But anyway, why is it there?"

The King

We continued walking and Durin said, "Everyone in Idonea has gold in their eyes. It comes from living on a planet with light from two suns."

"Wow. It's kind of cool, really. Does the gold stay forever?"

"Well, it takes a while to show up. Newborns do not show the gold until a week or two after they are born, depending on how much exposure to the suns they have had. Likewise, if someone were to leave Idonea, the gold would, in time, begin to fade."

"Hmm…But you have to have been born here? I guess my eyes won't do that?" I laughed to myself. "That's too bad, I guess. It would've been pretty cool to be the only girl on Earth with gold in her eyes."

"On Earth?" Durin laughed. "When do you plan on making an actual successful escape attempt?"

I looked sideways at him while we walked and said, "So, Rali didn't tell you that he is letting me go home?"

He stopped walking and I turned to face him.

"He is?"

"Yes."

"Why? When are you leaving? Are you leaving?"

"Of course I'm leaving. I can't stay here."

I started walking again and headed towards the lyptra. Durin caught up with me and said, "Why can't you stay here?"

I laughed. "Durin, this isn't my home."

"It could be."

Then something he had said earlier stopped me. "Durin, why did you say 'an actual successful escape attempt'? How did you know I had tried to escape?"

He cleared his throat and answered, "The guard told me. He uh…saw the Hyrokkin bringing you in from the courtyard. Said you had climbed out of your balcony."

"Hmm… I guess I wasn't as stealthy as I thought." I sighed and pushed the button on the lyptra. Yes, I had finally conquered the intimidating lyptras. He followed me into it and I pushed the button for the lowest floor. I was headed for the courtyards.

We rode silently on the lyptra. I knew Durin was watching me, but I didn't want to talk about staying or leaving. I just wanted to enjoy some fresh air and see as much of Idonea as I could while I was still there.

I exited the lyptra and Durin followed me.

"Where are we going?"

"I am going outside for some air. Where are you going?" I asked him.

"Wherever you are."

"Ah." I smiled at him, glad for his company.

We got a lot of stares walking out to the courtyards together but I didn't care. We walked out the main entrance and I headed for the stream I had seen a few days before.

When we got there, Durin continued our previous conversation, even though I had hoped he wouldn't.

"Why is Rali letting you leave?" he asked me.

I thought a minute before answering. "I think he finally realizes that I don't belong here. I need to be with my family and my friends."

"I cannot believe he is letting you go just like that. I never would. When will you go?"

"Five more days."

"Five days? Is that all the time I have with you? That is not enough!"

"What would be enough for you?" I joked.

"Well...five years maybe. No, five hundred years."

I laughed. "You are quite the charmer, General Durin."

"I am not trying to charm you, Annie. I am completely serious. I have never been this serious. Will you not consider staying?"

"Durin, there's no reason for me to stay, and every reason for me to go."

"What if I gave you a reason to stay?"

I turned to face him. "And what would that be?"

He turned away, and then after a moment, looked back at me.

"Annie, I...I think I am in love with you."

I just stared at him. No words, nothing. Just stared.

"What?" is what finally came out. "What did you just say?"

"I said I think--"

"Yeah, I heard you."

"Then why did you ask--"

"Never mind."

I turned back to look at the pretty stream flowing by with the gold and white fish swimming in it. What was I supposed to say to that? I knew he didn't actually mean it. He couldn't. I decided it was best to not say anything right then. He spoke first.

"I did not mean to upset you," he said. He seemed a bit dejected.

"Durin, I'm not upset. I'm just...surprised. I mean, you barely even know me. I'm flattered, truly, but you can't really mean that. Anyway, I am going to leave soon. Please don't put your hopes on me. Let's just enjoy this time we have together. Let's have a good time, okay?"

He didn't look at me for a minute so I stepped in front of him and forced him to make eye contact with me.

"Let's be friends and have fun. All right?"

He looked into my eyes then and said, "No, Annie. I do not want to be friends." Then his hands were pulling me close and then next thing I knew...

Yep. We were kissing again. Only this time I couldn't pull away. I didn't want to pull away. I wanted to enjoy this. I forgot about everything--my home, my family, annoying Sindri--and just indulged in his deep, longing kiss. We must've stayed this way for quite some time, because when we finally parted, there were about ten people staring wide-eyed at our public display.

Oops.

We looked at our audience and then at each other.

"I think I should go now. I've had enough fresh air for now," I said to Durin.

He smiled. "Well, Annie. I, unfortunately, have a meeting to attend for which I am now late. But I will be coming by later in case you feel the need for some more...fresh air."

I giggled. Dammit, I giggled.

He turned to walk off and, as he left, he called over his shoulder, "I will see you later...friend."

By this point, my thigh and my side were pretty achy, so I slowly headed back up to my room. I needed some rest after my eventful morning. I walked into the palace, got on and then off the lyptra, and then was back in my room. Freya was there waiting for me.

"Hi, Freya," I greeted her happily. "You know, you were right. I did have a good time." Freya looked up at me with a frown on her face. "You did want me to have a good time, didn't you?" I asked.

"Yes, I did."

"Then why do you look upset?"

She sighed loudly. "You are not having a good time with the right people."

"And just who are the right people?"

She walked away from me and over to the secret closet. She opened it and then busied herself inspecting the dresses inside. So I followed.

"Freya, who are the right people? Or do you mean the right person?"

She looked me in the eyes and said, "Annie, I know General Durin was looking for you, and I am pretty sure he found you by the look on your face."

What was the look on my face? I looked around for a reflective surface nearby but couldn't find anything at hand.

"Annie, the general is not...he is not worth chasing."

Again with the chasing? Were we five years old again when the girls chased the boys on the playground?

"Geez, why does everyone think I am chasing him? I'm not chasing anybody. And anyway, he is the one coming on to me," I told her.

"Well, you have to tell him to leave you alone," she demanded.

"Whoa, Freya. I don't have to do anything. And why is it such a big deal to you anyway? Why do you care who I hang out with while I'm here?"

"I just do not want you to...to get hurt," she said then. She actually looked concerned.

"I won't get hurt, Freya. I am here for just a little longer. I won't have time to get hurt. I am just enjoying myself, not falling in love."

She looked away from me and back to the dresses.

"But maybe you should," she said quietly.

"What? Maybe I should what? Fall in love? You just told me not to."

"Not to fall in love with General Durin...but maybe..."

"Ah, yes. You want me to fall in love with Rali. You want him to sweep me off my feet, carry me off into the sunset, and live happily ever after. Well, I'm sorry, Freya, but that is not in my plans. I am simply going to have a nice stay here, and then go back home. So stop trying to play matchmaker." I walked away from her and went searching for some pain medication. Not only were my wounds hurting, but I was starting to develop a headache, thanks to Freya.

"But, Annie," she started, "if you just spend some more time with him, get to know him better, you might--"

"Freya, that's enough. I am going home in five days. I am not going to fall in love with Rali. I am not going to marry him and be the queen. You cannot tell me what I should or should not do. I am not your daughter!"

The look she flashed me then was one of anger and sorrow and shock. I felt like a total jerk.

My shoulders slumped. "Freya, I'm sorry. I didn't mean to say...I wasn't thinking. I'm sorry. I'm...I'm feeling some pain from my wounds right now, and that isn't helping. But, no excuses. I shouldn't have said that."

She walked over to my bedside table, picked up a bottle and handed it to me. "Your pain medication is in here. If you don't want to fall asleep, just take half of one pill."

I took the bottle, thanked her, and watched her walk out of the room. I sighed. I wasn't doing too well with my 'number three goal' of being nice to her. She had been so good to me, and I would try to make it up to her after she had some time to herself.

The King

I took half of a pain pill and laid down on the couch with a borrowed book from the Royal library. After a couple of minutes, I began feeling a bit drowsy from the meds. I laid the book on a table and closed my eyes.

I thought about my family. I thought about my father. I had been fourteen when he died. I could still clearly remember my mom sitting on the edge of my bed when I woke up that rainy summer morning. I could still hear her crying quietly. I could hear her telling me that Daddy had been in a car wreck on his way to work. I remembered her pulling me into her arms and stroking my hair. We had stayed that way for a long time. She held me and cried, and I held her while my brain tried to comprehend what she had told me. It had taken a couple of days for me to really accept that my father was gone. And I was very angry. It wasn't fair for me to lose my daddy while other kids still had theirs. My daddy was the best. My daddy should've been around forever.

I rolled over onto my non-injured side and tried not to think about my father... That didn't work. So I got off the couch and walked over to the balcony. I looked out to the village and remembered that I had wanted to go visit there. The medication had dulled my pain, so I figured this was as good a time as any.

I grabbed my shoes and walked out my door. I headed down the hallway to the lyptra, but didn't make it that far before I heard voices. One was Rali's, and the other voices belonged to men that I didn't know. I walked towards the place where I heard the voices coming from so I could listen in...just in case it was interesting.

I approached the doorway to the room where the men were meeting and I could hear them discussing Helgrind and the Hyrokkin. Rali seemed to be silent most of the time, only commenting on what the other men were telling him. One man said, "They are weak. They cannot hurt us. We need not busy our guards with something so unnecessary." Then another one said, "And no damage has been done. No one is even aware of their occasional trespassing. Your Highness, I think we should do nothing further that might cause a panic or make the women feel unsafe. The Hyrokkin will not hurt us if we just let them be." My fists clenched hearing that untruthful information. I thought about the pain I had felt as the Hyrokkin's dagger had pierced my thigh, and the wound that had been burned into my side. I was angry that the leaders of this kingdom didn't see those monsters as dangerous. And I wanted to contradict them.

"Oh, I'm pretty sure you're wrong." I had walked right into the room and opened my big mouth. I wanted them to know the truth. There I was with about eight men in uniform (the Royal Army leaders I guessed) and Rali, looking at me in shock. They looked from me, to Rali, and then back to me. Then one of them said to me, "I am sorry, My Lady, but I don't think you should be here. If you would please--"

Rali interrupted him. "No, it is all right." Then he looked at me. "Please, Annie, continue."

I walked toward Rali. The men were standing in a dark room with one light shining over a table that had a large map of the kingdom. I walked up to it, stood next to Rali and noticed something on the map. There were little markers placed at every point where Hyrokkin had been spotted. "It seems that the Hyrokkin have mainly kept to the outskirts of the kingdom, right?"

"That is mostly accurate," said Rali.

"Yes, mostly accurate because that has recently changed. A few days ago, Rali...um, Your Highness, you were called to the council chambers because of a sighting close to the palace." I pointed to one of the markers and looked at him for confirmation. He nodded. "Okay, well not long after, they made it all the way to the courtyards. Isn't that right?" I looked back at Rali. And all the other men looked at him too. There wasn't a marker on the map for that one.

He stood still for a moment as if he was considering what he should say, and then said, "Yes. You are correct."

A few of the men looked confused but most seemed to be on the same page, so I continued.

"Well, I think you should be considering that they might get even closer next time. And maybe in greater numbers. It should also be noted that these Hyrokkin are not weak and they most definitely can hurt you, whether provoked or not." I looked around. "And which one of you said they wouldn't hurt us if we let them be?" I looked at the group of men and one of the taller ones slowly raised his hand as if he were hesitant to admit he had said that. I looked straight at him, "I didn't bother them. I let them be." Then I lifted my skirt up to reveal my wounded thigh...yes, I was showing almost my entire leg to Idonea's army leaders. There was a very audible gasp and a few of the men looked away out of gentlemanly respect, but not the one I was addressing. "I've got an even better one above my waist, wanna see it?"

Rali chuckled and said, "I think he got your point, Annie."

I let go of my skirt but didn't stop glaring at the man who had said they wouldn't harm anyone.

Rali cleared his throat to get the men's attention.

"Annie has a point, whether I agree with her way of making it or not. She is right. And I am rather disappointed that none of my own military leaders will step forward and admit the truth. The Hyrokkin are after something and may not stop coming until they get it. Annie was almost killed the other night..." he paused for a moment before continuing. "The Hyrokkin should and will be considered our enemy. Any one of them spotted on our planet should be dealt with immediately. They must be captured and made to answer for their crime. We will station more guards in the village, alongside the river, and outside the palace gates. We will find out how and where they are getting in. We will stop them before they can get close enough to harm anyone else. They know the rules, they must follow them."

I looked sideways at Rali and got a bit of a thrill seeing him be so authoritative.

"And just where do you suggest we acquire all this extra security?" asked a familiar voice. I looked in the voice's direction as Durin stepped out of the shadow and into our circle around the map table. Made sense that he would be there, but why hadn't he shown himself earlier? I'm sure I looked a bit surprised but he didn't see it. He didn't even look at me then. He was looking straight at Rali.

"We have plenty of guards in the palace-some that spend their days patrolling levels that have only a few tenants. Their abilities and strengths are being wasted there. We will reassign them to a position where they can do some real good," Rali said.

"Well, Sir," Durin said, "I think that if we begin to remove guards from the palace, our people, especially our ladies, may begin to feel the panic and vulnerability that was mentioned by Captain Tourn a moment ago."

"It didn't do me, a lady, any good to have them in the palace when I was attacked," I countered.

"I am fairly confident that most ladies of Idonea do not climb out of their balconies," Durin said.

Durin:1, Annie:0

Then Durin turned back to the men in the room. "There is no reason to remove any guard from their current position in the palace. It would only cause unnecessary worry." He looked right at Rali and said, "As the leader of your army, I recommend no immediate change from the way things are currently run."

Rali looked directly at Durin. "As leader of this kingdom I have to disagree. General Durin, you will tell your guards on levels nine, eleven, and fourteen that their duties now lie in guarding the roads from the village to the palace. Any courtier who requests a personal bodyguard will be denied, and Annie," he looked at me, "would you be willing to give your personal guards up for the cause? They have not done a very good job anyway."

I put on my most serious face and said, "It would be my honor."

"All right then. It is done. General Durin, I leave it up to you to find any more guards that can be moved outside the palace. We will meet tomorrow afternoon to discuss your progress. Gentlemen, thank you for your time, but I must leave now." He turned to me. "Annie?"

"Um...yes?"

"Shall we?" He held his arm out and I linked my arm through it. He led me out the door, into the hallway, away from eight surprised men, and one angry general.

Chapter 17

"Well, that was impressive," said Rali as we walked down the hallway.

"What?"

"I cannot say that I have ever seen a woman willing to reveal so much of herself just to make a point." He smiled at me.

"Oh, well...yeah. Sorry about that. I guess I should have been a bit more prudent. But what that guy said made me mad." I scowled again just thinking about it.

"Yes. I will admit, some of the men in there are not always worthy of my attention. I usually do not listen to much of anything they have to say. Some of them did not earn their positions because of battles they have won, or even because of their intelligence or talents. But they are from powerful families--"

"Yeah, I've heard about the kind of pull a 'powerful family' can have around here. You know, that just doesn't seem right to me. You're the king, aren't you? Can't you fire some of those guys and get some better qualified soldiers working for you?" I asked.

He laughed. "If only it were that easy, Annie. This is the way things have been done for years. It is not worth causing a riot to change it."

"I think that is just an excuse. 'This is the way things have been done'. So what? If you don't like it, change it. That's your prerogative."

He stopped walking, so I stopped, too. He looked at me for a moment without speaking. He wasn't just looking at me though, he was searching me. Searching my eyes for...I don't know what. But I was suddenly hypnotized again.

I didn't know how long we stood that way until I finally snapped out of the trance and stepped back.

"What?" I asked him.

He shook his head. "Nothing." He looked away for a second and then said, "I want to show you something. A place I think you will like." He took my hand and led me to some steps leading down to our right and a doorway with two doors at the foot of the stairs.

"What is it? Another library?" I joked.

He looked back at me as he pushed open the door and we entered a garden. But not in the courtyards. We were still up twenty floors. The beautiful outdoor park was situated in the air between two different wings of the palace. There were tall green trees lining either side and colorful flowers grew here and there. I could see benches placed in the shade provided by the tall trees - and the whole place was carpeted with lush green grass. I gasped.

"Wow," I said quietly to myself. I took a few steps onto the grass and was so glad I chose not to put my shoes on. The grass was so soft underneath my bare toes. If I had been alone I may have just laid myself down right there on the grass. But since I wasn't, I had to contain myself.

"What do you think?" asked Rali.

"I think it's beautiful." I walked even further into the small park and stopped under the shade of a particularly gorgeous oak tree. It was lofty with broad, jade-colored leaves that rustled as the breeze blew through the strong branches.

Rali walked over to me and said, "My father gave this to my mother."

"The tree?"

"No," he laughed. "The park."

"He gave her a whole park? Wow. How nice of him."

"Yes. My mother loved being outside, but did not always enjoy the bright sunlight shining from two suns," he explained.

"I can't blame her for that."

"So, my father had this constructed for her just a few years after they were married. She spent a lot of time here. I would often find her sitting here..." Rali walked a short distance to a chair and small table under another shady tree. "Sometimes she would be out here with my father, or maybe one of her ladies-in-waiting; but, usually, she preferred to spend her time here alone. It was her own little escape from the palace, built right in the middle of the palace." He smiled.

"That's lovely," I said. And I meant it.

Rali turned to face me and said, "I want to give it to you, now."

"I'm sorry, what?"

"I want this park to be yours. It can be your escape, your retreat when you feel the need to get away. There is plenty of shade for sitting and reading a good book, or you could just take a nice stroll through the lane," he said. Then his tone turned very serious. "Just, please, do not climb over the side." He hid a tiny grin, but not very well.

"Wait, you are seriously giving this park to me? Like...it's mine?" I narrowed my eyes at him as if that might help me understand this a little better.

Rali nodded. "Yes. It is yours."

"But...I'm not...I mean, I don't live here. I'm leaving soon. How can I own this park if I'm not even here?"

"Good question," he said and began strolling between the trees.

I followed him. "Rali, you can't bribe me to get me to stay. There are parks on Earth that I can enjoy, you know."

"Yes, do you own any of them?" he asked.

"Um...no."

"And did your boyfriend ever offer to give you your own park?"

"Well, no, but--"

"Has General Durin?"

"Wha...of course not," I said.

"Ah. Well, I guess this would make me...better." He looked sideways at me, grinned, put both hands behind his back, and strutted on down the lane.

I just stared after him for a moment trying to decide whether to be angry or pleased.

I chose the latter.

I quickened my pace to catch up with the 'very proud of himself' king.

"I wanted to let you know I have decided to accept your gift, even though it will only be mine for a short time."

"It will still be yours even if you leave," he informed me.

"Well, why would you do that? Surely, you would want to give it to Sin...to whoever you choose as your queen." I prayed he hadn't heard my slip up.

"I have no wish to give it to anyone except you, not even...whoever I choose as my queen." He smiled.

"Well, at least promise me you will let other people come here if they want to. This place is too beautiful to keep private."

"All right, I promise that if you leave, it will become open to the public."

"You should probably stop saying 'if'. It's going to happen. I will be leaving," I told him again.

"You keep saying that, and yet, I believe you less and less each time," he said.

"Well, that's your problem and there's nothing I can do about it."

Rali looked at me with a furrowed brow.

We walked on for a moment in silence. I knew he was hoping I would stay, and I didn't want to disappoint him. After all, I was discovering how much I actually admired this man. Now that I wasn't focused on hating him quite so much. But I couldn't stay on Idonea just to make him happy. I had other things to consider before him. My family, my friends...Jake...

I shook my head. I didn't want to think about any of that right then in that beautiful moment while walking in my park. So I decided to take that opportunity I had of being alone with Rali to find out more about him and his family.

"So, Rali, tell me more about your parents. What were they like?"

"Well, my father was a good king. At least he tried to be. He preferred quiet, small gatherings to the grand parties he was often required to attend as royalty. He would tell me that if he had not already known he was meant for my mother and she for him before the whole 'courting' period began during his reign, he would have detested every moment, and possibly stayed unmarried. If that were allowed."

"So, he and your mother were already in love?"

He hesitated. "I do not know if one could say they were in love, but they made a very good couple. He admired her and she admired him as well. But she was not desirous of the life of a queen. Still, my father pursued her and chose her at the Kostera."

"Were any of the other girls mad about that? Or any of the courtiers?"

"I am sure some of the other girls had to have been upset. But my mother was from a... Well, she was brought up by a--"

"A powerful family?" I finished for him.

"Yes," he admitted and he kind of flinched then. "So there was not much argument when she was chosen in the end."

"You said your father knew they were meant for each other, but she didn't want to be queen. Did she end up being happy?"

"Oh, I think she was happy. My father did anything in his power to make her happy, like build this park for her. He kept the Royal balls and festivities to a minimum so they could live as quietly as possible together. Yes, I believe she was happy. Through their many years together they became the best of friends. They were rarely apart. In fact, after he died, she went into a kind of seclusion. She lived only one year longer than he did." His pace had slowed a bit at that point.

"It must have been hard for you to have lost both your parents in one year," I said, thinking of my own experience of losing even one parent.

"Yes it was." I looked up at his face and saw a flash of anger, as if he was remembering his father's untimely death. We walked a few more steps before he continued. "I was twenty one when my mother died. And although I was considered of a fine age to be ruling the kingdom on my own, I missed having the council and advice from my parents." He looked at me and smiled a bit sadly.

We turned around as we approached the end of the lane.

"So, if you were officially 'The king' when you were twenty one...twelve years ago, right?"

"Right."

"Okay, then, why are you just now looking for your queen? Isn't that something a new king would want to do right away? You know, find his bride and start making little heirs to the throne?" I read a lot of historical fiction, so I was basically an expert on such topics.

"'Make little heirs to the throne'? Is that what kings are supposed to do?" he laughed.

"Well, among other things, of course, like declaring war, waving from balconies, and invading nearby countries," I informed him.

He laughed. "Well, I am glad you have finally arrived so that I may start doing my job correctly."

"Glad to be of service." I smiled up at him. "Anyway, back to my question. Why have you waited so long?"

He was thoughtful for a moment. "Well, Annie. I guess you could say I just want to be sure. I want to be sure I have found the right woman for me, and for this kingdom."

"Ha. Then I guess I'm out."

"Why do you say that?"

"Well, let's see. Your army leaders don't like me, the courtiers and powerful families, I'm sure, are not crazy about me. I've single-handedly made it possible for Hyrokkin to get into the palace...do you need more examples?"

"No, I think those will do nicely. Thank you for helping me."

"Anytime. Just trying to make it easier for you to narrow down your list of 'Hopefuls'."

"That's very thoughtful. And so selfless. Hmm...thoughtful and selfless. Could be considered two good qualities of a queen."

"Well, two good qualities can't possibly be enough."

"All right then. I'll tell you more. You are courageous, and--"

"What? No I'm not."

"You climbed out of your balcony and down the side of the palace. You talked back to armed Hyrokkin-so I'm thinking that wise may not be one of your attributes-you held your ground and spoke your mind to a group of my army leaders. Yes, you are courageous. You are also--"

"I was terrified to climb down the wall, and I was just angry with the Hyrokkin and your army men. I don't think any of that could be considered 'courageous'."

"Well, I do, and I am the king, so what I say goes. It's my prerogative, remember?" he said.

"Well, fine, but that's still only three."

"Oh, I have more. I'll have to say all of this quickly before you have time to interrupt me, so--"

"What do you mean before I--"

He stopped me with only a look.

"Ah, yes. Continue."

"Thank you. As I mentioned before, you speak your mind. Also, you care about others, otherwise you wouldn't have said anything in that meeting today about protecting the kingdom and keeping the Hyrokkin away. You are a fighter, as

I have learned on many occasions, whether you were fighting me, or Hyrokkin, or an imprudent lieutenant. As far as what is more pleasing for me, personally, well, you are very funny and make me laugh. You are entirely too beautiful for this place--"

"Wouldn't that be a negative?"

"And you do what you think you must. Even when asked not to."

"You are referring to me interrupting just then, aren't you?"

"Yes. And that leads me to another good quality. You are very clever and intelligent." Then he was silent for a minute.

"Are you done now? I would hate to interrupt."

"Yes, I am finished," he said.

"All right then."

We walked in silence for a moment before he said, "Do you have nothing to say in reply?"

"No. It is all pretty much true. Can't argue."

"Ah. Yes, notice I did not mention 'humility' as one of your qualities."

"Humility is overrated." I looked up at him and smiled. He smiled back.

We continued walking down the lane, back toward the entrance to the palace. When we approached the doors, I turned to Rali. "Thank you. Really and truly, thank you for this gift. I am sure I will spend time here every day until I go home."

He looked a bit disappointed but managed to smile at me. "I still have time to change your mind."

"My mind won't be changed, Rali. I need to go home."

"Annie, can't you just try to--"

"Rali, don't. I can't. And I won't. My family needs me-"

"I need you." Rali grabbed my hands and stepped closer to me. "Annie, there is a reason I brought you here. You know I have been watching you, learning about you while you were on Earth. I have so much to share with you, so much to show you..."

"Like what? What can you show me that would convince me to stay? What could you tell me?"

He was quiet.

"There is nothing you can do to change my mind," I said. "I'm sorry."

I turned and walked towards the door and had my hand on the doorknob when I heard him say it.

"Annie, I love you."

I froze. My feet felt glued to the ground. I now had two men confess their love for me today. But only one of them had meant it. And that was why I pushed open the door, forced my feet off the ground, and walked back into the palace without turning to look at him. Rali had meant it. And I didn't have any idea what to do with that. I walked back through the hallways as quickly as I could. I had to get away. I began to run towards my room. What Rali had just told me scared me more than anything else ever had. I was terrified, because when he told me that he loved me, I knew it was very possible that I was in love with him, too.

Chapter 18

When I got back to my room, there was a cold lunch of chicken with vegetables waiting for me. But no Freya anywhere. I walked to the tray of food and was surprised to find that I didn't have an appetite. That was a first for me. I went to the closet to get some more comfortable lounging - around clothes for the afternoon. My plan was to stay in my room for the rest of the day. I didn't want to go anywhere, or see anybody. I had some thinking to do.

And some apologizing.

I took off my feela and my dress, and pulled on some grey stretch pants and a long black cotton shirt. Then I walked over to the door to Freya's own room next to mine, and knocked.

"Freya? Are you in there?"

No answer.

"Look, I'm really sorry. I know you are just trying to help. Please come out and talk to me."

I heard some rustling around in the room, and then Freya's small footsteps heading towards the door. I stepped back as the door opened and she entered my bedroom with her head down. "My Lady, I must apologize for earlier. It is not my place to tell you how to live your life and who you should or should not love. If you would like for a new lady-in-waiting to take my place, I would understand."

My mouth dropped open. Wasn't she supposed to be mad at me? I had behaved like a jerk, not Freya.

"Freya, what are you talking about? No, I don't want a new lady-in-waiting, that's ridiculous. Anyway, you were just trying to give me some advice, and there's nothing wrong with that. I shouldn't have reacted the way I did. It was wrong of me, and I apologize. You don't owe me an apology, really," I told her.

She looked up and let out a huge sigh of relief. "Oh, thank goodness. I was sure you would want me to go."

"Don't ever think that, Freya. What would I do without you?"

She smiled and we hugged.

"Oh, Freya. We can't fight. I'm not here much longer, so let's be friends, okay?"

"Yes, ma'am," she said. "Though I will have to disagree with what you said about not being here much longer."

"Geez, you and Rali both. I just can't convince you guys, I guess. You two can console each other when I actually do leave."

"Whatever you say," she said and then smiled. "So, Annie, what are your plans for the rest of the day? I see you have already changed clothes. Can I assume you plan to stay in for now?"

"Yes. I would like to just lay low for a while and rest my poor wounds. Is that all right with you, Freya? Or did you have any special dinners or balls or dances planned for me to go to that I didn't know about?" I smiled at her and she shook her head.

"No. You have my permission to rest this afternoon."

"Thank you. You are very kind."

I crawled into my bed, took the other half of my pain pill, and lay down. I closed my eyes while listening to Freya bustle around the room, removing the food cart, folding linens, doing some general cleaning. It was a nice sound that helped me drift off to sleep.

I dreamed of my father again.

"Daddy?"

"Yes, Annie?"

"Tell me more about the star that can take us all to Annieland."

"Annieland? Oh, yes," he chuckled, "Annieland. How could I forget?"

My father had been on the couch reading the newspaper when I jumped up next to him.

"Well, let's see. This magic star, like I told you, could take you anywhere you wanted to go. Even if it was a place really far away."

"How did it do that? Would someone have to hold on real tight? Or did it have a seat on it? Did it have a steering wheel?"

He laughed. "No, it didn't have any of those things. The star itself didn't go anywhere. It was the power coming from the star that would launch a person through the air, to wherever they wanted to go."

"Wouldn't that be scary?" I asked him.

"Well, I imagine it would happen really quickly. The person might not even realize they were being transported anywhere until they arrived."

"Hmm...that's pretty fast."

"Yes."

"Well, okay then. Tell me what happens after the magic star power takes me and you and mommy and Jane to Annieland," I begged him.

"Annieland. Well, I think you should tell me about Annieland. I mean, it is your planet after all. What do you think it is like?" he asked me.

"Oh it's a beautiful place, Daddy. You will love it. We can go on lots of walks and we can live in a really big house there--since it's my planet and all--and you and mommy won't have to go to work. You can just stay home and play with me all day long." I smiled.

"That sounds wonderful," he told me. "What else?"

"Well, if we decide we want people to come visit us, you know, like Gramma and Grampa, we can send the magic star to bring them to us."

"That is very thoughtful of us."

"I think so, too, Daddy. We can send them letters on the magic star, too. Hey Daddy?"

"Yes?"

"What is the magic star called? Does it have a name or will we just call it the magic star?"

"Oh yes, it does have a name. It's a tricky name, but you are such a smart girl that I bet you can say it just fine."

"What is it?"
"It is called the Sidas Array."

I sat straight up in my bed, waking up right in the middle of my dream. "The Sidas Array," I said to myself. That's why it had sounded familiar when the Hyrokkin told me about it. My father had told me about it first. When I was a child.

"Did you say something, Annie?" asked Freya. She came closer to me and asked, "Are you all right?"

I looked at her with my eyes wide. "The Sidas Array. That is the name of the magic star."

She looked at me uncertainly and said, "That is what powers the Bridge, yes. But you knew that already. What is wrong? Did you have a nightmare? Can I get you something?"

"No...wait, yes. Rali. I need to talk to Rali." I got out of bed quickly, ran to my closet and pulled on a long blue tunic with silver beading over the jeans I had worn the first day I arrived. I pulled my hair into a messy bun and hurried towards the door.

"Freya, where would the king be right now? I need to talk to him."

"Well, I don't really know--"

"Is he in a meeting? What time is it?"

"It is after dinner time already. You slept for quite a while. Perhaps you should stay and eat something before--"

"No, this is important. I have to find him."

I marched through the doorway and into the hall. I decided to head for his room first, and if he wasn't there, maybe one of the guards would know where I could find him. I walked past quite a few courtiers who didn't seem to approve of my outfit by the way they stuck their noses up at me. I rolled my eyes. *Whatever.* I went up and up the curving hallway until I reached the door I had entered that night with the Hyrokkin. The door was closed but there were no guards. Apparently Rali had sacrificed his guards for the cause of patrolling the paths to the palace as well; so, of course, I just opened the door. I went up the steps as quickly as I could and tried not to think about what had happened there a few nights earlier. I reached the top step and headed to the bedroom door.

"I have to find out how my dad knew about the Sidas Array," I said to myself. "Surely Rali will know."

Something was going on that I needed to find out about. How was my father connected to all of this? Had he been trying to tell me about Idonea when I was little? How did he know? How much did he know? How much could Rali tell me of all this?

"Rali? Are you there?" I reached the door and pushed it open. The lights were dim and there was a fire roaring in his fireplace. I stepped in and called again. "Rali? I need to ask you about something. Are you here?"

Then I got an answer to my question...but not from Rali.

"He will be returning shortly. Would you like me to give him a message?"

And there she was. Reclining on one of Rali's luxurious couches. She was wearing a long, ivory - colored silk tunic that made her bronze skin look radiant. It looked just like the tunic I had worn when I was there. I knew it was Rali's. Sindri's face was lit up by the light of the fire, and her dark hair fell softly over her shoulders. She was in his room, on his couch, wearing only his shirt. And he would be here with her, with Sindri, exquisite Sindri. My heart fell. My stomach turned. I had to leave before Rali saw me there.

"Oh, umm...no. I just wanted to ask him something. But I don't...umm..." I didn't know how to make this any less awkward, so I just stepped back out of the room while Sindri watched me with a triumphant smile on her face. I closed the door, turned, and walked away. I headed back to my room in a daze. I couldn't stop seeing her there. I couldn't stop seeing him going back to his room to be with her. I shook my head to try to get the sickening images out, but all I accomplished by doing that was to make myself really dizzy.

I stopped walking and leaned against the wall. I was breathing pretty heavily and needed to calm myself down. I decided to do some mental 'self-talk'. I told myself, "It's okay, Annie. You are going home soon. You don't care about all of this nonsense." But then I reminded my 'self-talk' that Rali had said he loved me. My self-talk replied with, "He wants you to stay. He will say anything to keep you here so he doesn't have to admit he made a mistake in bringing you here in the first place."

My 'self-talk' was probably right. But I didn't feel any better. In fact I felt pretty miserable. I needed to distract myself. I needed to focus on the reason I had gone searching for Rali in the first place: the Sidas Array and how my father knew about it.

I took a few deep breaths and headed slowly back to my room. Maybe I could see if Freya knew anything about it. Or maybe spend some time searching the library. I was trying really hard to turn my attention to that mission. But it was no use. I couldn't concentrate when all I could see was images of her on his couch. My heart pounded, tears threatened to fall.

At that moment, I was sad, and I wanted to be alone. So I decided to go to my park. First, I stopped in my room to change (the denim was not being that nice to my wounds) and to let Freya know where I would be.

"Are you all right? Did you find the king?" Freya asked me. She looked concerned.

"Oh, he wasn't in his room. But it's not a big deal. I can talk to him tomorrow." I smiled at her and pretended all was well with the world. "I just want to put on something a little more loose fitting and then go stroll around and enjoy the evening."

"Do you need for me to go with you?" she asked.

"No, it's fine, thank you. I will just be in the park."

"All right then. If you do not mind, I might go down to the village while you are gone and see about some new materials for your wardrobe." She looked excited at the prospect. She was still holding on to some hope that I might be sticking around Idonea for a while. Normally, I would have argued with her. But I didn't feel like it at the moment.

"That sounds like a wonderful idea, Freya. Have a good time. I'll see you later." I had changed into a loose, jade green dress with a matching feela. No shoes. I walked out the door and headed to my park, which I had decided to name Annieland.

When I got there, I slowly walked down the lane, breathing in the fresh Idonea air; and I dreamed about being back home. I wondered what my friends and family were doing at that very moment. I wondered if they were thinking about me, wondering if they would ever see me again. "I'll be home soon," I whispered to the air.

I walked over to the chair and table where Rali had said his mother used to sit when she visited her park--now Annieland. I sat down and imagined what she must have felt like as Queen of Idonea. I was glad that her husband had built this park as an escape for her. I imagined it must have been so nice for her to have this place to go to when she needed to pretend for a moment that she did not share in the responsibility of running an entire kingdom. What a stressful life it must have been. Lucky for me, I would never have to worry about that.

Lucky, lucky me.

I supposed I really should be feeling sorry for Sindri. Once she and Rali were married, she would be the queen. She would be an example for women everywhere in Idonea. That puts a lot of pressure on a person.

I was so lucky.

Poor Sindri would have to go everywhere with the king. Attend meetings, balls, dinners--all those royal things that kings and queens had to go to.

Lucky me.

Poor Sindri would have to support Rali in his decisions as king, hold his hand when he was upset, stand beside him through thick and thin, be there for him every day and every night just to love him and be his friend.

Poor, poor Sindri.

I cringed. I was so jealous I could taste it. I felt the bile rising in my throat. I had to stop thinking about it. Being alone in my park wasn't doing me any good. I needed a hot bath and another pain pill just to knock me out for the night. *Good plan, Annie.*

I rose from the bench and walked back inside the palace.

"There you are," called Durin from down the hall. "I had just been to your room and no one was there."

Durin. Good, handsome, strong, Durin. Sure, he had kind of thrown me under the bus earlier that day in the meeting, but that was understandable, wasn't it? He had to be tough in front of the men. And, anyway, he was gorgeous. He could get away with a lot. And he was quite a sight for sore eyes at the moment.

"Hi, Durin. Yeah, I was just walking in the park, but I think I'm going back to my room now."

"Allow me to accompany you." He held out his arm and I took it.

"You said you were walking in the park? Is that the queen's park?" he asked me.

"Well, I guess it was. Technically it is my park now," I told him.

"How is that?"

"Oh, Rali gave it to me."

Durin stopped walking and stood in front of me. "He gave it to you? Why?"

"He was just trying to be nice, that's all."

"I think he is being a little too nice," said Durin tensely.

I laughed. "Don't worry. He isn't always that nice to me. I won't be jumping into bed with him any time soon." Not like someone else would be...or already had.

"That is good to hear."

We continued walking to my room and when we got there I realized Freya was probably still out in the village. I couldn't very well invite the general into my room without a chaperone...could I? I stopped in front of my door and looked up at Durin.

"Everything all right?" he asked me.

"Um...yes, fine. I was just thinking that maybe we should go for a walk or something."

"Go for a walk? Right now? I would rather just stay in. Shall we fix some tea and just talk?"

Sure... 'talk'. But you know what? Rali wasn't alone in his room. Rali wasn't off sulking about me somewhere. He wasn't thinking about me or how I felt about his relationship with Sindri. So why should I sit around and cry about him? Why shouldn't I have a grand old time while I was here? After all, this was my vacation, right?

"Ok, Durin. Let's stay in. That sounds like a great idea." I opened the door and he followed me into the room. He looked around and opted to take a seat on the couch.

"So, do you actually want some tea? I don't know where Freya keeps it, but I could find some."

He laughed. "No. Do not worry about it. Come and sit down with me for a while. I want to hear about Earth."

I walked over to the couch and sat down. I pulled both my legs up underneath me and got comfortable. "What do you want to know?"

"Start with what you like to do there. What do you do for fun?" he asked me.

"Oh, well...I like to go out to eat with friends, or read, or...well, I guess that's about it. I'm not the most exciting person you will find. Maybe Rali will kidnap someone more adventurous next time. Then you can hear some more thrilling stories."

"I do not care to hear anyone else's stories. I care to hear yours. So…let me see here. When you go back to Earth, you will enjoy going to eat with your friends?" he asked me.

"Uh...yes."

"Hmm... Seems like you could do that here with me. And when you go back to Earth you will...read?"

I'm pretty smart, so I figured out where he was going with this.

"Yes, Durin, I will read. And yes, I know I can read here, too, and probably do anything here that I could do on Earth." He opened his mouth to say something but I stopped him by continuing with, "but I can't do any of those things here with my family and my friends from Earth, now, can I?"

"Maybe you could all visit each other. Maybe Rali would go for that. And then would you stay?"

"You pose an interesting question, General. Maybe if it were like a road trip. Maybe if I could just drive across town to see them. But traveling across the universe is, perhaps, a little much."

"Perhaps. Well, I still have some time to change your mind, have I not?"

Geez, were Durin and Rali reading from the same book or something?

"Sure. And good luck with that," I said to him. I rose from the couch and walked to the balcony. It was a clear night and I could see lights on the pathways down to the village. I wondered if Rali had taken Sindri on another date before I had...interrupted. I wondered why Rali was going to such extremes to keep me here when he was clearly in love with her and not with me. And then I wondered why, when I had this gorgeous man in my room, all I could think about was Rali, and how I was pretty sure I had been falling in love with him. Was I still? Could I? After walking in and seeing Sindri lying on his couch, could I still fall for Rali?

Man, I had issues.

"Are you all right, my dear?" asked Durin as he walked onto the balcony behind me.

"Huh? Oh, yeah. I'm fine. Just getting a bit tired, I guess. The pain pills I've been taking can make me pretty drowsy." I smiled at him. Wow, he really was amazing. Those dark blue eyes, the strong jaw, the inviting lips...

But he wasn't Rali. I hated to do it, but I had to send Durin away. I couldn't lead him on like that. If I weren't going to stay on Idonea for Rali, I definitely wouldn't be staying for Durin.

"I think I need to get some more rest. I'm still recovering, you know."

He stepped back from me and studied me for a moment. Then he smiled.

"You are trying to get rid of me."

"No, I'm not. I'm seriously tired," I told him as convincingly as I could.

"Hmm... No. I do not believe you."

I walked back inside my room and said, "I'm sorry if you don't believe me, but I can't help that."

He followed me in and grabbed my arm to turn me towards him.

"You cannot get rid of me that easily, My Lady."

"Durin, I'm not--"

He interrupted my sentence with a kiss. It was a sweet, light kiss. It was gentle. He pulled away and looked at me. "Annie, please. I do not have a lot of time left with you. Please let me stay a little longer."

I couldn't look away from his dark eyes. He was pleading. He wanted to stay with me. He wanted to be there with me. Not anyone else. Not Sindri. But me. I leaned into his body and kissed him back. He wrapped his arms around me and we melted into each other's embrace. It was a moment of need, a moment of trying to fill an empty void.

But the more we kissed, the emptier I felt. I felt wrong, somehow. I was about to step out of this moment when I heard the door to my room open.

"Annie? Are you..."

I unlocked my lips from Durin's and slowly turned to face Rali who was standing in my doorway. His eyes widened in surprise. But then they narrowed as his body tensed. He was angry. And all I could do was stare at him. I was still in Durin's arms when Rali stepped back into the hallway and closed the door behind him. And that's when my body started working again.

"Rali?" I said quietly, still in a bit of shock over what had just happened. I backed away from Durin and limped towards the door. I had to explain to him. "Rali, wait," I said a little louder. I was almost to the door when I was yanked back in the other direction.

"Ow. Hey, let go," I ordered Durin. He had a strong hold on my arm and I couldn't free myself from him. "Durin, let me go."

"No."

"What? What's wrong with you?"

I looked at Durin and his eyes were even darker now. He looked determined.

"Durin? What...?"

"I am not letting you go, now or ever. You are mine, not Rali's. I am the better man. I deserve to have the best, not him." His voice was so low he was almost growling.

"Durin, listen. I don't know what kind of contest you and Rali have going on, but I am not the prize. Please, let go," I pleaded.

Instead of doing that, he grabbed and held my other arm. He pulled me towards him and I couldn't stop it.

"Durin...Durin, what are you doing?" My heart pounded. He was one of the strongest men I had ever been around. I wouldn't be able to fight him off. I tried talking to him some more.

"Okay, Durin. I know you are mad. I'm sorry. Let's go back and sit on the couch and talk some more. Okay?"

"I do not want to talk. I am tired of talking. We are not friends, Annie, remember? I wanted more from you. I wanted what Rali could not have. But now, neither of us will have you."

Okay, now I was terrified.

"Listen to me, Durin. You don't want to hurt me. You know why? Because I love you. I do. I should have said it earlier, I was just...I was just scared is all. Durin?"

I didn't even recognize the man in front of me anymore. Durin was gone and in his place was a hungry monster. And I was his meal just waiting to be devoured. He pulled me to his lips and began kissing me again. Only it was rough this time. His strong hands squeezed my arms. His face was pressed against mine so that I could hardly even breathe.

"Durin, stop!"

He was squeezing me so hard. I tried pulling away, I tried kicking, I tried pushing, but I couldn't make any progress against the beast I was fighting.

"Just a goodbye kiss for me. Rali will not get one," he growled. He ripped my feela off in one swipe and while his hands were busy with that, I used mine to try scratching his eyes out. I made a nice groove down one side of his face, but that was all I could do. It made him pretty mad, though. He hit me in the face then and I fell to the ground. I tried to get up but he grabbed my side and reached up the inside of my dress all the way to the stitched - up wound ...and ripped. My old wound had been made new again, and I couldn't breathe from the pain. I rolled over onto my back and stared up at the face of death. He had once been handsome. He had once been fun and charming. Now he was the last thing I would ever see. He bent down over me and wrapped both of his powerful hands around my neck.

"Durin, don't," was the last thing I whispered to him.

The last thing he said to me was, "I have to."

Chapter 19

Tears flowed down my cheeks as I felt Durin put more pressure around my neck. I thought about my family, but mostly, I thought of Rali. I regretted that the last he would see of me was when I was with Durin. I regretted that I had just realized my feelings for him and had never been able to tell him. I cried while Durin tried to kill me.

Then there was a smash of glass, a grunt came out of Durin's mouth, and suddenly I could breathe again. Durin fell over to the side, and I saw Freya standing above me holding half of a glass vase. The other half was in pieces on the floor.

"Annie? Annie, are you all right? Oh dear, Annie?" she cried.

I coughed the most painful coughs I've ever felt in my life. "Freya," I whispered, because that was all I could do, "Freya, I'm not okay. Get a doctor. I'm bleeding. My wound, it's..."

Then Freya followed my glance down to my side and gasped. There was a small pool of blood forming from my reopened wound. I was getting dizzy. "Freya, hurry."

Just then, Durin pushed himself up onto his feet and staggered a few steps backwards. He put his hands up to his head which was trickling blood. Freya showed no sign of fear and held up the jagged glass vase she still held in her hands.

"You come near her and I will slit your throat," she hissed at him. He looked at her, tiny little Freya, and then down at me, still lying on the floor.

Through gritted teeth he said, "He loves her. Not you. You had better get that in your pretty little head. He is lying to you. Do you know why he really brought you here? Has he told you about your father?"

"I'm calling the guard." Freya told him.

He laughed eerily and then made his way to the door. Over his shoulder he said, "I would have loved you, Annie."

Freya aimed the sharp glass at him until he was in the hallway with the door closed behind him. I didn't care where he went, as long as he was gone. Freya dropped the vase, grabbed a blanket from the couch and rushed back to my side.

"Here, Annie. Hold this to your side. I will get the doctor. I must be sure there is a guard to stay with you in case the general returns." Freya got up to leave and I called to her to come back.

"Freya, don't tell Rali. Not yet. Please, just get a doctor as quietly as you can." I didn't want to deal with Rali yet. I only wanted to worry about surviving before having to think about him. And I knew that, after what he had seen earlier, he was not happy with me. No, I wasn't ready to face him. And after what Durin had just said about Rali lying to me, I wasn't sure I *wanted* to face him.

Freya hurried out the door, and almost immediately came back with a guard. Then she quickly left again. I looked over at the guard who seemed a little nervous to be in my bedroom. But when he walked closer, I saw that it was Arthur.

"Arthur," I whispered as loudly as I could.

He came right to my side when he saw that I was wounded, and knelt down. "My Lady, what has happened? How can I help?" he asked.

"Just stay here and keep talking to me. Freya has gone to get a doctor."

"How did this happen? Did someone hurt you?" Arthur looked angry. And he was a big guy. I wouldn't want him to be mad at me ever.

"Arthur, I can't explain it all right now, but please, just talk to me. Tell me something. Tell me about you. You have a family?"

Arthur seemed a little confused as to why I wanted to know about his family while I was laying there bleeding to death.

"Please talk, Arthur. It will soothe me."

"Okay, ma'am. Uh...my family. Yes, I have a wife and two daughters."

"How old?" I asked.

"Inga is eight and Beyla is five."

"That's lovely. I would like to meet them someday." I tried to smile at him, but I was in too much pain. It probably came out looking more like a grimace.

"Yes. We shall have you over for dinner soon, if you would like."

"Yes, that would be..." I was getting really fuzzy and weak. "It would..."

"My Lady? Stay here with me. Listen to me, stay here."

"But I can't. I have to go..." Everything was fading. I was losing a lot of blood. Was this what delirious felt like?

"No, you do not. You do not have to go. You must stay here with me," said Arthur.

"But, Rali...I can't...I want to, but..."

My eyes started to close, but I saw Freya come running back in with the doctor that I was beginning to become very familiar with. Freya rushed up to my side as Arthur rose to his feet and backed away.

"Annie, the doctor is here. Now open your eyes." Then she proceeded to smack my face around a bit.

"Ow, Freya. What are you doing? I have to go to sleep now," I told her drowsily.

"No ma'am. The doctor needs you to drink this medicine. It will help you heal from the inside while he stitches you back up on the outside. It worked well on you before." Then she called Arthur back over and had him lift my head and shoulders from the floor just enough so I could drink the doctor's medicine. It was warm and tasted like metal. Yech. It was nasty stuff. But I drank it all down. I knew it was either that or have Freya smack me around some more. After I drank the medicine, I stayed on the floor while the doctor worked his magic on my side...again.

The doctor told me, "It is not as bad as the first time, however, because the wound was not cauterized like last time, you have lost more blood. I have stitched you up, and the tonic you drank will speed up your healing. But you must take extra care. You have lost a lot of blood and will be weak."

"What about my neck? I can't talk very well."

He ran his hand lightly across my throat and examined it. "It is bruised, and your throat will be sore. But again, it should heal quickly." Then he looked at Freya and said, "I will clean the wound, and help you get her changed. But then she must go straight to bed and is not to leave it for any reason until I say she may get up."

"When? How long will that be?" I asked the doctor.

"I cannot be sure. More than a day, though."

I was really going to have to stop getting into trouble. It was taking all the fun out of my vacation which was growing shorter with each of my little escapades.

"Okay, Doc."

Freya and the doctor got me cleaned up and into a loose cotton nightgown. With their help (and the help of some wonderful pain meds-I was surely going to be an addict soon) I got into my bed, and was quickly fast asleep. I slept so hard that I didn't even dream. I just slept and slept while my body worked to heal itself.

I woke up the next day and the rays from two suns were streaming in through my balcony. The sheer drapes were gently waving in the breeze. Birds were singing outside...and Freya was snoring inside. She was asleep in an armchair that she had pulled up to my bed. She had on her same clothes from the night before, and in one hand, she held a small dagger. Little, tiny, fierce Freya, who had saved my life the night before. How would I ever thank her?

I tried to sit up, but quickly decided against it when I felt a surge of pain from my new old wound.

"Oooow," I said too loudly.

Freya woke up immediately and jumped to her feet. "Leave her alone!" she yelled to no one in particular.

"Freya, it's okay. It was just me. Sorry."

She looked down at me lying on the bed and put the dagger aside before she came over to me. "Annie? How are you feeling? Are you hurting? I can get the doctor." She started walking toward the door before I could reply.

"Freya, please. Just wait a minute," I told her. She came back to me.

"What is it? What can I get you?" she asked.

"A glass of water, please."

She walked into the bathroom and came back with my request. I drank it slowly. My throat was still pretty sore. It still hurt to talk, but I had things I needed to say to Freya.

She sat next to me on the bed, examined my neck, and pushed some of my hair back behind one ear.

"Freya," I whispered.

"Yes, Annie?"

"I am so, so thankful that you are here. You saved my life. Thank you. I don't know how I will ever repay you."

She smiled and said, "I am just happy that I came back when I did. If I had arrived just one minute later, I...I," she started to tear up. I took her hand in mine and squeezed it. Neither of us wanted to say what could have happened if she had been just one minute later. She collected herself and then continued.

"Well, I think I will go and get the doctor now. You slept all night and practically all day. He will want to check your wounds. Will you be all right? I will be gone only for a minute. Shall I get a guard?" she asked.

"No, I will be fine," I said. Then I reconsidered. "You could hand me that dagger, though."

She did. And as she walked towards the door to get the doctor, she said, "Oh, and I know exactly how you can repay me." She looked over her shoulder at me. "Stay here and marry the king." Then she grinned and walked out the door.

I sighed.

Stay and marry Rali. There were two things wrong with that. One, I needed to go home to where I belonged and wasn't attacked by monsters or angry soldiers every day. Two, even if I did stay, it was clear that Rali and Sindri were supposed to be together. And I was sure after what Rali had seen in my room, he wouldn't want to marry me, anyway. Or even talk to me. The funny thing was, not long before, I couldn't have cared less if Rali wanted to talk to me or not. But now, things had changed. I wanted him to talk to me. I wanted him to *want* to talk to me...

I wanted him to want to marry me.

But even if he had wanted to marry me, then what? I couldn't very well marry him and live on Idonea forever...could I? Of course not. That was ridiculous. Right?

Yes. Just plain ridiculous. I was from Earth and I should stay on Earth. But then...the dream I had had. The memory of my father telling me about the Sidas Array. Was there something to that? I still needed to find out more about it. I didn't know if I could talk to Rali about it...or anyone. I didn't even know if Rali would tell me anything if I asked, or if he would tell me the truth. Why hadn't he told me anything already? What was he waiting for?

Maybe when I healed, I could do some research in the library. I hoped I got a good report from the doctor and would be able to get out and about a bit before having to go home.

Huh...that was strange. I had just thought of it as having to go home. Not getting to go home.

That's new.

The door opened and Freya came in followed by the doctor, who was quickly becoming a dear friend of mine.

"How is my favorite patient today?" he asked.

"I'm only your favorite because I keep you in business. I'm alive, so that's good. It's kinda hard to move, though," I told him.

"Yes, well, then do not move," he laughed.

I frowned at him.

Freya laughed then. "I am so sorry, doctor. She is not the most cooperative patient you will ever have." She smiled at me.

The doctor checked out my side and said it looked good. I didn't agree, but I wasn't the doctor. It looked pretty gross to me. He also pointed out that I had developed a bit of a black eye. Fabulous. Must have been where Durin hit me. I was getting more and more colorful by the minute.

"I am going to give you more of my healing tonic--"

"Yuck," I said.

"--and you should be able to get up in the morning," the doctor said.

"In the morning? But that's a whole day wasted." I cried. Wow, I really wasn't very cooperative.

Freya said, "You have already slept through most of the day. The suns will soon be setting. There is not much you could do today, anyway."

I thought I could probably have gone to the library. But oh well. I could do that the next morning.

The doctor gave me the tonic and I drank it as quickly as my poor sore throat would let me. I didn't want to savor the metallic taste at all if I could help it. Then he gave Freya a bottle with some more pain pills in it and he left for the night. He said he would come by in the morning to be sure I was healed enough to get out of bed. I decided I would put all my mental energy into healing. Maybe if I urged my body enough, it would listen. Worth a try.

The doctor left, and it was just me and dear Freya again. She brought one of my books over to me and made a pot of coffee.

"Oh, Freya, you are the best. Thank you."

"You are most welcome." She helped prop me up on my pillows, set a mug of coffee on my bedside table, turned on my lamp, and then went over to the couch where she could work on a new dress she was making.

And keep an eye on me.

I sat comfortably--well, relatively comfortably--in my bed while reading *Jane Eyre*. I was just to the part where Jane had her first encounter with Mr. Rochester, when Rali came storming into my room. It startled me so much that I nearly threw my book in the air.

Freya jumped up and then immediately bowed her head. "Your Highness. We were not expecting...um," she looked over at me. "I think maybe, if you could come back--"

"Silence, Freya. I am not here to talk to you," he growled. His eyes were on me the whole time. His green eyes were turbulent, like waves in the middle of a storm. He stood a few feet inside the door, not near enough to see any of my wounds. And my black eye was on my right side, not directly in his view. I tried to keep it that way. I still wasn't ready to deal with him...though it seemed he was quite ready to deal with me.

"Can I help you?" I said as normally as I could, though it came out as just a loud whisper. But he didn't seem to notice.

"'Can I help you' Really? Is that all you can say?" he asked.

"Pretty much."

"You... I just don't understand you." He began pacing at the end of my bed, and it was tough to keep slightly turning my head so he couldn't get a good glimpse at my eye.

He continued, "After everything that has happened, Annie. After all I have done. And you told me you were not chasing him." He stopped pacing and looked at me. "You told me that. You lied to me." He began to pace again. "And then I just went on making a fool of myself. I gave you my mother's park, I told you about my family. I told you... I told you that I loved you."

I glanced at Freya who was doing her best to keep sewing, but her eyes got really wide when Rali admitted that last part.

I tried to think of what I could say. But what could I say? Anyway, he surely hadn't meant it when he said he loved me. Just a few hours later he was with Sindri. So how could he come in here and yell at me?

"Rali, I can't talk about this right now. Please, just leave me alone." I knew he wouldn't, but I thought I'd try.

"Leave you alone? Why? You expecting a visitor soon? Should I clear out before your dear sweet general gets here and sees me? We would not want to upset him now, would we?"

"Please, Rali," I could feel the tears. "Please, I can't talk right now. I need to..." And then I started coughing because of how much I had been straining my voice to convince him there was nothing wrong.

Freya got up and handed me my mug of hot coffee. I sipped it and the heat felt good on my throat. Then I tried again.

"Rali, I'm sorry. This is not what you think..." More coughing.

"You are right. It is not what I think. I thought you cared for me. I thought you might... I thought..." he looked down at the floor and then back up at me. "Never mind what I thought. I was wrong. This will not work." Then he turned and walked towards the door. And I watched him.

"Your Highness, wait," called Freya.

I tried to tell her to stop but I coughed instead.

"Your Highness, she has been hurt. Durin…he tried to kill her."

That stopped him. He whirled around and looked at Freya, searching her face to see if she might be lying. Then he walked slowly over to the end of my bed. All I could do was look right back at him. It hurt too much to say anything.

"Annie? Is this true?"

He walked closer to me and I could tell the very moment that he knew it was true. He saw my eye and the bruising around my neck. He walked to my bed and sat down next to me. He gently put his hands on my face and looked closely at my eye and my neck.

"Why did he do this?" he asked me. His voice was hard and emotionless.

I took another sip of coffee and said, "He was mad. When you came in and saw us, I went after you, to explain, and he didn't like that. He said that if he couldn't have me, that you couldn't either."

Rali told me to rest my voice for a moment. He called Freya over and asked her how badly I had been hurt. She told him the extent of my wounds. He looked back at me in amazement. "Well, Annie. You are just the woman that keeps on kicking, aren't you?" He forced a small smile even though he didn't really seem to be in a joking kind of mood. "Are you in pain? Are you comfortable?"

"Yes, I am heavily medicated, so I am fine. The doctor said I can get out of bed in the morning."

Rali seemed to be thinking for a moment and then said, "Freya, how was the doctor called without my being notified?"

She looked guilty and then said, "I went directly to him myself. I asked him not to tell anyone just yet. It is my fault, sir."

"Freya," said Rali, "you should have come right to me. I should have been told--"

"Rali, don't be mad at her," I said. "I asked her not to tell you. And, anyway, she is the reason I am still here. She saved my life, Rali. She came in and smashed a vase on Durin's head."

He looked at Freya, grabbed her hand and held it in his, and said to her, "Did you? Thank you, Freya. I am indebted to you."

"Oh, Sir, I am just glad I was here."

Rali let go of her hand and looked back at me. "Annie, do you know where Durin is now?"

I shook my head.

Rali thought for a moment and then said, "He must be found. He must be punished." He got back up from the bed. "Annie, I must go and talk to the council. I will come check on you as soon as I can." Then he turned to Freya. "Freya? Please continue your loving care of our little troublemaker."

Then he was gone. Freya and I both watched him as he left. Freya looked at me and I knew what she was going to say before she even said it.

"How come you never told me that he said he loved you?"

I sighed. "Freya, he didn't...well, he did say it, but I don't think he meant it."

"What? Are you demented?" She pretty much yelled.

"Jury's still out."

"Are you not hearing him? Are you not seeing how much he cares for you?" she asked.

"Well, Freya, it's not that simple. There's a lot more going on." I took a long sip of my coffee and put the mug back on the table. Then I began to readjust my covers and my pillows when I realized Freya was tapping her foot on the floor.

"Oh, right, you probably want me to elaborate."

"Yes, ma'am. If you do not mind."

"Of course not. After all, I do owe you one." I smiled at her. She just continued tapping her foot. "Okay, well, here's the thing. Last night when I went to find Rali... remember?"

"Yes."

"Well, I went to his room first, and he wasn't there...but someone else was." I looked at her to see if she knew who I was talking about. She thought for a moment, then her eyes got wide and she said, "No...you do not mean..."

"Yes, I do. Sindri was there. And you know what she was wearing?"

"...nothing?" she said nervously.

"Ha! No. But pretty much. She had on one of Rali's shirts. She was lying very seductively on his couch. Like a lioness waiting to pounce." I shivered.

Freya shivered.

"So, it's pretty obvious to me that, even though Rali may say he has feelings for me, he will be choosing Sindri at the Kostera, and they will live happily ever after. She knows it, he knows it, and I know it. So, all I need to do is survive the next few days--which doesn't seem like it should be too hard of a task, but you never know with me--and then I will go home, and live a normal life." I snuggled back into my pillows, pulled my covers up, and picked up my book.

Then Freya grabbed my book and pulled it away from me.

"Hey! Gimme." I reached for it but she was too far away.

"If you were not already so injured, I would smack you with this book," she said.

"Geez...you're mean sometimes."

"And you are stupid sometimes. When you saw Sindri in his room, was he there with her?"

"Well...no...but--"

"Then how do you know they did anything? How do you know they had plans to be there together? Or that he ever saw her in his room? Chances are, she went there hoping to seduce him, he never showed up, and then she left. But she is probably relishing the fact that you saw her there, and that would almost be enough for her." Then Freya came close to me and narrowed her eyes. "Do not let her win. Do not let her think she has defeated you. She has not won anything yet. And if you have anything to say about it, she will not win at all."

I just stared at Freya for a moment and then said, "Wow. You can be a real bitch sometimes." Then I smiled. "I like it."

She laughed and gave me my book. "Well, I just want you to think about it. Things are not always as they seem."

"Sure, Freya. Whatever you say." I opened my book and tried to read some more. But my mind was too busy with other things. I thought about what Freya had said about Sindri. It was true that I hadn't actually seen Rali with her. But she had said he would be back. So that meant he had to have been there at some point, right? Surely Sindri wouldn't have gone there, put on his shirt, and waited there for him on his couch. That would be silly. No, she had to have been with him earlier, or later, or both. That was the only thing that made sense. Even if I didn't like it. But, I realized, it didn't matter whether I liked it or not, because I was going home in a few days. I couldn't stay on Idonea. I wouldn't stay on Idonea. The best thing was for me to go. I would miss Freya, and I would miss Rali. But they would go on with their lives, and so would I. And we would all be fine. Just fine.

I managed to read my book for a while before Rali came back. He walked in and came right to my bedside.

"How are you feeling?" he asked.

"Fine. Tired. I just took a pill, so I will probably be asleep soon. You came back just in time." I smiled at him and he smiled back.

"Well, I am glad you feel all right." Then he looked at Freya who was cleaning out the coffee pot. "Freya? May I have a minute alone with Annie?"

"Of course, Your Highness." She bowed her head and then went into her room.

Rali looked at me when she had closed the door. He took my hands in his and said, "Annie, listen. I do not know what feelings you had for Durin and I do not care." Then he looked away for a moment. When he looked back he said, "Okay, maybe I did care, but not anymore. I am sorry I got so upset with you. It was none of my business. I just keep messing things up for you. Maybe if I had done things differently...maybe I should have--"

"Rali, don't. Don't blame yourself for any of this. This was all Durin. Not you, not me...well, maybe a little me," I shrugged. "But mostly Durin."

We were quiet for a moment and then Rali looked into my eyes. "Annie, did you...love him?"

I shook my head. "No, Rali. I didn't. I see now that it was stupid of me to even like him." I looked up at Rali and said, "Believe it or not, right before you walked in, I was trying to get rid of him."

"Really?" He seemed skeptical, but I couldn't blame him. Not after what he had seen.

"Really and truly. Scout's honor."

"Who is Scout?"

"No one. Never mind. Anyway, Rali, I was trying to make him leave because...because while he was with me in my room, all I could think about was...you."

Rali sat back and actually looked surprised. He thought for a moment and then smiled. "You like me," he said.

I couldn't help it. I laughed.

"Ow, Rali, don't make me laugh, it hurts."

"I am not trying to be funny."

"I know you're not trying to. You just are."

"Funny?"

"Yes. Very. And very cute."

He smiled again. "I like this conversation. What other things do you like about me?"

"Oh, Rali. As much as I would like to continue praising you, I am feeling my medicine working now. I will be asleep in about thirty seconds."

His smile faded. "Oh, all right. I will get Freya, then." He sat for another moment and he was still holding onto my hands.

Finally, he got up to fetch Freya when I found myself pulling him back. "Wait, don't go."

"But I have to get Freya so she can keep an eye on you tonight."

"No." I didn't want him to leave. I didn't want to be away from him. "Stay. Stay with me."

He looked at me and then looked towards the door to Freya's room. "Are you sure you want me rather than Freya?"

"Please, Rali. Don't go."

He sat back down and began to settle into the chair by my bed. I shook my head and said, "I need you closer to me. Just...I just want you to hold me for a while. Please..." And then there were tears falling down my cheeks.

Rali walked to the other side of my bed, removed his boots, and climbed in next to me. He put one arm under my head, and the other across my waist, below my wound. I curled up into his body. I melted into his warmth. I had never felt so comfortable, so safe, so...loved. I drifted off listening to the sound of his breathing, and feeling the warmth of his body against mine.

The last thing he said before I fell asleep was, "I will hold you whenever, wherever. I love you."

Chapter 20

    I had never slept so well in my life. Despite all my cuts and bruises, I slept comfortably, and soundly. I dreamed of my father again. Only it was more like a lot of little dreams in one. There were scenes of the two of us walking in the park, and then scenes with just him as he sat on the couch and read a book or read the newspaper. There was a short dream of my mother and father whispering to each other at the kitchen table while my little sister and I peeked at them from the hallway. Right before I woke up, I was dreaming of my family riding in the car on our way to my grandparent's house. We were all singing Christmas carols. They were happy dreams.

The King

    I opened my eyes and stretched my body, which felt a whole lot better after so much rest...and medicine. I looked beside me and realized I was alone. But I could still see a slight indentation in the pillow next to mine. I ran my hand over it and remembered falling asleep in his arms. It had been beautiful. I looked around the room and didn't see Freya anywhere. I pushed the covers off of myself and slowly let my legs fall over the side of the bed while I sat up. I was sore, but I could manage this movement pretty well. So I decided to get on my feet. And I did. I walked towards the balcony and found that I could walk quite easily. I stepped over to the railing and breathed in the fresh morning Idonean air. The breeze blew through my hair and made it flutter around my face. I could see a few guards walking the pathways from the village to the palace. It must have been pretty early, because they were the only people I saw up and about.

    I turned to walk back inside, but stopped myself. I went back to the railing and looked out over the kingdom. I imagined what it might be like to wake up to this every morning. I wondered what it might be like to be queen of this land. I imagined myself looking out over my people. Standing by Rali's side. I smiled, but then quickly tried to wipe those thoughts out of my mind. I still had other things to consider, such as being at home with my family, finding out how my father knew about the Sidas Array--and there was still that nagging little reminder in the back of my mind that Sindri had been nearly naked in Rali's room just a couple of nights earlier. I didn't want to think about the two of them together. Even though I knew I was falling for Rali, I couldn't be sure he felt the same. From what I had seen and heard, it seemed that he and Sindri had already been matched up, like Rali's father and mother before him. That was how things were done. I was just there to have some fun until I left. *Yes. Remember that, Annie...*

I went back in my room and decided to take a nice hot shower before beginning my day. As I walked towards the bathroom, I heard Freya's door open and close. She saw my empty bed before she saw me and called my name a bit frantically.

"Annie?" she said.

"I'm here, Freya. I'm going to take a shower."

She looked over to where I was and looked relieved.

"How are you feeling? You look much better this morning." She smiled as she walked toward me.

"I feel much better. I slept really well."

She grinned at me. "Oh, yes. I bet you both did."

"Freya. Don't start."

"Do you believe me now?" she asked.

"What do you mean?"

"I told you he cares for you. I told you he meant it when he said he loved you. So, do you believe me now?" she smiled.

I sighed. "Freya, I am going to take a shower. I'll deal with you later." I shot a quick smile at her before I went into the bathroom.

I emerged from the steaming shower feeling healthier and stronger than I had felt in quite a while. I put on a fluffy robe and walked back into my bedroom. I could smell freshly brewed coffee and I saw some of my favorite breakfast foods waiting on the table. The eggs were fluffy and the croissants crusty. I decided I would worry about my hair and make-up after I ate. Freya brought my coffee to the table as I sat down to my plate of deliciousness. I would miss being served good meals three times a day.

I sighed. I was having a good time here, but I knew I couldn't stay. I decided I would go talk to Rali about my father after breakfast. I needed to find out more about my family connection...or if there even was one.

As I took my first bite of croissant, Freya brought a folded piece of paper to me. "This was on the table by the door," she said.

I opened it up. It was from Rali.

Annie,
I am sorry you will have to awaken to find that I have left.
I have urgent matters to attend, but would like to see you later this evening if you would oblige me.
I will send the doctor this morning and hopefully he will determine that you have healed enough to go on a little outing with me.
Get some rest, enjoy your day, and please...don't climb out any windows until we can discuss it beforehand.
Rali

An outing, huh? I wondered where he wanted to take me. I was disappointed that I wouldn't get to learn anything about my father from him right away, but was looking forward to whatever he had planned for the evening.

"So, what did he say?" asked Freya, who knew exactly what he had said because she was (not so slyly) reading the letter over my shoulder the whole time.

"Oh, he wants to take me somewhere this evening, I guess."

Freya smiled. She was loving this. She would be tickled pink if I stayed on Idonea and became queen. I was sorry I would have to disappoint her.

Would I have to disappoint her?

It was then that someone knocked on my door. Freya answered to find a servant carrying an enormous bouquet of white flowers.

"Oh my, Annie," said Freya as she directed the servant to put the flowers on my table. "These are gorgeous! I am sure they must be from the king."

I smiled at the warm gesture from Rali. There was a small pink card visible in the flower arrangement and once the servant left the room, I quickly grabbed the card, eager to read more kind words from Rali.

"He is really going all out today," I said to Freya as I looked at the card. But I was wrong. The flowers weren't from Rali.

My dear,
These flowers are my way of saying I am sorry.
I can be a very jealous man. I just care for you a great deal and want more for you than Rali can offer. He does not love you. He is not trustworthy and knows more than he is willing to tell you. I would never lie to you and I never meant to hurt you.
Please accept my apology. I will see you again soon.
Yours forever,
Durin

"What the...? Is he insane?" I threw the card on the floor and picked up the vase of flowers.

"What are you doing? What is wrong?" asked Freya.

I walked towards the balcony and said, "They're from Durin. That miserable, no good, mental case sent me flowers to make up for trying to kill me."

"What?" yelled Freya. "But...hey! What are you doing?"

I walked all the way to the railing of the balcony, looked down to be sure it was clear, and I dropped the vase and flowers over the edge. I watched as the beautifully horrid bouquet dropped straight down to the courtyard. It was a long way down, but I could see the vase break into pieces when it reached the ground and all of the flowers were scattered. A nearby guard in the courtyard heard it and rushed over. He saw the mess and looked up. I just smiled and waved and then went back into my room, wiped my hands off on a towel, and continued eating my breakfast. Not many things could ruin my appetite, though his card was pushing it.

Freya had picked up the card but I snatched it out of her hands before she had a chance to read it. I didn't want her to see the things Durin had said about Rali. I wanted to consider those things on my own. Freya gave me a questioning look when I grabbed the card but I just shook my head and tore the card into pieces.

"It's rubbish, Freya. It's just him saying he's sorry and he wants to see me again soon."

"What is he thinking? That you will see the flowers, forget about what he did to you, and go running into his arms?"

"Apparently," I said.

"Well, you need to tell this to the king. He should know that the general plans to be seeing you again soon. You need protection."

"Rali is busy today with an urgent matter, but I will tell him about it when I see him tonight," I told Freya. She seemed satisfied with that, though a little nervous. She walked over to my bedside table and opened the drawer. She took out the small dagger and brought it to me.

"Keep this with you always," she told me.

I sighed. "Yes, ma'am."

She sat down across from me while I finished my breakfast.

I took my last bite and said, "Freya, if I go back, I'm going to miss you. I'm going to miss you a lot."

"If you go back?"

"I mean when I go back. *When.*"

"Mm-hmm. That is not what you said."

"My mistake." I didn't want to get her hopes up. I was still pretty sure it would be best for me to return to my family.

"I do not think it was a mistake. And neither do you."

"Right, Freya. Sure. Anyway, what am I wearing today? Let's get dressed."

She seemed excited about picking out the day's attire and scurried over to the closet. She looked at the contents for a moment and then pulled out a long, fitted sea green tunic with dark blue edging, and matching dark blue leggings. Casual, yet sophisticated.

"You are so good at this fashion thing, Freya. I might just bring you back to Earth with me," I told her.

"Oh, I am not going anywhere. I guess you will just have to stay here with me," she said.

I wanted to smile and joke with her about this because that made it easier, but I couldn't just keep teasing until the minute before I left.

If I left.

"Freya, please don't get your hopes up. I really should go home. My family needs me and must be so worried. I have to go back to them. Okay, Freya? I am leaving in three days. Do you understand?

She just stared at me blankly.

"Freya? Do you understand what I just said?"

No reply.

"Are you upset with me?"

Silence.

"Freya, say something."

She blinked, looked down and then back up at me. She said, "Okay, My Lady. Whatever you say."

My Lady? So we were back to that now? Fine.

"Thank you, Freya. Now, let's do my hair. Nothing fancy."

"Yes, My Lady."

Freya quickly, but beautifully, dried my hair and pulled it back into a loose knot with a few small braids wrapped around it.

"Thank you, Freya."

"You're welcome, My Lady."

I rolled my eyes.

The doctor came in then and did a quick examination. My wounds were healing nicely, and I was not in much pain. He gave Freya some low dose pain medication to keep for me in case I needed it. Besides my slight limp, the doctor said I was good to go. I was glad I had the all clear for my date with Rali that evening.

After the doctor left, I told Freya I wanted to go get some books from the library.

"I am going with you," Freya said,

"I really don't mind going alone. I might be there for a while," I told her. I was actually wanting to do some research on my own.

"Do you really think I am going to let you go anywhere by yourself? That...that maniac is out there somewhere and will be looking for you. I am sure he would just love to find you all by your lonesome sitting in a library with no one around. I am sorry, but I am not going to let that happen," said Freya.

"I will take the dagger you gave me. I'll be fine--"

"Don't you argue with me. I am coming with you. It is not a request." Freya marched over to me, took my arm in hers, and we walked to the door together, side by side.

"All right then. Let's go." I was still going to look for information that might help me, I was just going to have to do it with Freya looking over my shoulder...but I was kind of getting used to that.

We walked out the door, and I noticed two Royal Bodyguards posted right outside in the hallway. As we turned to walk towards the lyptra, they followed us. One of them was Arthur.

"Hi, Arthur," I said to him as we walked.

He nodded but said nothing.

"I hate to be rude, but...why are you following us?" I asked him.

"We are under orders by King Valiar to go with you wherever you go if you leave your room," he answered very officially.

I stopped walking and turned to face Arthur and the other guard.

"Are you kidding me right now?"

Arthur and the other guard looked at each other and then at me.

"No...no ma'am. We are not," said Arthur.

Freya grabbed my arm again and said, "Come on. It is just fine. The king wants to be sure you are safe."

I turned around and continued walking with Freya. "Geez, I can't get any privacy in this place."

Freya said, "As soon as the general is found and imprisoned, I am sure you will have more freedom."

"Well, when will that be? And, hey, speaking of that, is anyone even looking for him? I haven't heard anyone say anything about trying to find that creep."

"What do you think the king meant by an urgent matter?" Freya said. "And yesterday when he left your room, he went straight to the council and a search began immediately afterwards."

That shut me up for a second. But only a second.

"Oh, right, well...good." Yeah. Tell 'em, Annie.

Our little party of four rode down the lyptra, exited, and headed for the library. I was glad Freya knew how to get there because I would've gotten lost, I was sure.

As we turned a corner, I saw a beautiful, middle-aged woman with dark hair piled high on her head. She was walking in our direction and stopped when she saw us. Her eyes went wide and then suddenly narrowed. She started walking towards us again, but this time she seemed to be on a mission. She was coming straight towards me. I slowed down and finally just stopped walking altogether to avoid a collision with this irate woman who I had never seen before in my life.

"You," she growled at me.

"Me?" I squeaked. I looked around and she most definitely was referring to me.

She stopped right in front of me. She was so close I could see the fine lines forming at the corners of her eyes. I could swear flames shot out of her lips when she spoke to me. "You do not belong here. Who do you think you are?" she spit at me.

"Annie. Annie Watts. And you would be?"

"Do not play innocent with me. You are trying to ruin everything. You are trying to seduce him and by doing so, bring down the kingdom."

"I'm sorry, what? How am I going to do that, exactly? And who am I seducing?" I asked her.

Freya spoke up and said to the woman, "Dagny, this is not the time nor the--"

"Shut up. You should not have even been allowed back here."

"Hey!" I yelled. "Don't talk to her like that. Who the hell are you? And what is your problem?"

She directed her anger back at me again. "The king is going to marry my daughter. You are wasting your time."

Ah. I now assumed I had the pleasure of speaking to the mother of Sindri. What a treat.

"Oh, okay. I see. Well if Rali and your daughter are, in fact, headed down the aisle, why are you mad at me?" I asked her.

She continued to fume but didn't respond immediately.

"Listen," I said, "I would love to continue this chat with you, but, as you said, I am wasting my time here, and apparently, you have a wedding to plan. So, I will be off. Have a wonderful day." I began to walk around her when she grabbed my arm and turned me back to face her. I could see the gold shining in her eyes.

"I have seen how he looks at you. I have seen the attention he has been giving to you. But do not be fooled. You are like a new toy. You are different and exciting." Then she put her face right in front of mine. "But the novelty will wear off. And he will choose my daughter. They were meant for each other. They belong together. Do not forget it." She stepped back from me then, gave me one last fiery glare, and then walked past me.

* * *

I watched her as she walked around the corner and then let out the breath I realized I had been holding.

"Well, that was unexpected." I looked at Freya and she had her hands balled into tense little fists. She was gritting her teeth and shaking.

"Freya?" I said softly to her. "Freya, calm down. Are you okay? Can I get you something? Take a breath, Freya. Take a few breaths."

She listened and took some deep, calming breaths. She uncurled her hands and seemed to relax.

"I am sorry, Annie. That woman just...she just infuriates me. Always has," Freya said.

"I'm gonna take a shot in the dark here, but I'm guessing that Dagny is the one that led the effort to get you kicked out of here?" I asked her.

"Yes, ma'am," she answered.

"Ah. Well, that makes sense. Are you going to be okay? Do we need to go back?"

"No, no. I am fine. We should go find some books for you." She took a few more deep breaths and we continued to the library.

As I walked through the library doors and searched for something helpful, I began to realize what it would mean for Freya when I left. She would be here to see Rali marry Sindri, and would have to bear the gloating of that awful Dagny who will have gotten everything she wanted. Dagny had had Freya and her daughter, Katrin, banished because they were in the way of her own ambitions, and of Sindri's. Now she will have gotten rid of me and the path made clear for her to be mother of the new Queen of Idonea.

Ugh. Queen of Idonea. Sindri didn't deserve that. She didn't deserve someone like Rali. She deserved someone more like...Durin. Now there was a fine match. If only the two of them could fall in love and move away to Helgrind together. That would be nice.

    I was sorry for Freya. Although I couldn't stay just for her, I did wish there was something I could do to ensure her continued presence in the palace if that was what she wanted. I figured I could think about that later. But in the meantime, it was becoming very tempting for me to stay just to keep Sindri away from Rali. If he were to choose me over her...

    I sighed.

    Anyway, back to my research.

    After perusing the books for a while, I couldn't find anything that might help and I remembered Rali mentioning that most historical or important documents had been moved to a safer location. So I grabbed a few books solely for entertainment value and headed back to find Freya.

    "All right, Freya. You still here somewhere? Sorry I took so long," I called out.

    "I am still here. Did you find anything good?" she asked me. She had been sitting near a window, reading a book while I wandered the library all morning.

    "Oh, I found a few things. Ready to go back?"

    "Yes, ma'am," she said. The guards had been standing in the doorway the whole time and followed us out the door as we left.

    Our walk back was uneventful and there were no further gifts from Durin waiting for me when I got back. I sat down on my couch and opened up one of my new selections from the library and did a bit of reading before lunch. After eating, I took half a pain pill and drifted off to sleep.

"Annie. Annie, are you awake?" My father's voice woke me.

"Yes, Dad." I was in my bed at home and I was about thirteen-years old. I turned onto my side to peek at my alarm clock. It read 12:40 am.

"Annie, I want to tell you something," he whispered.

I sat up. "Is it a secret?"

He thought for a quick moment. "Yes, it is kind of a secret."

"Is it just between you and me, Dad?" I whispered back to him.

"Yes, sweetie. Just you and me. Now listen, I need you to know something. I need you to know that...if something ever happens..." he hesitated.

"If what happens?"

"If I ever have to go away, or if something happens to me and I can't come back to you, I need you to know that you will be okay."

I didn't know what he was trying to tell me. Or why he was trying to tell it to me.

"Where are you going?" I asked.

"I'm not going anywhere. I plan to be with you forever. But, sweetie, if something were to happen and I couldn't be there, you need to know that you…that you will be cared for." He glanced at my bedroom door and then back to me. I couldn't tell for sure, but it almost looked like his hands were shaking.

"Yes, Mom will take care of me. But just don't go anywhere, okay Dad?"

He smiled at me. "I will always be with you. Always. Even if you can't see me. We have all of our stories to keep us close. We have Annieland, right?"

"Right. If we are ever apart, we can close our eyes, and meet in Annieland."

"Okay, sweetie. I like that." He gave me a hug, and then stayed with me until I fell back to sleep.

When I woke up from my dream, tears rolled down my cheeks.

Chapter 21

Rali had sent a message for me to be ready just before dinner. We were going out to the village to eat. I was finally going to be able to see the village up close and spend some time there. I was also looking forward to asking Rali what he knew about my father and how my father might've known about the Sidas Array.

And maybe, just maybe, I was excited about spending time with Rali. Before I left to go back to Earth.

Freya had chosen a beautiful dress for the occasion. It was a pale pink silk and chiffon dress. It was strapless with gold jewels sewn across the top. The bottom layer was the silk, and it was fitted to my torso; but, over that, the chiffon flowed freely all the way to the floor. The feela was gold lace and was narrow across the front, covering only a bit of my skin right below my collar bone, leaving my shoulders bare. The sleeves of the feela stopped right above my elbows. The shoes, which I would take off as soon as I could, were tall and golden. If someone had told me they were made of pure gold, I would've believed them.

Freya thought I should leave my hair down. She brushed it and left it loose and wavy. I put only the slightest bit of make up on, but Freya insisted on a bit of gold dust on my eyelids, and a pink lip gloss that matched my dress. I walked over to the full length mirror in my room to examine the final product.

Good Lord Almighty. I would definitely be giving Sindri some competition in the looks department. I smiled at my reflection, and may or may not have given myself a little wink.

"You look...just beautiful, Annie," said Freya. Was that a tear in her eye?

"It's all your doing, Freya. Thank you."

There was a knock on the door and Freya went to answer it. Arthur was standing there and informed me that it would be his duty--and honor--to escort me to my waiting carriage. I smiled and walked over to the door. I turned to Freya before I left and said, "Try not to miss me too much."

Arthur and I walked down the hallway and boarded the lyptra.

"So, Arthur, when do I get to meet your family?" I asked him.

"You want to meet my family, My Lady?" he asked.

"Of course. I told you that the other night, remember?"

"I do remember. I guess I am just a little surprised that you remember. You were a little..." he hesitated.

"Oh, I remember just fine. And I want to meet your wife and daughters. Maybe tomorrow?" I had two more full days left in Idonea after tonight. I wanted to cram in as much as I could.

"Well, that would be all right with me. I will take you there myself tomorrow evening."

"That would be lovely." I smiled at him and then the doors to the lyptra opened. I took a step forward and tripped on those dam shoes, catching myself on Arthur's arm which kept me from falling on my face.

"Ugh, these shoes!" I griped. "Who invented these horrid high heels anyway? They should all be sent to Helgrind and burned!"

Arthur started to laugh at my outburst about something as silly as shoes. I looked up at him, folded my arms across my chest, and grinned.

He stopped laughing. "What?" he asked me.

"I told you I would do it," I said as we started walking out of the palace and down the pathway.

"Do what, My Lady?"

"I made you laugh out loud. I'm just sorry it took me so long," I said, remembering back to the day he walked me down the aisle to 'meet' the king.

He laughed again and so did I.

We continued walking down the pathway, and I could see the lights of the village not too far off. But in front of that, at the end of the pathway, was my waiting carriage. It was pulled by two large black horses with long black manes. The carriage itself was open and would seat two people in its dark blue-cushioned seats. The wheels were, of course, golden; and the outside of the carriage was dark blue with silver and gold embellishments.

Rali appeared from the other side of the carriage wearing fitted black leather pants, a midnight blue tunic, and the same long black vest with the gold embroidery that he had worn at the ball. He walked toward me with a masculine elegance. He stepped with a regal air about him. Those green and gold eyes sparkled in the artificial palace lights. His smile was warm...and it was for me. Yes, this was the most attractive man I had ever seen in my life.

"Annie, you look beautiful," he said as he approached me.

"So do you," I said without thinking. "I mean...thank you. You look very nice, too." *Nice save.*

He smiled and held out his hand. I looked up at Arthur, whose arm I was still holding, and said, "Thank you, Arthur. I will see you tomorrow."

Arthur looked at me and seemed embarrassed that I had said that in front of Rali.

"Oh yeah, Rali," I decided to explain, "I am meeting Arthur's family tomorrow. I am really looking forward to it. Good night, Arthur." I stepped towards Rali and he helped me into the carriage.

Rali looked back at Arthur once I was sitting in the cushioned seat and Arthur looked down at the ground, avoiding Rali's eyes. He told Rali, "It was her idea, Sir."

Rali chuckled and said, "I am sure it was. Good night, Arthur."

Arthur gave a small bow and walked back towards the palace while Rali climbed into the carriage next to me. He grabbed the reins, gave a little flick, and off we went.

I sat back to enjoy the scenery. The suns were setting, I could see the river flowing off to the right of us, and the village was straight ahead.

"So, Rali," I said, "You all can travel between planets on a light beam but you still use a horse and carriage? Seems kinda strange, don't you think?"

He smiled. "While we have the ability to do many things, we do not always choose to do them. Idonea is a small planet, and we would rather not jump from one location to another. Most of us like to enjoy the journey as much as the destination. We do not want to miss anything."

"I like that. Everything moves so quickly where I live. The cars, the people...everything. No one stops to enjoy the moment they are in. They are always rushing toward the next big thing," I said.

"Well then, I am glad you prefer the way of life on Idonea. Maybe you will stay after all."

"I didn't say I prefer it. Just that I like it. But I like a lot of things," I said.

"Like what?" he asked me.

"Well, I like coffee. I like drinking coffee while reading, as you know. I also like being barefoot and I like meeting new people. I like dogs and chocolate and eating just about anything. I like--"

"Me?" asked Rali.

"Well, I thought we already established that yesterday."

"I made an observation yesterday, but you never confirmed it," he said matter-of-factly.

"Did I deny it?" I asked.

He thought for a moment. "No you did not."

"Well, there ya go."

He looked sideways at me. "That is still not a confirmation."

"Guess you'll just have to figure it out for yourself, then." When I glanced at him, I realized just how close we were in that little carriage. We were so close we were practically in the same seat. I could see the individual strands of his black hair. I could see the gold in his eyes. I could see his inviting lips…they were moving closer. I quickly turned away and focused my gaze on the road in front of us.

"So." I cleared my throat. "Where are we going, Your Highness?"

He was quiet for a short moment and then answered, "I thought we would eat at one of my favorite restaurants in the village. It is small but very popular and it has the best food you will ever taste."

"My mouth is already watering."

"It is a good thing we will be there shortly."

The road became a little narrower as we entered the village. Rali pulled on the reins and the horses came to a stop. Rali exited the carriage, handed the reins to a waiting servant, came around to my side and helped me out onto the ground.

We walked through the village, hand in hand. Rali pointed out different shops and stores while we strolled along. We were watched by every pair of eyes that we passed. It was like we were celebrities. It actually made me a little uncomfortable so I tried to pretend Rali and I were the only people in the village as we walked. It was easy to do once I focused on my partner and all he was telling me about the kingdom as we made our way to dinner. He had just been in the middle of telling me about some of the special vegetables grown on the farms and sold there in the village when a small child ran up and bumped into me. I think I had startled him as much as he had startled me.

"Oh, are you okay?" I asked the boy who looked about six-years old.

He stepped back and looked up at me. "Sorry, ma'am," he said.

I smiled at him and bent down so I could be on the same level. "What's your name?"

He looked down at the ground shyly and put his hands behind his back. He said quietly, "Linny."

"Linny? I like that name. How old are you, Linny?" I asked him.

"Linny. Come here!" I heard a woman call. I looked up and saw a pretty young woman running up to the boy. She caught up to him, took his arm and said to me while bowing her head, "I am so sorry, My Lady. He was not watching where he was going. It will not happen again. I am sorry."

She started to pull him away when I stood up and told her, "Oh, it's okay. There's no harm done. He was just running around like all little boys should. Please don't be upset with him. If anything, I got in his way. So if someone must be in trouble, it should be me." I looked down at Linny standing next to his mother and gave him a little wink. He smiled and then looked back down at the ground again.

The woman lifted her head and looked at me in astonishment. She said, "Well no, no one is in trouble. Thank you, ma'am. I am glad you were not hurt."

"Not at all," I said to her. Then I looked back at the boy. "Linny, it was nice to meet you. I hope I run into you again sometime." I held my hand out to him and he hesitated only a moment before reaching out and shaking it. Then he grabbed his mother's skirt. She smiled at him, then at me, and thanked me one more time before they walked off together.

"What a cutie," I said as Rali and I continued walking.

"So, you like children? You are very good with them," Rali said.

"Thanks. Yes, I do like children. I like that they have the ability to keep us 'grown-ups' from taking things too seriously sometimes."

Rali laughed.

"Do you like children?" I asked him.

"Of course, I do. And do you not remember? You are the one that informed me that it is my job to create many little heirs to the throne."

We laughed.

"You know, I don't remember seeing many children running around the palace, now that I think of it," I said.

"Well, most of the courtiers send their children to a kind of boarding school when they are of school age. They are gone for weeks at a time and come home for visits during breaks," Rali told me.

"How sad. Those poor children. Don't they miss their moms and dads?"

"I would imagine they do at first. But then they must get used to it after a while. I haven't heard any complaints, anyway."

"Of course you haven't. No one wants to say anything negative to the king."

He gave me a puzzled look. "Why not? If someone in my kingdom does not like how something is done, shouldn't they be able to come to me?"

"Well, they should be, I guess. But do they? And anyway, isn't it really those powerful families that run the place?"

He seemed annoyed with me for saying that. "They do not run the place, as you say. However they do voice concerns and suggestions at council meetings."

"Ah. And are these suggestions voted on? How do new laws and regulations get passed around here?"

"I meet with my council, which includes members of these families and some of my higher-ranked military men. We discuss the best options from things as trivial as when the next ball will be held, to bigger issues such as what to do with the Hyrokkin."

"And who makes the final decision on such matters?" I asked him.

"Well, I do, of course."

"Okay. And what if the council doesn't like your decision on something?"

"Well, it does not really matter if they do or not. I have final say on how things are done and, so far, no complaints. I must be a very good king." He stuck his chin high in the air and began to strut.

"Ha! I guess. And a very humble king, as well."

"Yes, yes. Very much so, My Lady. We must have humility in common."

We walked a few more yards and stopped in front of a small cafe where people were seated both inside and outside to eat. I could smell the food being prepared inside, and it made my stomach growl. A man who appeared to be the host or the owner of the establishment scurried up to us and bowed.

"Good evening, Your Highness. We are so happy that you have come to dine here tonight. Will you be eating inside or outside on this fine evening?"

Rali looked at me to answer that question.

"It is so nice outside right now. Let's eat out here," I said eagerly.

"Outside it is, My Lady," said the host. He took a quick scan of the tables on the patio when I realized all the tables were full. I was about to tell him we could eat inside instead when he hurried over to a couple at a nearby table and informed them that the king was here and asked them to please take their meal and finish it elsewhere. I was horrified! I rushed over.

"Oh, please, no. Please let them finish. I had no intention of forcing anyone from their seats." I looked at the confused and now nervous couple who had, only a moment ago, been enjoying a nice quiet dinner to themselves. I said to them, "I am so sorry. We can eat inside or come back later, right Rali?" I glanced at him still standing at the entrance to the cafe. He looked like he was holding back a laugh, but managed to say, "Absolutely. We can do some more sight-seeing and check back later."

I looked back at the couple. "Please, stay here and enjoy your dinner. And don't hurry. We will take our time. I'm so sorry we disturbed you." I turned back to the host and said, "If you would please hold a table for us, we will come back in an hour or so."

"Yes...yes ma'am," said the host.

"Thank you. You are very kind."

Before I walked off, I told the couple, "Again, please take your time. There are other tables we can choose from as well, and I will feel just awful if I come back and find out you felt rushed through your dinner."

They both smiled at me and the man said, "Thank you, My Lady. We will stay and relax for a bit." Then he grinned at the woman across from him and said to me, "We are celebrating tonight."

"Oh, how fun! May I ask why?"

He looked at his partner again and she nodded her permission to him. He informed me that she had just agreed to marry him.

"That is so wonderful. Congratulations." I turned to Rali and said, "They're engaged! Isn't that exciting?" He nodded and smiled.

"What are your names?" I asked them.

"I am Asa and this is my...fiancée, Liah." They smiled at each other.

"Well, Asa and Liah, congratulations again. I'm Annie and I wish you both the best. It was so nice to meet you. Maybe we will see you again later. Have a wonderful night of celebrating."

They thanked me and then I walked back to Rali, took his hand, and led him on down the path for another stroll before dinner.

We had walked silently for a few moments when I realized he was looking at me. So I looked up at him.

"What?" I asked.

"Nothing," he said. "Just wondering how you do it."

"Do what?"

"Well, how you manage to make everyone you meet fall in love with you so quickly and easily," he answered.

"Do not," I replied maturely.

"Do not be upset. That is a good thing."

"Whether or not it's a good thing, it's not a true thing."

"Oh, it is very true. For example, Freya adored you right from the start, and--"

"She didn't adore me. I guess she liked me all right."

"She adored you. And stop interrupting."

"Oh, right. Sorry."

He sighed and then continued. "Arthur is already eager to introduce you to his family. The little boy and his mom--and now this couple you just met-- are all enchanted by you. That is impressive."

I waited a moment before saying anything. I wanted to be sure he was finished before I replied. God forbid I interrupt again.

"Well, I can counter by naming many people who do not like me in the least."

"All right then. Go."

"Okay. Well, there's...um..."

Rali smiled. "See? I told you there--"

"Wait! I've got one." I interrupted...of course. "Sindri's mother. She absolutely despises me." I grinned at him, proud of my small victory.

"Sindri's mother? When did you meet her?" he asked.

"Oh, well. We didn't officially meet. She saw me earlier in the hall and...um...let me know that I am not her favorite person."

"Ah. Yes, Dagny can be a bit...direct."

"So, you know her well?"

He was silent.

"I guess you would, seeing as how she will be your mother-in-law soon." I glanced sideways at him to see his reaction.

It wasn't what I expected. I don't really know what I expected, but it wasn't at all what he ended up doing. Rali stopped walking and turned to face me.

"Is that what she told you? Or is that what you think?" he asked me seriously.

"Uh...well, both," I said nervously.

He studied my face and didn't say anything. He let go of my hand and continued walking down the path. I waited a moment to see if he would stop and come back, but he just kept walking. So I hurried to catch up.

"What? What's wrong? I mean, it's true, isn't it? You and Sindri? Everyone knows it."

He stopped again and faced me. "Everyone? Who is everyone exactly? Sindri's mother? Probably Sindri herself?

That does not sound like everyone to me." His eyes flashed with anger.

"Well, it's not just them," I said even though I knew it pretty much was. "Maggie knows it."

"Ha!" Rali laughed and crossed his arms over his chest. "Yes, Sindri's little sister. I'm sure she is not biased at all."

"Well...Durin said--"

"I do not want to hear anything that man said. I am sure he told you many things to make you desire him over me. He would tell you whatever you wanted or needed to hear just to side with him, just to choose him, just to...to..." He trailed off and looked away. I knew I shouldn't have brought up Durin. I had only wanted to make my point. And I ended up just making Rali furious with me. Nice going, Annie.

"Rali, I'm sorry. I shouldn't have said that. We were having such a nice time. Let's just forget I said anything, okay?"

Rali took a deep breath. He looked down at the ground and then at me. "All right. We will forget it." Then he started walking down the path without me again. Guess it took him longer than a few seconds to forget things.

I caught up with him and walked beside him in silence for a while. We made our way down to the river. It was flowing gently and silently. There was a bench nearby and I walked over to it and sat down. Rali followed and sat next to me which made me feel a little bit better.

We sat for few minutes just enjoying the beautiful evening. There were a few other people walking along the river that night. Some in groups of three or four, some hand in hand. They all strolled by happily, talking to each other, laughing, smiling. It was nice to see.

I had to work up my courage before I finally said anything to break the silence between Rali and myself.

"Rali?"

"Yes," he said while still looking out at the river.

"Are you...still mad at me?"

He looked at me then. His green eyes were cool. "I am not mad at you. Why would you think I was mad at you?"

I raised my eyebrows at him and then gestured toward the path we had just come from. "Weren't you there, too? Do you not remember what just happened?"

He sighed and said, "I'm not mad at you. I just wish that...I wanted things to be different."

"Different how?" I asked him.

He was quiet and then said, "I wanted you to feel differently about being here. I wanted you to feel differently ...about me."

I was sad for him then. I believed then that he had actually expected that I would instantly have fallen in love with Idonea and with him when I had been brought here in the first place. But I hadn't. Not in the beginning. And then he had had to watch me with Durin. That could not have been fun. I remembered the feeling I had felt as I walked in and saw Sindri in Rali's room that night. It had made me physically ill. I still got a bit queasy when I thought about it.

"Rali, when I first got here, when I realized that I had been kidnapped--by you--and taken from my home, I was furious. You couldn't have believed that I would have been able to brush all that aside and be happy that I was going to get to live in a pretty palace and be courted by a king. It's not that easy."

He looked at me thoughtfully.

"You can't just force something on someone and expect them to like it," I said. "This was all new to me. It still is."

"But you are enjoying yourself more now--"

"Yes, because I have a choice now. The moment you told me I could go home...it changed things for me. This is like a nice vacation for me now. I am not here to get involved in matters of the kingdom. I am not here to try to win the heart of a king." I looked him in the eyes and said, "I am not here to fall in love and get married."

He looked away and back towards the river. "All right, Annie. I understand." He cleared his throat and stood up.

He stood there gazing at the flowing water for a few minutes. And I sat there gazing at him. He seemed to be mulling over some thoughts in his head. He was very serious. I thought maybe he was beginning to understand that I couldn't stay there. Maybe he was finally comprehending that becoming queen of that world was not every woman's ambition. And I think that it hurt him to realize those things.

And honestly, it was hurting me, too.

After a while he turned back to me, put a smile on his face and asked me, "Shall we check and see if a table is available yet?"

"That sounds great," I replied. I got up from the bench and put my arm through his.

We walked silently back to the cafe. Things had changed between us now. It was different. It was cold and lonely. I didn't like it.

When we returned to the cafe, there was a table being held outside for us. It was not the same one from earlier-- that couple was still there celebrating and I waved at them. I thanked the host for saving us a table and then Rali and I were seated. We looked at the menu and Rali made a few suggestions for me. I chose the roast duck with garlic potatoes and vegetables. When the waiter left the table to put in our order, I looked at Rali.

"So...are we just not talking anymore now? Because that's gonna make for a really boring dinner, don't you think?"

"Okay. What would you like to talk about?" he asked.

"Hmm...well, actually, I did have something I wanted to ask you about."

"What would that be?"

"Well, see, it's about my father. I think he may have somehow known about you guys."

"Who is you guys?"

"You guys, you know. All of you here on Idonea. Or maybe he didn't know about Idonea, but I think he knew about the Sidas Array."

Rali took a drink from his water glass before saying, "Oh really? What makes you say that?"

He didn't look at me but just past me. He didn't seem at all interested in what I was saying. But as much as I hated myself for it, I had to find out if there was any truth to what Durin had said in his letter.

"Well, I remembered something he said to me once when I was young. See, he died when I was fourteen--"

"Yes, a car accident if I recall."

I stared wide eyed at him. "How did you know that?" I asked him.

"I told you. I know a lot about you. So what did your father say to you?"

I blinked a few times before answering. "He told me a story about a magic star that could take someone far into space, wherever they want to go."

"Well, that sounds like a nice story that anyone might tell. It doesn't mean he knew about the--"

"He had a name for it. He called it the Sidas Array. He knew about it."

Rali paused for a moment and seemed to be thinking over something. "I think maybe you are remembering things inaccurately."

"So you don't think it's possible that my father knew about it?"

He took another sip of water. "No. I do not."

I slumped back into my chair. One of two things was happening. Either Rali was being honest with me, which meant my father had just coincidentally made up a correct name of a magical star. Or, Durin had been telling the truth and Rali was lying. I wanted to believe that Rali was the honest one, but the problem was my father. I just couldn't believe that, after everything he had told me, my father didn't know about this place. He had been telling me about it my whole childhood, it seemed.

I gave Rali another shot. "Don't you think someone on Earth might know something about it? Or this place? I mean, a bunch of people disappearing overnight? Someone had to know something, right? Who's to say someone didn't write something down about it? Or tell people about it? It gets passed down, other people hear about it....maybe it's just possible that my father had been told about it by someone in his family, or maybe read about it somewhere. Don't you think there's even that small possibility--"

"No, I do not," he said quickly.

His quick reply and obvious desire to get past this topic just confirmed for me that he did in fact think it was possible. And maybe even knew it was possible. And it made me upset that he wouldn't be honest with me about it. It was starting to look like Durin was right. And that was disturbing.

We sat in a frigid silence until our dinner arrived.

"Thank you," I said to the waiter who delivered our delicious-smelling food. "This looks wonderful," I told Rali, trying to bring some easy conversation back to our date. He nodded and then began eating quickly.

"In a hurry to get home?" I asked him. "Not having a good time? So sorry. Maybe you should've brought someone else."

He slammed his hand down on the table and I jumped. "I did not want to bring anyone else! No one but you. Do you still not see that?"

I sat in stunned silence and didn't know how to respond. But that worked out just fine because he wasn't finished.

"You let other people tell you how things are and how things will be. Maybe you should think for yourself," he said. Then he leaned across the table and said quietly, "Maybe you should stop thinking about what is comfortable and easy, all those things that left you searching the skies for a better option. Maybe you should look in front of you and think about what is new and real."

What he said reminded me of Sindri's mother telling me that my newness would soon wear off and that Rali would ultimately choose her daughter.

I responded. "I am thinking for myself. I know what is real here. You think it is exciting to have something new and different. But how long will that keep you interested? A few weeks? Maybe a few months? And then what? Will you go back to what you already know and love?"

He looked confused. I continued, "I know that you and Sindri are meant for each other. I know you are going to choose her and live happily with her as your queen. I saw you leave the palace together the other night and I saw her in your room before...or after...or...well, I saw her in there lying on your couch. So don't try to fool me into thinking I am your one and only true love when I've seen with my own eyes that it isn't the truth, Rali. Stop lying to me."

I realized I had tears in my eyes, so I quickly looked down and tried to wipe them away inconspicuously.

Rali sat back and said nothing.

So did I.

He thought for a minute and then said, "So, you saw me take Sindri out on a date."

"Yes."

"And you saw her in my room, lying on my couch. Was I there?"

"No, she was alone...at the moment."

"So, you have gathered from this evidence that she and I are in love and will soon be happily wed?"

"Well… and you kissed her goodnight after your date, and many people believe that you two are meant to be together."

"Hmm... Quite a case you have presented. But there is one thing you are missing." He leaned toward me and looked me in the eye. "You never asked me how I feel about Sindri. You never asked me about my date with Sindri or the night she was in my room. You have never even cared to find out my opinion of the whole matter, have you?"

"Well...no."

"Why not? Don't you think that might be important? Asking the other party involved in this supposed engagement?"

"I don't know if you will tell me the truth. It's pretty obvious that, so far, you haven't. So why should I ask you? I can't trust you."

After a cold, quiet minute he stood up from the table and said, "We should go."

"Go where?" I asked.

"Back home...to the palace. I think we are finished here."

"Oh....well, fine."

I got up and followed him back to the carriage, leaving my barely touched dinner on the table.

When we got back to the carriage, Rali helped me in and then climbed behind me. He took the reins and the horses began the walk back to the palace.

It was a miserable ride back. I fought tears the whole time. Neither of us said a word. There wasn't anything to say. I was going home in a couple of days and Rali would marry Sindri. We would both forget that this had happened, that I had been brought to Idonea; and I would buy my bookstore, marry Jake, and drink coffee.

I knew Rali was lying to me, hiding something from me. But what I didn't know was if I was more upset about that or more upset that I would soon be leaving him and he would be marrying Sindri.

When we got back to the palace, Rali walked with me all the way to my room. We got to the door when he grabbed my arm and turned me to face him.

"Annie, will you not ask me?"

"Ask you what?"

"Ask me if I love Sindri. Ask me who I want to be with. Ask me if I want you to leave."

His grip was tight on my arm, and it was beginning to hurt. He pulled me even closer. "Ask me!" he demanded.

I looked deep into those eyes. I never wanted to look away. "I...I can't ask you," I whispered as the tears finally fell.

He tightened his grip. "Why not?"

"Because...whatever the answers are, I don't want to know."

He let go of my arm and took a step back. We stared at each other for a long moment.

"I'm sorry, Rali," I finally said. "I have to go home."

The King

    I turned to walk into my room, but before I stepped through the door he said, "Do you love me?"

    I couldn't look at him. I just stood there in my doorway and said, "I'm sorry." I stepped inside, closed the door, sank to the floor and cried.

Chapter 22

Freya was by my side in an instant. I barely made it into my room when I couldn't hold in the sobs any longer. Freya held my head in her lap and softly stroked my hair.

"It is all right, my dear. It is okay. Just cry it all out. When you feel better, we can talk," she said to me.

I continued to cry for a while longer until I finally calmed myself down. Freya fixed some soothing lavender tea and walked me over to the couch. She asked if I wanted her to prepare a hot bath, but, at that moment, I needed to talk - I needed to sort things out. And I wanted Freya to help me.

I filled her in on everything Rali and I had said to each other during our date. I told her how awful I had been and the horrible things I had said.

"Why did I say those things, Freya? Why would I tell him I couldn't trust him? And I have been taking everyone else's word over his. Even Durin's. Why would I do that? What's wrong with me?" I cried.

"Oh, my dear Annie. It is very obvious to me why you have said and done these things," said Freya.

"Well, would you mind filling me in? I'm feeling a little lost at the moment."

She chuckled. "Annie, it is simple. You are in love with the king. You do not want to leave--"

"Yes, I do. I need to go home--"

"You said 'need'. You have been saying that for a while now. But what do you want, Annie?"

My mind flashed back to the pub where Erika and I spent an evening after work. She had asked me the very same question. I didn't fully know the answer then… But I did now.

I knew what I wanted. I wanted to be with Rali. I wanted to stay on Idonea with him. Of course, I still wanted to see my family again, but it was getting harder and harder to say that I wanted that more. What I didn't want, was to have to choose. I told Freya this, and she nodded.

"Yes, it is a tough place to be in. Choosing between love and family. It is not an easy choice."

I sighed. "Well, after the things I said, I'm sure it doesn't matter anymore, anyway."

"What do you mean?" asked Freya.

"Well, I was kind of a jerk. I'm sure he will want to pick Sindri over me now. She would never say mean things to him. She adores him."

Freya grabbed my ear-yes, my ear-and pulled me across the couch where she put her face in front of mine.

"Ooo ow! Freya! What is wrong with you? Let go!"

"Listen to me, Annie. Stop screaming!"

"Ow. I will if you let go!"

She did. I rubbed my poor ear and gave her the meanest look I could muster.

"Now, be quiet and listen to me. If you ever again say that the king would choose Sindri over you, I will grab your other ear and drag you from here to Earth myself!" said Freya. "Good Lord, Annie. You are the dumbest smart person I have ever met in my entire life." She got off the couch and walked into the bathroom. I heard her turn on the bathwater. She came back in the room and got a nightgown out of my closet.

"What are you doing?" I asked.

"I am getting your bath ready. You are going to take a bath, wash away all those negative thoughts, and then you are going to go to sleep. You have one more day here before the Kostera when the king will choose his bride. You are going to be clean and rested, and we are going to enjoy the day whether you like it or not. Now get in there and get in the bathtub!" she commanded.

I had no choice. "Yes, ma'am." I scurried into the bathroom and got into the warm water as soon as the tub was filled. Freya came in and told me that she, too, was going to get ready for bed and that I would see her in the morning.

"Okay, Freya. Good night," I called to her.

"Hmph," was her reply.

After I got out of the bath and dried myself off, I put on my nightgown and crawled into my bed. I thought about the choice I needed to make. The choice between being on earth with my family and friends, or being on Idonea with Rali. I couldn't imagine never seeing my family again, but it made me physically ill when I thought of leaving Rali. I knew in my heart that he preferred me over Sindri. I didn't need to ask him to confirm that. But I couldn't get over having seen her there. In his room. He hadn't acted surprised when I mentioned it. He knew she had been there. And somehow it was hard for me to think that any man would've kicked her out of their bedroom looking the way she had. Then there were the questions that he wouldn't answer. Why had he brought me here, really? What wasn't he telling me about my father? Why wouldn't or couldn't he be honest with me?

I turned onto my back and stared at the ceiling. I had one more day before the Kostera. I would have to talk to Rali at some point. But what would I tell him? That I loved him but still had to go home? That I didn't love him?

I rolled back onto my side and closed my eyes. I turned my thoughts to other things to help me fall asleep. I thought about meeting Arthur's family the next day. I thought about what I might want to do or see in the morning. Maybe I would visit Maggie. I hadn't seen her for a few days.

After a little while, I finally drifted off to sleep.

When I woke up, breakfast was waiting for me and Freya was getting my clothes ready.

"Good morning, Freya. You gonna yell at me some more?"

"That depends. Are you going to say any more dumb things today?" she asked.

"I sure hope not. My ear is still sore from yesterday." I smiled at her, got out of bed, and started on my breakfast.

"So, what would you like to do today?" she asked me.

"Well, this evening I am going to Arthur's house to meet his wife and kids, but before that I am free and clear. I figure I should find Rali and talk to him at some point."

"What are you going to tell him?"

I sighed. "I don't really know yet."

"Well, you will probably have to wait until this afternoon to talk to him. Today the king and his council are meeting about the state of the kingdom. They meet once a quarter. It keeps the king and his council members busy almost all day," Freya told me.

I was disappointed, but I figured it would be good to have more time to figure out exactly what I wanted to say to him.

I finished my breakfast and got dressed. Freya picked out a midnight blue cotton dress with a sky blue feela. I walked right past the shoes. Then Freya put my hair in a high, curled ponytail.

"All right, I'm good. Where to, first?" I asked. But she didn't get to answer because there was a knock on the door. Freya answered it and Maggie came walking into my room.

"Hi, Maggie. How funny. I was just thinking last night that I should visit you today. I guess you had the same thought?" I asked her.

"Hi, Annie. Yes, I guess I kind of did. Only I did not think of it until a few moments ago." She had a handkerchief in her hands and was wringing it nervously.

"Is everything okay, Maggie?"

"Yes. Everything is fine. I just...I wanted to know something and was hoping you could tell me."

"Well, that depends, I suppose. What do you need to know?"

"Where do I start?" Maggie began, "My sister's room is right next to mine, and I heard voices in there late last night. My mother was in there with her and Sindri was very upset."

I really didn't want to hear about Sindri at the moment, but it seemed that Maggie really needed to get something off her chest. "Okay, what happened? Why was she upset?"

"Well, they were talking about...you."

"What about me?"

"Oh, they were griping and moaning about you and the king. They knew that you two had left together last night. They think that you are putting spells on him, or seducing him, or promising him riches or something if he chooses you over Sindri to become his queen."

I laughed. "What? That's ridiculous. Are they insane?" Then I stopped laughing abruptly. "Oh, sorry. I didn't mean to insult your family," I lied. I absolutely had meant to insult them. I just probably shouldn't insult them to her face.

"No, it is okay. I am here because...well, I want to know what really is happening with you and the king. See, I am really tired of...of being Sindri's slave." Maggie began to tear up. I walked over to her and guided her to the couch to sit down. Freya brought her a tissue.

"Do you remember, Annie, the other day when I told you about the man I was seeing?" asked Maggie.

"Yes. Yes I do. He is a captain, right?"

"Yes. Well, I had left the palace to meet him a few nights ago. I have had to meet him in secret because I knew Sindri and my mother would be upset if I were not entirely focused on my sister right now. Well, Sindri came looking for me that night because she needed me to help her sneak into the king's room. But she could not find me and was furious. When she found out where I had been, she sent a letter to the captain telling him that I was already engaged to another man and that he had to leave me alone or the king would have him banished. I have not seen him since." Maggie began to cry and I put my arm around her shoulder.

"Wow, Maggie. I am so sorry. Your sister should not have done something so cruel," I told her.

"And the thing is, I have always been there for her. I have done everything for her; and now, she treats me like this."

"Maggie, maybe I can help you find the captain. We can explain what happened. Please let me help you," I pleaded.

Maggie looked up at me with her tear - stained face. "That is not why I am here. I am here to help you."

"What? How? I'm not the one who needs help. Let me help you find the captain--"

She stood up and wiped her face with her hand. She had a new look of determination.

"No. Annie, I want to tell you something. I do not know what your feelings are for the king, but I want to tell you that he does not love my sister. I am afraid, though, that if he has no other option available to him, he will marry her. He has to marry someone. That is the law. Idonea needs heirs, so the king must marry."

"Well, aren't there a lot of 'Hopefuls' that would marry him?" There had been about thirty of them at the ball.

Maggie explained, "It has been known since the beginning of this king's reign that that he would choose Sindri whenever he was ready to marry. The Lange family is the wealthiest and most powerful. It just makes sense. Sindri has always expected that she would be queen. No other girl here would dare try to take the king away from her. It's all a big show, really. And then you came along. The king brought you here himself. Well, Sindri has hated you since Day One. She has been doing her best to keep herself first in the king's eyes ...but she has failed. He does not love her."

"What? How do you know this?" I asked her. I tried not to seem too excited about this possible turn of events.

"The night that I was not available to help Sindri, she sneaked into his room herself. She made a fire and waited for him to come and find her." Maggie lowered her voice to a whisper and said, "She even told me that she stripped off all of her clothes and then put one of his shirts on. She thought she could seduce him and get him to promise his love to her in exchange for...well, her skills." Maggie and I both made a sick face. Then she continued, "But it didn't work out the way she wanted. I heard her telling my mother that when the king found her in his room he asked her to leave."

"Seriously?" I said.

"Yes. But she would not. She climbed into his bed and tried to get him to join her."

"What did he do?" I asked.

Maggie said, "He told her that as much as he admired her persistence, he was not in love with her and would not share his bed with her."

I stared at her for a moment...and then started to chuckle. So did Freya. We looked at each other and mouthed *admired her persistence*. We were so on the same wavelength, Freya and I.

Then I turned back to Maggie and said, "Well that is unfortunate for her. But what do you want me to do with that?"

"I want you to marry the king," she said.

"Huh?"

"Yes. The king loves you. Everyone knows it."

And this whole time I had thought everyone knew the king loved Sindri. I was starting to wonder which "everyone" I should be trusting.

Maggie continued, "My sister and mother were beside themselves last night after hearing that you and he had gone out to the village. I think they are planning something, but I do not know what. They do not want you here. They have expected their whole lives that Sindri would be the next queen. You should be careful."

I thought about how Dagny had gotten Freya and her daughter banished from the palace and knew that what Maggie was saying could be true. But what was I supposed to do about it?

I thanked Maggie for telling me, and asked her for a moment alone to think. Maggie understood and left me alone with Freya.

As soon as she left, I walked out to the balcony and Freya followed.

"Okay, Freya. What do I do?" I asked her.

"Well," she shrugged. "I think maybe you were right before."

"What do you mean?"

"When you said you should go home and live your life and let the king live his. Yes. Absolutely. I mean, after what Maggie has said about her sister, I think it would be very good for our kingdom to have Sindri as our queen."

"What?"

"Yes. She is very clever, sneaking into the king's room like that, sending the false letter to the captain. And she is very determined. She wouldn't leave the king's room even after he showed no interest. Yes, that is exactly what Idonea needs."

"Freya, I--"

"Oh, I am not finished. I have not even mentioned how great this will be for the king. This will provide him with the opportunity to learn how to deal with a wife he doesn't love… or even like, maybe. He will not share his bed with her, so it will be quite an interesting challenge for him to produce any children. It will definitely perfect his problem-solving skills. Perhaps he will take a mistress. It is not uncommon--"

"Okay, Freya."

"Stop interrupting, I have not told you what you will get out of all of this."

I sighed. "What, Freya? What will I get out of all of this?"

She looked me in the eyes. "Nothing."

I wasn't expecting that answer.

"You will go home, hug your mother, your sister, your friends, and be happy for a time. But then you will remember, and you will wonder whether you made the right choice. I know how you love the king even if you will not admit it to me or even to yourself. You do not just love him. You yearn for him. You have yearned for him your whole life, have you not? Can you see that now? You have told me about your feelings on Earth. Something always missing…always wondering what more life could offer you. Well, have you wondered what more life could offer you since you got here?"

I was silent.

"No, you have not. Because what you have been missing is right here. His name is Ralnnulf Aerick Valiar. And you need him just as much as he needs you."

I turned away from her and looked out over the kingdom. What Freya had said was…well it was true. I couldn't deny it no matter how hard I tried. I didn't want to leave Rali. I couldn't leave Rali. Going back home, to Earth, wouldn't change that. I would live the rest of my life feeling only partly there. Despite the unanswered questions, I knew I was in love and I didn't want to lose that.

No, I couldn't go home now.

"Freya," I said.

"Yes, Annie?"

"Where are the king's council chambers located, exactly?"

"Why?" she asked.

I walked back into the room and headed for the door. "Because I need to speak to Rali immediately."

Freya smiled, clasped her hands together and followed behind me. "I will take you there myself."

She led me down the hallway and after a couple of minutes and a few turns, Freya stopped in front of a wide door.

"They are in there," she said and pointed to the door.

"Okay. Thank you, Freya." I turned towards the door and was about to knock, but before I did, I turned back to Freya and gave her a big tight hug. Then I let her go, stepped back and looked at her smiling face. "Here I go," I told her. Then I turned back to the door and knocked. I heard heavy footsteps coming to the door and a large bodyguard opened the door. He just stared at me. So I spoke up first.

"Um...hi. I need to speak to the king, please."

He kept staring and didn't move. Men's voices came from inside the room. I tried again.

"Please, it is urgent. Can you please tell the king that I need a moment with him?"

The guard looked me up and down, and took a step backwards into the room. He turned away from me and toward the men in the council room.

"Your Royal Highness," he said, "There is a woman at the door who says she needs a moment with you."

Then I heard Rali answer him, but I couldn't see him around this massive wall of a man.

"I am in a meeting right now, it will have to wait," I heard him say.

The guard started to turn back around to me but before he could I said, "Tell him it's Annie."

The guard faced me and said, "The king is in a meeting, he is not to be--"

"Yes, I heard him, but this is important." I yelled without really meaning to. But it worked. Rali heard me.

"Annie?" I heard him say.

"Rali. Yes, it's me."

"Let her come in," he said to the guard.

The King

The guard slowly stepped to the side and I walked past him into the council chambers. The room was long and narrow with a table that went almost from end to end. Every seat around the table was filled by a member of the council. I recognized a few of them, but I didn't focus too long on anyone except Rali. He was seated at the head of the table and stood as I entered.

"I'm sorry to interrupt, but I really need a moment of your time," I said to him.

"Of course," he said. Then he turned to the men at the table. "Excuse me, gentlemen. I will only be a moment." He then motioned for me to follow him. He headed to a door on the other side of the room. I followed him to it and he held the door open for me. We both walked into the smaller adjoining room containing a small table and a few chairs.

Rali closed the door behind us and said, "What is wrong, Annie? Has something happened?"

"No. Nothing is wrong." Then I stopped. Here he was, standing in front of me. The man I had fallen in love with - and I knew that now. I wanted to stay here with him, and not because it was exciting, not because it would make Sindri furious, but because I loved him and I needed him. But in that very moment, I had no idea what to say to him.

He cocked his head and said, "I thought you said it was important. What did you need?"

I hesitated for a moment and he started to speak again. "Annie, if you do not need me right now, I really should--"

"Rali, wait," I said.

He took a step toward me. "What?"

I took a step toward him and said, "I need to ask you something. I should've asked you this before, and I'm sorry I didn't."

"What do you want to know?"

"Do you love Sindri?" I asked.

He smiled warmly at me, took another step forward and said, "No, I do not."

"Who do you want to be with?"

"I want to be with you, Annie." Another step.

"Do you want me to leave?"

"No. I want you to stay here with me and never leave my side."

He took one more step and we were within inches of each other.

"Now I have a question for you, Annie Watts," he said. "Do you love me?"

I reached up and put my hands on both sides of his face and whispered, "Yes." I pulled his face towards mine and he didn't fight me. Our lips met, I wrapped my arms around his neck and his arms were around my waist. We kissed each other gently, but passionately. It wasn't lustful, it wasn't greedy. It was perfect. This was what I had been missing. This was what I had been looking for. Feeling safe and adored in the arms of the man I loved.

We could have stayed that way for hours, but were interrupted by a council member that I had met, but whose name I couldn't remember. Alfred? Albert? Whoever he was, he opened the door and said, "Your Highness, we really need to..." And then he stopped when he saw what was keeping His Highness so busy. "Oh, I am sorry." He began to close the door again and Rali called after him, "We will be there shortly, Albrecht."

Ah! Albrecht! So close. Wait, what?

"What was that? We will be there shortly? Who's we?" I asked him.

He laughed. "We. You and me."

"But why am I going to your meeting?"

The King

"Did you not hear what I just said? I do not want you to ever leave my side. Now come on." He grabbed my hand and led me back through the door and into the council room.

Chapter 23

    We walked back into the council room hand in hand. Rali instructed one of the guards to bring an extra chair to the head of the table. I was to be seated right next to Rali, in front of all of his council members. If Sindri didn't hate me already, she surely would as soon as she heard about this. But I didn't care. It wasn't my goal to make anyone hate me or be envious of me. I had Rali's love, and that was all I needed.

    As we sat down, we, naturally, were given a few strange and confused looks. Rali addressed this by saying, "Gentlemen of the council, this is Annie Watts. She will be sitting in on our meeting today to learn more about the kingdom and how it is run. So, let's all be on our best behavior. Albrecht? Shall we continue?"

    "Yes. Of course, Sir. We were just beginning to discuss the state of our military and some of the new posts that have been assigned. Colonel? Please give us a general summary," said Albrecht. This began an easy discourse among some of the members. I just sat back in my chair and tried to listen and learn all I could. I was starting to realize that these were things that might affect me in the future. If I were to be queen, I would need to know the basics of this place.

During a bit of a lull in the discussion, I leaned over to Rali and whispered, "Did Sindri ever come to any of these meetings with you? You know, try to learn about how to run the kingdom?"

He whispered back, "No. Why?"

I shrugged and said, "Oh, no reason. Just wondering. Guess this makes me...better."

Rali began to chuckle and some of the men shot disapproving looks in our direction.

The council talked about many subjects that concerned the kingdom and I learned a lot. When they began discussing the Hyrokkin, I tried to focus and take note of anything important they said. Since I had had my own experience with the monsters I wanted to know all I could about them. Some of the army leaders proposed an attack on the planet of Helgrind. They wanted the Hyrokkin to know they could not continue to trespass on Idonea or to attempt to steal the Sidas Array. I was even able to impress some of the men by sharing a little of my experience, and I could describe the gloves the Hyrokkin had used to hold me without burning me. I suggested that the Idoneans try to figure out what material the gloves contained in order to build shields or armor with it and protect themselves from the Hyrokkin flame. I received a few nods of approval and a hand squeeze under the table from Rali. I felt all giddy inside, like I was fifteen again.

Not all of the council members were in favor of an attack. This included the man to whom I had bared my wounded leg at the earlier meeting. These men were very determined to keep the Idonean army off of Helgrind, and keep them all on Idonea to protect the people. Rali was leaning towards the side of the men who wanted to attack. But no final decision was being made.

After meeting most of the morning, the men took a break for the lunch hour. Rali and I got up from our seats and were discussing what we wanted to do for lunch, when I heard a familiar voice. A voice that made me cringe. It made my wounds start to hurt again, and my throat dried up so that I could barely speak.

"Are we breaking for lunch already? But I just got here."

I looked over to the doorway, and there was Durin. He waltzed into the room as if nothing had happened. As if he hadn't ever attacked me, or tried to choke the life out of me. My legs went numb and I dropped into my chair. Rali followed my gaze to the doorway. It was hard to describe the look on his face when he saw Durin. It wasn't anger. It wasn't fury, as one might have expected (me, for example). It was... calm. Composed. Durin's and Rali's eyes met, and Rali began to walk across the room toward him. His walk was controlled and steady.

"Hello, Your Highness. Sorry I am late. Your guards did not want to let me in for some reason," said Durin.

Rali just continued toward him.

"If you do not mind, could you please remind them that the General of your Army deserves their respect? It was quite an inconvenience for me to be denied--"

He wasn't able to finish his sentence because Rali's grip around his neck made it impossible for him to breathe...so talking was out of the question. Rali picked him up with one hand on Durin's throat and the other held tight to his jacket collar. Rali slammed Durin up against the wall, and brought his face right up to Durin's.

"You do not deserve their respect after all you have done," he said through gritted teeth. Now his anger was coming out. And we all witnessed it.

It was magnificent.

"You are no longer welcome here. You are hereby stripped of your title as General of the King's Army, and you are to remove yourself from the palace immediately." The words practically blazed out of Rali's mouth.

"Where...where will I go?" choked Durin.

Rali let go of Durin and he fell to the floor, landing with his legs sprawled in front of him and his back against the wall.

"The guards will take you from here. You are to be detained until the council and I can discuss your fate," Rali told him.

Durin struggled to his feet, brushing off his pants and jacket. Two guards approached him and bound his hands behind his back. They began to lead him out the door; and as they did, Durin looked at me and said, "Is he still lying to you about your father? That is why you are here. The king knew your--"

"Guards, take him away, now!" yelled Rali.

"You know so little, Princess. You may be in for a shock."

And with that, Durin was led out the door. I didn't know where he was being taken, and I didn't care. I didn't ever want to see him again.

Rali was by my side quickly. "Are you all right?" he asked me.

I looked up at him. "I'm absolutely fine. But I didn't just slam a full grown man against a wall. Are you all right?"

He took a few deep breaths. "Yes. I actually feel a lot better now that I got to choke some of the life out of him."

Many of the council members were standing around and whispering to each other in groups. Rali turned to them and suggested they waste no more time getting to lunch because the council would reconvene in an hour. They filed out of the room and Rali sat down in the chair next to me.

We sat in silence for a few moments until what had just happened sank in for us both.

"Thank you, Rali," I finally said. "You have no idea how nice it feels to have you as my protector."

He smiled at me, reached up and ran one hand down the side of my cheek. "You will always have me to protect you."

I smiled. And then, as much as I hated to do it, I had to ask him about what Durin had said.

"Rali? What did he mean? What do I not know about that might shock me?"

Rali sat back, and let out a heavy sigh. "Annie, there is a lot I need to tell you. I have been wanting to tell you since you got here. But I had to be sure, first. I did not want to bring up anything that was...unnecessary."

I was so confused. "Unnecessary? Like what? Why would something be unnecessary?"

"Well, if you were to go home, for instance, and never want to think about me or Idonea again, then none of this would matter."

"Okay, so since it looks like I will be here for a while, are you going to fill me in?" I asked.

He grinned, "So, you are going to be here for a while, huh? Not going anywhere?"

"Oh, shut up. I think we both know you wouldn't survive the loss of me. I am just doing you a favor," I said.

"I appreciate it very much."

"Great. Now, anyway, we have one hour. So, tell me what I need to know."

"It will take longer than an hour. But for now, I need to tell you about Durin."

"Ugh. Just hearing that name makes me cringe."

"Well, he is not my favorite either, but it might help to know a little of his history and how he and I are connected."

"All right. Go ahead."

"Well, as you know, Durin was quite young to hold such a high position in my army. He is only a couple of years older than I am."

"Yes, he told me that he earned the position, even though it did help that he was from a powerful family." I remembered him telling me as much at the ball.

"Oh, he did not earn it. He was given the position purely because of his family connection."

"Wow. Must be a pretty important family."

"Uh...yes. The most important, actually," Rali said.

I thought for a second and then I started to catch on. "So, are you saying...is Durin related to you?"

"He is my brother. Well, my half-brother."

I sat back in my chair and let that sink in. "Okay, wow. Explain, please," I said.

"Soon after my parents were married, my father...well, my mother wasn't his only lover."

I shook my head. *Men.*

Rali continued, "He and another woman had a child – Durin - a couple of years before I was born."

"Did many people know about it?" I asked.

"No. And many still do not. As far as I can tell, only my parents, a few close servants, myself, Durin, and Durin's mother ever knew about it. And now, you."

"Is Durin's mother still around?"

He looked at me and hesitated for a moment. "Yes. She has been given many honors and much wealth for her silence. She was married off to a very high ranking officer and only a few years later, they had a daughter. Durin's mother demanded that her daughter be promised to the king's legitimate first born son, or she would let everyone know about the king's bastard child. She would try to get her son an equal claim to the throne if she could not get her daughter there."

"Oh. My. Lord. You mean Dagny. She was your father's lover? She is Durin's mother? And your father promised her that you would marry her daughter, Sindri."

"Yes."

"Wow, again."

"Yes...wow."

This was a lot of new information to take in. No wonder Durin had tried so hard to win me over or get rid of me. And Dagny had made a deal with Rali's unfaithful father that she expected would be kept, even though Rali's father wasn't around anymore. This made so much sense as some of the Durin puzzle pieces began to fall into place. Though it was all quite insane.

"So, basically, if you marry me instead of Sindri, you will be breaking your father's promise, and Dagny may go public with Durin's parentage?" I asked him.

"Basically, yes."

"And you still want me to stay?"

He laughed. "Of course. Even if Dagny does decide to share the news with the world, not much harm can be done. No one would believe her anyway. They would wonder why she waited so long to say anything."

"Well, can't she demand that Durin be given his position back? Or be given your position?"

"Demand to whom? Me? I am not likely to give in to her demands. I have done nothing wrong that I need to answer for."

"Well, you fell in love with me instead of her daughter, and she considers that to be very wrong," I pointed out.

"She can think what she wants. I do not care. She cannot ruin my happiness now that I have you." He leaned forward and kissed me. Then he got up from his chair. "So, what shall we have for lunch? We could eat in the dining hall, or in my room or yours. What do you want to do?"

I stood up also. "I don't care what we do, as long as you don't pretend like you have told me all there is to know."

"What?"

"There is a lot more, I'm sure. And I have a lot of questions. So when will you fill me in?"

He smiled. "Yes, there is more. But can we just relax and enjoy each other's company for a while? We have a lifetime to talk."

I smiled at the thought of that. A lifetime to talk with Rali. I guess it would be all right to just enjoy some time together...not talking.

"Okay, Your Highness. You win. But we are eating in my room. Freya will be there and honestly, I don't think we should be alone right now."

He grinned. "You do not trust me?"

"Oh, that's not it at all." I grabbed his hand and looked up at him. "It's me I don't trust."

He laughed as we walked out of the council chambers and down the hall towards my room.

Freya was in my room when we arrived and ordered our lunch to be served there. She somehow didn't seem too surprised to see me walking in with Rali. The three of us said a few words to each other before she went into her own room so Rali and I could eat privately...though she did leave the connecting door between our rooms open.

Rali and I ate our lunch quickly and then walked over to the balcony to talk for a few minutes before heading back to finish up the council meeting.

"Tell me what happens at the Kostera tomorrow. I am sure it will be a big event," I said to Rali.

"Oh, it is a huge event. Every person in the kingdom gets involved. Even the villagers. They have parties and festivals all day long; and, here in the palace, we feast and dance and celebrate as well."

"Okay, but how does it all start? And when do you make your big announcement? I am just dying to know who the next queen will be," I said.

Rali laughed. "If you do not already know, then you are not as smart as I thought you were, and I might have to change my mind."

"Ha! Right. You wouldn't. Not when you can have someone as fascinating as Annie Watts." I smiled at him and he smiled back. But then his expression changed slightly and he looked out over the kingdom.

"What? I was just kidding. I'm sure I'm not that fascinating."

"No, it is not that. And, yes you are. But I was just thinking about tomorrow. Annie...before the announcement is made, before I make it all official...are you sure?" he asked me.

I turned to him and he also turned to face me. "Rali, I have given this a lot of thought. I have fought with myself over this for some time now, whether I realized it or not. It is hard to imagine being so far from Earth and my family and my old life. I will really miss it," I said. Then I stepped towards Rali and put my arms around his waist. "But that doesn't even compare to how much I would miss you. This is my new home. You are my new family. And there is nowhere else I would rather be. So, to answer your question, yes, I am sure."

He must have believed what I said because the following kiss was strong and intense. We were wrapped up in each other, emotionally and physically. It would've taken a crowbar to separate us. Instead, it was Freya's voice calling into my room to inform us that our lunch break was over that got us to unlatch ourselves from each other.

I began smoothing my hair and walked into my room to check myself in the mirror quickly before heading back to the meeting. Rali followed me in and stood behind me. I looked at our reflection in the mirror. Yep. We were one good - looking couple, if I did say so myself.

"Annie, I want to give you something," Rali said.

I turned around. "Oh, I like you. Not even officially engaged yet and already giving me presents. Nice."

He laughed. "Well, actually, what I am giving you will take care of that."

"Huh?" That seemed to be my go-to response these days.

And then Rali held out his hand, and in it was a ring. It wasn't anything extravagant, but it was beautiful. It was a thin gold band with small sapphires set along one side.

"It was one of my mother's rings. I chose this one because I thought you would like it more than the typical engagement rings here. They can get quite large and showy and...obnoxious, really. This one seemed more like you. Unpretentious, natural, and unmistakably beautiful."

"Do you carry this with you everywhere or something? When did you have time to go get it?"

When I think back to this moment, I realize that I was totally ruining the most beautiful proposal with my annoying questions.

Rali answered, "I picked this ring out for you the day I brought you here and have had it with me since then. Just in case."

I smiled and looked up to meet his gaze. "You've known all along, haven't you? You've never doubted it."

He laughed, took my hand in his and said, "Miss Anne Watts, before I make my announcement tomorrow, I would like to check with you first. Will you stay here with me? Will you marry me and be my wife and the Queen of Idonea?"

The tears started to fill my eyes as I nodded my head. "Yes. Of course. Yes."

He put the ring on my finger and it fit perfectly.

Wow. This was really happening. I couldn't believe it. Two weeks before, I was walking down the street wondering how I was going to keep avoiding proposals from Jake and trying to figure out what else was out there for me, and now, I was engaged to a king...on an entirely different planet.

I did not see that coming. It all seemed to be happening so quickly, but it also seemed so right. So I wasn't too concerned with the fast pace of it all.

I grabbed Rali and hugged him as tightly as I could. I was happy. I was safe. I was loved. In that moment, everything was perfect.

I let go of him, stepped back, and...yawned. Oh, great way to ruin the moment again.

He laughed. "Bored with me already?"

"No. Sorry. I'm just...tired, I guess."

"Well, you have had a long and eventful morning. We both have. Now, unfortunately for me, I have no choice in the matter and I have to go back to the council meeting. However, you, my dear, are much more fortunate. You can stay here and rest," he said as we walked towards the door.

"But I want to go with you. I'll be fine, I'm fully awake, I'm not...not..." Yawn.

Dam.

"No ma'am. As your king and your future husband, I command that you stay in and rest this afternoon. I will come by after the meeting is over."

"Fine. But don't start thinking I'm gonna let you order me around when we are married," I said.

He chuckled. "I am afraid it may be the other way around."

I smacked him on the arm as he walked out the door and he turned around to sneak in one last kiss before he left.

I closed the door behind him and stood there for a moment just listening to his footsteps walking away. After they had faded completely, I walked back into my room...no, I floated back into my room. This was perfection. This was happiness. I didn't even notice Freya walk into my room. I was too wrapped up in my own thoughts. I went to my closet, changed into some black stretch pants and a blue t-shirt, and walked over to my bed to lie down for a bit...as my fiancé had commanded.

Ah, my fiancé. I climbed into my bed, and as I was pulling my covers up over my legs, I noticed Freya as she stepped up to my bedside.

"Oh, hi Freya. I'm just gonna rest for a bit. Okay?"

She cocked her head to one side, crossed her arms over her chest and said, "Really? You are just going to come in here, lock lips with the king for an hour, have a ring appear on your finger, and then go to bed? Oh, child, I do not think so. Now tell me everything, and I mean everything."

I had to laugh. I sat up in the bed and propped myself up with some pillows. "Fine. But then I'm going to take a nap. I've got a busy life ahead of me and I should get some rest."

Freya grinned and I filled her in on everything that had happened that morning. As I came to the part about the proposal, Freya teared up. After I had told her everything, she hugged me tightly and let a few of her tears fall.

"So, Annie, you are happy now?" she asked me.

I smiled. "Yes. Very happy." Then I thought about my family back on Earth and my expression must have changed.

"What is it?" asked Freya.

"Well, I just...I will miss my family. I wish I could talk to them again. That would make my happiness totally complete, I guess."

"Oh, I am sure that can be done," said Freya casually.

"Wait, what? How? When?" I sat straight up, fully focused on what Freya was saying.

"Well, I'm sure the king will tell you. I think he wanted to see if you would choose him before he told you about everything there is to know about this place."

"Yeah, he mentioned there were a few things he wanted to tell me. Do you think I will be able to see my family again?"

"I am not completely sure about seeing them, but you should at least be able to talk to them. People on Idonea have the ability to communicate with those on Earth, and the other way around," Freya said.

"What? Really? But, that would mean that there are people on Earth who know about this place." I thought about my father, and I knew that what Rali needed to tell me concerned him. I was eager for Rali's meeting to be over so I

The King

could ask him about it. And maybe he could settle some of these doubts I was still having because of Durin's accusations.

I began to yawn again and Freya said we could talk more later. I laid down in my bed and drifted off to sleep, wondering what I would soon learn about my father.

It was a few hours later when I awoke. I got out of bed and changed into a simple green cotton dress and white feela. I pulled my hair back into a loose, messy bun and went looking for Freya. She came through the door just as I was about to knock on it.

"Ah, you are up. I have a message for you. One of the king's guards came by...Arthur? And said he is sorry, but because of preparations for the Kostera tomorrow, he and his wife are very busy and will have to postpone your visit. He said he will check with you later to find a better time, and that his wife is very eager to meet you."

"Oh. Okay. That's fine, I guess. Thank you, Freya." There was some free time I needed to fill. And I knew who I wanted to spend it with.

"Is the council meeting still going?" I asked Freya.

"As far as I know. I imagine the king would be here if it were over," she answered.

"That's one long meeting," I observed.

"They can take all day sometimes. Depends on what all needs to be discussed. And with the Kostera tomorrow, I imagine there is a lot to talk about."

"Yeah. I guess."

I sighed.

I decided I would spend the rest of the lovely afternoon in the...in my park. I grabbed a book, and headed out. Freya insisted that I take the dagger with me, just in case, but I told her I was pretty sure that as soon as I walked out the door, I would have two armed guards stuck to my side. And I was right. The guards outside my door followed right behind me the whole way to the park entrance. I asked them if they would please make themselves comfortable in a couple of chairs outside by the door. But they said they must be alert at all times and would stand inside the entrance.

All right then.

I walked out into my park, found a nice spot under a shady tree, and relaxed with my book for a while. I was just doing what I had been instructed to by the king, my future husband. I smiled to myself. I was pretty sure I could get used to this.

I read for a while and enjoyed the peace and quiet when I heard some footsteps behind me. I turned to see who was coming, hoping it would be Rali, but I was disappointed. Instead of him, it was Sindri who was coming towards me.

Fabulous.

"Hello, Sindri," I said as nicely as I could. After all, I am a generous soul and harbored no hard feelings. I knew where Rali's heart was. And it wasn't with her. I actually almost felt sorry for her. After dreaming her whole life that she would be the queen of this place, and having all of that taken away from her by...me. I started to get a little worried about being alone with her after that thought. But I reminded myself that the guards were right inside the door. All I had to do was scream if I needed them.

Sindri walked over to the table carrying a pitcher of tea and two glasses. "Hello," she said and sat down across from me. She looked a little nervous. Her hands were a bit shaky as she set down the tea and glasses. "I have brought us some refreshment."

Us? I was pretty sure I had been in my park by myself and hadn't asked for any company. But, oh well, I would let that slide.

She looked up at me, took a deep breath, and began.

"Annie, listen. I know you must despise me. I have been...well, I have not been very nice to you."

Well...yeah.

"I have come to offer you my friendship."

"Where is this coming from?" I asked. "Why are you wanting to be friends all of a sudden? Aren't we in a competition?"

She laughed. "You have already won the competition. If I am not mistaken, that is one of Rali's mother's rings on your left hand." She pointed to my hand which I, apparently, had not done a very good job of hiding.

I looked at the ring. "Well, that doesn't necessarily mean anything. Maybe it is just a parting gift." I wasn't sure if anyone was supposed to know about the engagement before the announcement at the Kostera the next day.

She laughed again. "It is alright, Annie. I am not upset. Well, I was upset. I am sure my sister told you. She is quite angry with me right now. I have not been kind to her lately, either." She looked down as if she were taking a moment to pray for forgiveness for her sins.

After a minute she looked back up, and poured some tea in both glasses.

"I'm not going to drink any of that. Do you think I'm an idiot?" I asked.

"That is too bad. It is quite refreshing." She took a small sip and smiled. I waited to see if she started convulsing or passed out. She seemed fine. But I still wasn't willing to risk it.

"You see, Annie, my mother had been promised that I...that I would marry the king and be the next Queen of Idonea. We both believed that this promise would be kept. So you can imagine how upset we were to find out that it, in fact, would not be kept."

I nodded sympathetically. Although I don't think she believed that I really cared...because I didn't.

She continued. "Well, after giving it some thought, I have realized that I can either continue to be mad about how things turned out, or I can try to make the best out of the situation and get on with my life. After all, there are many attractive and powerful men in this kingdom, and I would bet that one of them might be able to make me happy." She smiled and sat back in her chair. I guessed it was my turn to talk. I really didn't know what to say, because I couldn't tell if she was being honest...or what.

"Well, Sindri, I really appreciate you for coming out here to talk to me. I will admit, I was a little nervous at first that you might try to get rid of me while I'm out here all alone."

She laughed. "That would be a hard task to accomplish. Your guards are right inside the door, and I am pretty sure I would be the first person suspected if anything were to happen to you."

It disturbed me a bit that she seemed to have actually thought about this possibility. But she was right. This would not be the best place to try to get rid of me. We were the only two out here, so she would be the first suspect. It was light outside (though the suns were about to set and it was quickly getting darker), and my guards were right inside the door...at least they were when I had come out to the park. Were they still? I had no idea.

My throat started to tighten up just thinking about that.

"Well, Sindri, like I said, it was really nice for you to come and try to be my friend, but I think I should go back to my room now."

"But I am not finished."

I hesitated but stayed in my seat.

"I am just trying to be your friend. I know you must not trust what I am saying, but you do not have to accuse me of trying to poison you. I would never!"

I raised an eyebrow.

"No. It would be much more fun to knock you out with a tree branch." Sindri's eyes darted behind me. I turned quickly. I was looking into the malicious eyes of Durin. Before I could get out of my chair, he swung a branch at my head.

And everything went dark.

Chapter 24

I woke up on a cold hard floor, my head throbbing. I could hear Durin and Sindri talking. But their voices seemed so far away.

Durin said, "He will not find out. I took care of the guards, and they will not be talking to anyone."

Sindri said, "But what if someone saw me go out to the park? What do I say then?"

"You say that you went out there to take her some tea, but she was not there."

"Okay. I can do that. So when can we send her home?" asked Sindri.

Send me home? What does she mean?

"We have to wait until she wakes up. We cannot send her unconscious like this. She should be awake soon."

"And you are sure you know how to do this?"

Durin answered, "I am the son of the late king, and I have been taught everything my brother has been taught. Our mother demanded it."

Then I realized where I was. I was in the same room I was in when I first came to Idonea. I was in the room where the Bridge was activated and used to send or bring people back and forth. They were going to use it to send me back to Earth.

I tried to get up but my head was hammering. They both came rushing over to me when they heard me moving and Durin picked me up in his arms and stood me on my feet.

"Hello, princess. It feels nice to hold you again," he said.

I tried to wriggle out of his arms, but I was too weak, and my hands were bound behind my back. What had they done to me?

"What...what are you doing?" I asked.

"We are sending you home. Is that not what you have wanted ever since you got here?" said Durin.

"Rali. He will come. You will be punished," I said.

They both laughed.

Sindri walked up in front of me and said, "Annie. Rali's precious Annie. He is not coming. You sent him a message. He will know all about you soon. Poor man. He will be so heartbroken to learn that you decided to go back home."

"What? What do you mean? What message?" I asked.

Durin answered. "Well, it seems that you were quite upset with Rali when you found out he has been lying to you."

"You keep saying that. Lying to me about what?"

"Many things, my dear. But most importantly, he has been lying to you about your father," said Durin.

"My father?"

"Yes. See, he has not told you about your lineage. He has hidden from you your true past. He knows all about you, yet has refused to be honest with you. And once you figured that out, you decided you needed to leave. After all, you could never be with someone who would lie to you, now, could you?"

"How do I know that what you are saying isn't a lie? Why should I trust you?"

"Think about it, Annie. You know what I am saying is true. Your father told you things, things that not many people could know about. And Rali lied about it, did he not?"

"He didn't lie. He just...he just hasn't had the chance to tell me, yet. He said he--"

"He said he would tell you later. But why? Why wait? Why did he not tell you from the very beginning?"

I hated that what he was saying made sense and that I had wondered these same things myself. But that didn't matter to me then. Surely Rali had planned to tell me about my father when we had more time.

"So, you have sent a message to him saying that I left because I was upset that he didn't tell me the truth?"

"Yes, basically," said Durin.

I shook my head. "He won't believe that."

"Why should he not? He knows how much you loved your father and wanted to know about his connection to this place. In your message you make it quite clear that after you found out from Sindri's mother that Rali knew your father - yes, he knew your father – you were so upset about his deceit that you had to leave."

"What? I don't believe you."

Durin laughed. "Of course you do not believe me. It is a hard truth, but it is the truth."

"Rali knows I wouldn't believe anything Dagny says."

The King

"It doesn't matter if he thinks you believed it completely, but it is plausible that it would cast just enough doubt to make you decide he is not trustworthy. He also knows how much you wanted to go back home. All of this put together would make complete sense." Then he stepped closer to me and said, "Or perhaps you would rather tell him that you were really in love with me the whole time. After all, he saw the heat between us." He leaned in and kissed me. I reacted the only way I could think of.

I spit in his face.

He stepped back quickly and wiped the spit off of his face. Then he grinned at me. "Oh, I will really miss your pluck, princess."

"And I will miss getting the chance to spit in your face again. So, you've come up with this story. Why get rid of me? Then what? What is your plan?" I asked him. I thought using the old tactic of getting my captors to talk might give Rali enough time to figure out where I was and come save me. Because I had no idea how else I would be getting out of this situation.

"My plan? Oh it is a good one. It starts with sending you home. Do not worry. Your friends are waiting for you as we speak. We have been in contact with them and they cannot wait for you to get home."

"You have been in contact? With who? How?"

"We have always been able to communicate with people on Earth. And once we decided you had to go, I took it upon myself to let some...new friends on Earth know that you would be returning shortly. You see, you have been in the way since you got here. The king is supposed to marry Sindri, here. She will be the queen. She will have access to the council and will begin, one by one, turning them against her husband. It will not be hard, as I have already begun the process as the king's general. Also, we have my mother's word against the former, and now dead, king to help overthrow his second born, Rali."

"That's your plan? Really? That's all you could come up with?" I shook my head. "I'm not impressed," I said.

Durin grinned. "I have no desire to impress you anymore. All I want from you now is your absence. And I will achieve that soon. I thought, at first, that you and I might be a good match. That if you fell in love with me, Sindri and the king would be together, and you and I could live happily ever after." Durin's grin turned into a snarl. "But you did not choose wisely, my dear. So, you must go."

He started to push me toward the Bridge entrance. I tried stalling some more. "So, you send me back to Earth. Then what? Rali will just come to get me and bring me back. Then you're screwed. See why I'm not impressed?"

"Oh, Rali will not be coming after you. He will be too busy here. But even if he could come to you, your friends will be looking for him, and ready for him. They are not too happy after they heard how he has treated you during your stay here."

"What do you mean?" I asked.

"Well, look at all your wounds, your scars, this fresh bump on your head. It is a shame how he has beaten you and made you his slave."

"But you... He didn't do any of those things."

Durin laughed and said, "Be sure to stick with that story when you get home. That will really make it fun."

"You...you monster! You've told them that he did this?" I screamed at him.

"Well, of course. But do not worry. They will not get the chance to punish him there on Earth. He will be preoccupied on his own planet," Durin said.

I did not like the evil smile that was crawling across Durin's lips.

"Doing...what?" I asked, not sure I wanted to know the answer.

Durin began to pace in front of me while he told me his plans. "Well, you know our friends next door? You have met them."

"The Hyrokkin? Why? What do they have to do with this?"

"Oh, they have a lot to do with this. How do you think they keep getting on Idonea? Who do you think provides them with ships for transportation? How do you think they have been able to make it as close to the palace as they have?"

I looked at him and I knew. "You. You were the General of his Army. You were in charge of the guards and where they were posted, and what their assignments were. You have been letting them come here. You have been helping them come here. But why? Why would you do that?"

"Who do you think is going to help me take over this kingdom? The king's bodyguards? No, I need an army that will do my bidding. I need men behind me that will demand the will of the new king be done! I have been helping the Hyrokkin, and they will help me."

Then I knew how Durin had found out about the Hyrokkin attacking me. They had told him. It was Durin who had told them where to find the king's chambers. Durin was working with them the whole time. He was the Leader they had spoken of.

"They will not help you. You might get them here on Idonea, but who says they will listen to you after that? Why should they?"

"Because, I will ask for their obedience in exchange for something they have been after for quite some time." He walked over to the end of the Bridge.

"No," I whispered. "You can't. You can't let them have the Sidas Array. They will be able to go anywhere...even Earth." I was feeling sick to my stomach.

"Yes. I suppose they will. And under my command, my army and I will rule the universe. How do you feel about my plan now, princess?"

I growled. "You are evil! You won't get away with this. Rali will--"

"Rali will do nothing! He is weak. He does not know how to rule an army. I do. He should not be king of Idonea. I should. He is not worthy. He cannot take care of this kingdom the way I could."

"He took pretty good care of you in the council room this morning," I said.

I would never learn when to hold my tongue.

Durin slapped me across the face, leaving yet another mark that Rali could be blamed for. "I think it is time for you to go home."

He walked towards me and I tried to run for the door, but Sindri grabbed my bound hands. We both fell to the ground, and I wriggled free of her grip pretty easily. But I couldn't escape the grip that Durin had on my waist once he got to me. He picked me up and dragged me over to where the Bridge was activated. I fought him the whole way. I was still waiting for Rali to come through the door. I was still watching for him, holding on to the hope that he would rescue me. Wasn't that always how it happened in the movies? The poor damsel in distress who is about to be hurt or killed is rescued in the last scene by her hero? Yes, that is what was supposed to happen. But where was my hero?

Durin held me to him with one strong arm as he turned a few knobs, twisted some gears, and pushed some buttons which prepared the Bridge for my journey.

"All right, Annie. Now is when we must say goodbye. I am truly sorry that you chose him over me. Otherwise, this could have turned out so much differently for both of us."

"I would never choose you over Rali. You aren't good enough to lick his boots, you son of a b--"

"Hey, hey, now sweetheart." He ran a hand down one side of my face. "Do you really want our last words to each other to be so cruel?"

"Yes." I spit on him again.

That pretty much did it. As Durin lifted me into the waiting beam of the Bridge, I took one last look toward the door.

No Rali.

My hero was not coming. The last thing I saw on Idonea was Durin's wicked smile.

It was dark. I was alone. I was traveling through space, but could see and hear nothing. Was I even conscious? Was I dreaming? I was aware of myself, but that was it. I could see nothing around me, nor could I feel any movement. Was I moving? Had I arrived? Where was I going? Where had I been? I was slipping out. I was fading...but there! There was a light ahead. I was heading straight for it. It was so bright, it was almost blinding. I put my arm over my eyes as the light got closer and then fully enveloped me. It felt like I was falling, now. I could feel the wind. I could see the sky above me. I was falling. I was falling fast. I looked below me and saw grass and trees. Directly below me, coming up fast was a building. And I was about to fall right into it. And then suddenly, I slowed down. It was as if someone had pushed on the brakes and I slowed immediately. I floated down right through the roof of the building, and landed, not so softly, on a hard, white floor.

"Ow." I groaned. I had landed on my wounded side and was afraid damage had been done. I put my hands down on the floor and lifted my upper body up a little so I could look around. Everything was a little blurry, and so bright. The floors were white, the walls were white, and the people were dressed in white. The people? There were people here. Who were they? They were on the other side of the large room and their faces were blurry. Were they behind a wall? What was that? Glass? I tried to stand up, but I was still a little weak, so I just sat up and pulled my legs underneath me on the floor. My vision began to clear and I could see that I was in a sort of observation room. Behind me was a solid wall, but the other three walls were made of glass, or plastic, or some other transparent material. And there were people in white coats watching me on the other side of those walls. Some of them had clipboards, and a couple of others held video cameras. I felt like a fish in a bowl.

"Hello?" I said. "What...where am I?"

A door opened to my right, and a short man in a white coat stepped in. He closed the door behind him and began to slowly walk toward me.

"Hello, Anne. I am Dr. Fellows. I am here to help you. You are safe now," he said as he took a few cautious steps towards me.

"What? Safe? Where am I?"

"You are back home. You are back on Earth. Your friends on Idonea have sent you back home to us," the doctor said.

"My...my friends? No, I'm not...I need to go..."

"It's okay, Ms. Watts. I know it must have been bad there. Your friends told us everything. We can protect you now." The doctor had moved close enough to me to reach out and put his hand on my arm to help lift me up. He got me to my feet and I was a bit wobbly.

The doctor said, "You have been through a lot, I know, and you are weak from travel. But we will soon have you feeling much better." Dr. Fellows then turned and motioned to someone on the other side of the glass to come in with us. A tall, thin woman came through the door and walked toward me.

"Hi, sweetie. I am Dr. Harris. Will you come with me? We have a lot to discuss."

Sweetie? Oh, I did not like her.

"My name is Annie, not sweetie," I informed Dr. Harris.

"Of course, Annie. Now, let's go to your room, and we can talk while Dr. Fellows examines you."

"Examines me? Why? What is going on?" I was beginning to panic.

"Well, Swee...um, Annie, we need to be sure that you are healthy after what you have endured. We need to try to determine what damage has been done, both physically and mentally, and try to figure out the best way to get you back to your happy life here," said Dr. Harris.

"What I endured?" My mind was still a little foggy. I had a hard time getting my thoughts together. I knew I didn't want to be back on Earth. I needed to go back to Idonea.

The doctors began leading me towards the door through which they had entered earlier.

"Your friends told us about...your experience. We are so sorry. There is much to talk about when you feel up to it," Dr. Harris told me. "But for now, maybe you should just rest."

"You keep saying my friends. I don't know who you're talking about. I don't know what you mean. I don't..."

The doctors exchanged a worried look and Dr. Fellows said, "We know you have been through much trauma. You are showing signs of shock, and have most likely blocked out many of the things that happened to you on that planet. That is best for now. Our immediate goal is to make sure you are healthy physically, before beginning our psychological treatments."

I stopped walking. "What? I don't need psychological treatments. But I think maybe you guys do." I yanked my arms out of their grips and turned to face them. "Now, if someone would please tell me where I can catch the nearest cab, I have some work to do." I needed to find out who these people had been talking to, and how to get back to Idonea. There had to be a way. I turned away from the doctors and started walking down the hallway as if I knew exactly where I was going. But I didn't make it far before their hands were on me again.

"It's okay, Annie. We are going to help you. Now, please, just come with us to--"

"I'm not going anywhere with you. I am getting out of here. Now let go!" I tried getting out of their grips again, but this time they were prepared. Dr. Fellows wrapped both arms around me while Dr. Harris pulled out a syringe.

"What the...what is that?" I tried to move away but two more men in white coats came through a doorway and helped Dr. Fellows hold me still.

"Wait...Stop!" I kicked, I pulled and I put up quite a fight. But four against one, especially a travel - wearied one, were not the best odds. Dr. Harris inserted the syringe into my arm. The room became blurry and I was on the ground in seconds. Then it was dark again.

"Annie? Annie, can you hear me?" said a man's voice.

My eyes were closed. My eyelids were too heavy.

"Rali?" I whispered.

"What, Annie? What did you say? It's me. I'm here. I've missed you," said the voice again.

I put all the effort I could into opening my eyes. I saw light. And a face. I knew that face.

"Jake?" I said.

He smiled and wiped a tear from his eye. "Yes, Annie. It's me. I'm here. You're safe now. Thank God. I thought...I thought I'd never see you again." He had my hand in his. I looked around and saw that I was in another white room. Only this one was smaller and had a few tiny windows with bars. I tried to sit up but found I couldn't move.

"It's all right, Annie. These are just here for now, to keep you from hurting yourself," Jake said.

"What?" I looked down and realized that I couldn't move because I was lying in a bed with restraints across my chest, my waist, and my legs.

"The doctors will remove them when you are better. But for now, just rest. Just rest and get better, Annie."

"Get better? Am I ill?" I was so confused.

"You have been through a lot. And the doctors said it is best to keep you here under observation until they can help you deal with what has happened."

"What has happened? What do you mean? Why do people keep telling me that I have been through so much? How does anyone know? What the hell is happening?" I yelled.

My little outburst sent the white coats rushing in with another syringe.

"No, please, I'm fine. I'm just...Jake, please don't let them," I pleaded.

He looked at the doctors and said, "Please, just wait. I don't think she is going to hurt herself. I can help her to calm down."

The doctors looked at each other, then at me, and then walked away.

"Thank you, Jake."

He smiled and said, "No problem. I would rather have you awake and talking right now, anyway. I haven't been able to talk to you in so long. How are you feeling? Are you comfortable?"

"As comfortable as someone can be while lying on a bed and being held down by thick belts," I replied.

"Yeah. But the doctors mean well. They really do want to help."

"Sure. So they say. Listen, Jake, can you please tell me? What is everyone talking about? What do they think happened to me? Where does everyone think I have been this whole time?" I really hoped Jake could make things a little clearer for me.

He hesitated for a minute. "I really don't want to talk about this, Annie. The doctors said it could be painful to you if I--"

"I don't care what the doctors say, Jake. I need your help. Please. I need to know what they intend to do, and why." I squeezed his hand and hoped I could convince him to help me.

He looked around, and then leaned close to me. "They know that you were kidnapped by the king of the planet called Idonea. They know that he held you captive and forced you to...to..." he sat back again and stopped talking.

"To what, Jake?" I knew he wouldn't answer me, and I didn't need him to.

I sighed and laid my head back down on the pillow. Jake put his hand on the side of my face and began to brush some of my hair out of my eyes when he suddenly stopped and moved closer to my face.

"What? What's wrong?" I asked him.

He sat back a bit and said, "Well, it's your eyes. It looks like they…like they are sparkling. Like they have gold in them or something. That's weird. Maybe it's the lighting."

"What? Let me see. Get a mirror."

"I don't think they want you near any breakable glass."

"Get me a mirror, Jake. Get a mirror!" I yelled.

Then the voice of Dr. Fellows came on over some sort of intercom system and said, "Ms. Watts, if you can please calm yourself down, we will find something for you."

"I'm calm! Just get a mirror!" I screamed…calmly.

I relaxed my muscles and laid my head down on my pillow. I took a few deep breaths and closed my eyes. I needed to see. If what Jake had said was true, if there was gold in my eyes, then that would mean…

"Okay, Jake. I'm okay. Can you ask the doctor for a mirror, please? You can hold it. I just want to look."

Jake looked towards the door to the room and in walked the doctor with a small handheld mirror. I tried to put my hand out to grab it, but the feel of the restraining belt reminded me why that wouldn't work. Dr. Fellows handed the mirror to Jake who held it up to my face.

"Closer, Jake. I need it closer."

Jake obeyed.

I lifted my head as much as I could and opened my eyes wide as I glanced into the mirror. My mouth fell open.

"Oh. Oh my…" I said quietly. I dropped my head back onto the pillow. The gold specks that I had seen in Rali's eyes and in Durin's, the gold that appears only in the eyes of those born in Idonea…that same gold was now in my eyes.

"How could this be?" I whispered to myself.

"What? What is it, Annie?" asked Jake.

I just laid there and shut my eyes. Was this what Rali had been hiding from me? Was this what my father had been hinting at with his stories? Was he…was I from Idonea? There was no other explanation.

"It's…it's nothing, Jake. Just the lighting. You were right."

I didn't want to tell him what was going on. Not yet. I needed to find out more about how I had gotten back to Earth and what they planned to do with me.

"What else are they saying?" I asked Jake. "How do they know about Idonea?"

Jake looked toward the observation room and then leaned close to me and whispered, "There is a society…they have remained secret for many years, apparently. Once you were taken, they came forward with some information about this planet they believed you had been taken to. They are eager to meet with you when you are released."

"What else? What are the doctors saying happened to me?"

Jake shook his head and said, "I…I don't think I would be helping you heal by telling you--"

"Dammit, Jake! You've got to help me here! I have to know what they are planning to do! You have to get me out of here!" I yelled. I struggled with the restraints.

Wrong move, Annie. The white coats came back in and this time there was no arguing with them. They put me under again.

The next time I woke up, I was alone. Jake was no longer sitting by my side. I looked around and could tell that it was dark outside. A lamp on the other side of the room was all that lit the area. I tried again to sit up, but was still restrained by the belts. Dr. Fellows must have been watching me on a camera from an observation room or something, because he came in the room as soon as there was movement.

"Hello, Ms. Watts. How are you feeling?"

I didn't say anything. I just looked at his hands and checked for syringes.

He must've seen me because he said, "Oh, don't worry. I am not going to give you any shots right now. I am just here to check your vitals and make sure you are doing all right before I leave for the night. Dr. Thompson will be watching you when I leave. I will come back first thing in the morning."

"When will the restraints be removed?" I asked him.

He looked at me sympathetically. "As soon as we are sure that you will do no harm to yourself."

"But, I can tell you right now that I won't harm myself. What more do you need?"

He chuckled. "I can see that you are a strong woman. That is good. You will need a lot of strength to get through the next few weeks or so."

Next few weeks? But I needed to get out of there now. "Why weeks? Why do I need to be here? I'm fine."

"You may believe you are fine now, but that is just part of the shock you are experiencing. It is totally natural." He took a quick look at a chart on the bedside table and then turned to me and said, "You get a good night's rest, Ms. Watts. I will see you in the morning." Then he walked out of the room and closed the door.

I was left alone with my thoughts, and finally was not under the influence of whatever had been in Dr. Harris's syringe. It was time to think.

Here is what I knew. I was back on Earth in some sort of hospital. The people here had been told by someone on Idonea that I had had unspeakable things done to me on that planet. But why? And who had they...

Then I remembered something that had been said to me just before landing in that hospital. It was starting to come back. I had been with Durin and Sindri and they had said something about contacting Earth.

They had done this. They had told the doctors, or someone, that I experienced trauma while on Idonea. They were trying to appear as the good guys. But what would they gain from that? Why did they want the doctors to think that I had been harmed? Maybe they knew I would be detained? Maybe they knew I would try to fight them or argue with them...and I would seem crazy. Of course, that had to be it. If I continue to insist that I am fine, the doctors will keep me here longer. They believe that Durin and Sindri had been my friends on Idonea and that they had helped me escape back to earth. So the doctors believed whatever story was fed to them. Made sense.

So what was I going to do about it? I took inventory of the situation there, and on Idonea – as much as I knew of it.

I needed to figure out how to get back to Idonea. But before I could do that, I needed to get out of that hospital. If I kept up with my denial of any traumatic events, the doctors would keep injecting me with drugs, and keep me in restraints - and I would never get out.

No, I needed to cooperate. I had no intention of lying about what really happened on Idonea, I didn't want to pretend that Rali had been cruel to me. But maybe I could say just enough, nod my head at the right things, tear up at the right moments... Yes, I could put on a good enough show to convince the doctors I was healing. And then I could get on with the rest of my plan: Finding my way back to Idonea.

Durin and Sindri, at that very moment, were planning their attack on Rali with the help of the Hyrokkin army. I knew that Rali would not be able to come get me. Durin would be keeping him busy, and at some point would be handing the powerful Sidas Array over to the fire monsters. All hell would break loose if that were to happen.

I still had many unanswered questions about my father and what he knew about Idonea. Seeing the gold in my own eyes just created even more confusion in my mind. I needed to get in contact with this society that Jake mentioned. Would they be able to help me? Would they know a way back to Idonea?

I needed information. I needed to get out of the hospital. I was determined to get out as quickly as possible. I was determined to go back. Back to Idonea, back to the man I loved, back...to my home.

Carlee Boccacci

Acknowledgements

First, I have to thank Jackie. This book wouldn't be here if you had never told me to write the thing in the first place. You gave me the nudge I needed to start working towards my dream.

I would also like to thank:

My husband, Jay – You play with the kids so I can write, you let me bounce ideas off of you, and you give me the encouragement I need to keep going.

My kids, Marilee and Rafa – You two are the cutest things ever and you remind me how important the imagination is.

My parents, Steve and Kelley Vogt – You've always supported me no matter what the dream. And look, I actually followed through this time!

Erika Massey– You give me the advice I need and provide me with inspiration for my characters. This book wouldn't be here without your excitement and eagerness to read it. You are the Erika to my Annie. (And the Erika to my Carlee.)

My brother, Eric – I can't thank you enough for the artwork you do for my books. But also, thank you for actually liking what I write. You're a great sibling and a great friend!

Beth Castle – Where would this even be without you? Still sitting on my computer just waiting to be read. You gave me the push I needed and the motivation to get this out there to the readers. Thank you for making this happen.

Jeanette O'Hara – You think I'm good at things and you tell me so. You have no idea what a boost you are to my self-esteem. Thank you for thinking I'm cool.

William Bernhardt – This book is what it is because of your awesome teaching. (I hope you take that as a compliment.) Your workshops helped me get this novel into shape.

Teresa Miller – You are such an inspiration to me. I know I am so blessed to have been in your class. I learned so much about the art of writing from you and your encouraging words keep me going.

Tamara Grantham – Your comments, writing advice, and reviews have meant so much to me. I truly admire your work and I feel so special having your support.

Barry Friedman – I may not always take your advice, but just know that I always listen to it. Thank you for continuing to teach me even when I make it tough.

My writing group, Lynette Bennett, Warren Danskin, Maribeth Garrett, Sandra Parsons, Larry Yadon – Your suggestions and writing advice have helped me get where I am today. I absolutely love when we get together. You all really are the best!

My writing buddies, Cheryl Bucktooth, John Dixon, Lindy Echeverria, Nick Glasscock, Ambra King, Johnny Bryan Ward – Your comments and critiques on my writing have made me a better writer. I am so glad I have you all in this with me!

My first readers, Amy Bosen, Krystal Grizzle, Leesha Vogt – Thanks for being willing to read my first draft and then still being excited for the next one!

And last but not least, Luke Groom – There wouldn't be a "Sidas Array" without you. Thank you!

About the Author

Carlee Boccacci was born and raised in Tulsa, Oklahoma. She earned a Bachelor's Degree in Human Development and Family Science from Oklahoma State University. Carlee is married to Jay Boccacci. They have two children, Marilee and Rafael (Rafa). They also have two Golden Retrievers, Mika and Roger, and a Newfoundland named Smaug.
When Carlee isn't writing, she enjoys reading anything that sweeps her off into another world. She also loves movies and binge watching shows with her husband.
Keep up with her and news about her upcoming works on her website.
Carleeboccacci.com

Made in the USA
Coppell, TX
03 November 2019